Praise for *Almost Family*

"Hoffman never lets facts flatten characters; he has made them too human—too strong or too stubborn—for that." —*New Yorker*

"Everything in this book rings true—the dialogue, the cadences, the deft-touch observations, the best and worst of human nature." —*Atlanta Journal-Constitution*

"Hoffman has got it all exactly right: the interlocking of individual lives and great public events that made every Southerner feel as though he or she were living on the very edge of history, and the incredibly complicated web of intimacies and evasions that wove through the lives of blacks and whites." —Jonathan Yardley, *Washington Post*

"One of the successes of his book—a portrait of the 29-year relationship between Vivian Gold, an Alabama Jewish woman, and Nebraska Waters, the black woman she employs—is that it provokes thoughts and feelings about any such relationship in the reader's own life." —*New York Times Book Review*

"Hoffman has written an evocative novel of social history in which a racial theme becomes a metaphor for human experience." —*Newsday*

Chicken Dreaming Corn

Chicken Dreaming Corn

a novel

Roy Hoffman

The University of Georgia Press
Athens & London

Published by the University of Georgia Press
Athens, Georgia 30602
© 2004 by Roy Hoffman
All rights reserved
Designed by Anne Richmond Boston
Set in 10/14 Minion
Printed and bound by Maple-Vail

The paper in this book meets the guidelines for
permanence and durability of the Committee on
Production Guidelines for Book Longevity of the
Council on Library Resources.

Printed in the United States of America

08 07 06 05 04 C 5 4 3 2 1

Library of Congress Cataloging-in-Publication Data

Hoffman, Roy, 1953–
Chicken dreaming corn : a novel / [by] Roy Hoffman
p.   cm.
ISBN 0-8203-2668-2 (hardcover : alk. paper)
1. Jews—Alabama—Fiction. 2. Children of immigrants—Fiction.
3. Romanian Americans—Fiction. 4. Jewish families—Fiction.
5. Mobile (Ala.)—Fiction 6. Antisemitism—Fiction.
7. Immigrants—Fiction 8. Violence—Fiction. I. Title.
PS3558.O34634C48 2004
813'.54—dc22   2004007020

British Library Cataloging-in-Publication Data available

To my dad, Charles Hoffman,
Sage, kibitzer, storyteller of the past
and
My mom, Evelyn Hoffman,
In memory of her light and laughter

&

To my grandparents, in memory,
Morris and Mary Hoffman,
Aaron and Sadie Robinton,
who journeyed so far to find home

Contents

Author's Note ix

Part I: 1916–1918

The Land of Cotton 3
A Good Smoke 16
A Dream of Water 32
Lonesome Whistle 47

Part II: 1925–1930

Family Portraits 71
Night Fires 86
What You Pay 102
Free and Clear 115

Part III: 1931–1936

Easy Terms 133
French Quarter Blues 152
Georgia Sun 165
Rose Wine 183

Part IV: 1937–1945

Chicken Dreaming Corn 203
Over the Store 232

Acknowledgments 243

Author's Note

"Chicken dreaming corn" is an expression my Romanian Jewish grandmother used to refer to the yearnings of ordinary folks for something special or extraordinary. I recently learned that the saying in Romanian, *pasarea malai viseaza,* means "the bird dreams of corn," implying lofty expectations or unreachable goals, and that *malai* can mean maize, corn flour, or a type of brittle corn bread. *Malai* crumbs, more desirable to many birds than corn, might be hard to attain. I figure my grandmother gave an Alabama twist to the expression, especially since she and my grandfather opened their first place of business next door to Mobile Poultry Farm, "Dealers in Eggs and all kind of Live & Home-Dressed Poultry." This is one of the kernels of fact in a work of the imagination.

I

1916–1918

The Land of Cotton

Down the stairs from the bedrooms to the floor of his store, past the blouses and pants under dust covers waiting for day to begin, Morris Kleinman made his way to the front door thanking God, blessed be His name, for a regular night's sleep, his devoted Miriam, four healthy children, and strength enough, after a nagging cold, to be the first one up on Upper Dauphin Street wielding his broom against the walk in preparation for the Confederate Veteran's parade.

Above him the swallows looped their crazy script against the chalky Mobile sky. They circled above the Lebanese clothing store and Syrian pressing shop, turned and soared above the Greek bakery where Matranga was baking his New York twist bread that would sell, in today's busy crowd, for a nickel a loaf. As the Holy Cathedral bell gonged six times Father O'Connor scraped his way on one good leg toward the church steps, calling out to Morris, "May peace be with you," to which Morris called back, thinking of the silent, glaring Orthodox priest of his Romanian village, "Good morning, Monseignur, and *shalom* to you."

Horse hair, wood shavings, tobacco, goat droppings, melon rind, ashes, a lone shoelace—his broom whisked away last night's debris onto the wood-brick street. He reached down into the gutter and retrieved the shoelace, slipping it into his pocket for Miriam's scrap box; yesterday she'd kissed him when he salvaged an ivory button.

As he wheeled out the clothes racks he looked down the street, past the red-brick and stained-glass Cathedral, past the tattered Star Theater marquee and the humble mercantile storefronts of Habeeb and Zoghby and Kalifeh, toward Lower Dauphin where the likes of prosperous Greenbaum and Leinkauf were nowhere yet to be seen. *Oh,* he shook his head, the German Jewish merchants still blithely asleep in their canopied beds.

The ritual morning prayers humming at his lips, he turned to go back in, eyeing a crate to be opened. Facing east, *tallit* over his shoulders, he laced the prayer straps through his fingers and intoned the Hebrew, rocking gently, trying not to think about the work pants he'd ordered from Schwartz in Memphis or the dresses from Besser in New Orleans, *landsmen* with their own ties to the Carpathian vistas of Romania. The sun fanned out like palmetto leaves across the storefronts where cedar bread boxes awaited Smith's Bakery deliveries and, in the doorway of the Norwegian Seamen's Hall, men curled hoping for day jobs cleaning stables or lugging bananas from the docks. As Father O'Connor said his first "amen" in the incensed recesses of Holy Cathedral, Morris said his last "*o main*" standing behind the cash register of his store. He added a prayer for safekeeping of Papa, dwelling still with sister Golda, so far away. "You will join us here in Alabama," he vowed. "Soon."

He folded away his prayer shawl, picked up a crowbar and faced the shoulder-high crate: *Besser Fashions. New Orleans.* Thinking of his sons curled in a lazy cocoon, he went back upstairs.

In the front room, his own, Miriam lay curled in their bed before the French doors half-opened to the balcony. The collar of her embroidered gown came high on the neck, her dark hair coiled in a bun. Without turning she raised her hand to signal she was awake: the eyes and ears of the house even as she dozed in reverie, he knew, of the village lanes and kitchen tables of her Romanian home.

He passed his daughter's room. Lillian had kicked off the covers, her twelve-year-old legs sprawled to the far corners of the mattress, her gown twisted up to beyond her knees. The color was robust in her face, blessed be His Name, but after her rheumatic fever—three years ago, this day of the Confederates—who could ever be sure? He stole in and draped the sheet back over her.

He turned into the front room where baby Hannah snored in her bed. Just the other side of a muslin curtain dividing the room, ten-year-old Abraham and eight-year-old Herman lay elbow to shoulder, mouths open like fish. He leaned over and stroked the back of his hand over Abe's cheek; his son groaned. He wiggled his fingertip on the peach fuzz over the boy's upper lip; Abe brushed away the finger.

"*Gutte morgen, mein boychik,*" Morris whispered.

"Mornin'," Abe moaned back.

"*Langer loksh,*" he exhorted, using the nickname, "long legs," for his lanky son.

"No school today, Daddy."

"Up!"

"Sun's not even up."

"This son is the first who will make good at Barton?"

"Hm, mm."

"Who will make a good marriage to a nice *shuyna madele?*"

He nodded in the pillow.

"Who will help his Papa in the store?"

He was answered with a rising snore.

Morris laid his hand on the boy's shoulder and belted, "*Avraham!*"

The boy bolted upright, but Herman was already on his feet, slipping on his pants, dancing from side to side and bunching his fists like a boxer.

Miriam called out, "You will wake Hannah!"

"Abe will hush her," Morris answered.

"Oh, Daddy!" Abe protested, climbing out now, but Morris instructed, "Stay, you, with the baby."

Abe flopped back down and hugged on his pillow.

On the first landing, with Herman padding behind, Morris fingered up a cigar butt he'd stuck into an ash tray and chomped down on it.

"Daddy, are we Rebels?" Herman asked as they came to the crate.

"Today? Yes, we are Rebels."

Morris jockeyed the box out of the corner and wedged the crowbar into a crevice. Herman reached up and grabbed hold of the bar and lifted his feet off the ground. The boards groaned apart.

Morris lifted out the skirts one by one: pretty pale blues and checkered reds. "Besser," he addressed the spirit of his supplier in New Orleans, "now, you are making good business."

From in the back he pulled a skirt soiled on the side. Holding it close, he eyed the brown stain. "Besser," he fumed, "you try to sell to me this *drek*?"

"Daddy!"

From deep inside the crate came scratching and scuffling. Feathers flashed brightly, then exploded into wings.

"Gall durn bird!" Herman cried. "Shoo." A starling wove toward the eaves.

Morris found the bag of old shoes and brought one out, hurling it upwards. The starling dove away, arcing across overalls.

"Small blessings," Morris muttered as bird droppings missed the table and splashed against the floor. The starling turned back over his head and flew up the steps. Herman raced behind.

Into Lillian's room, back through Abe's and Herman's, the bird coursed. Herman grabbed up a broomstick and jumped onto the bed, dancing around Abe's pillow.

Abe sat up blearily. "What are you doing?"

"Is this fun!"

"Not fair."

"You're the one didn't get up." Herman poked wildly at the air.

"Daddy wouldn't let me!"

"In bed like a bum!" Morris yelled at him.

The bird swooped back into the dining room, veering by Morris's head, who cursed Besser like he was in the next room.

"Y'all leave Abe alone," Lillian said, coming from her room, jaw dropping at the spectacle of Daddy waving his arms in the air and turning in circles.

Morris ran toward the front of the apartment, throwing open the French doors. The starling looped back, veered toward Herman who shouted, "*Go on, git!*" before it banked and hurtled into the calm, bluing Alabama sky.

After drinking his black coffee and eating a bowl of *mamaligi* that Miriam had fixed—he still preferred to pasty Southern grits this hearty Romanian dish of cornmeal boiled down to yellow porridge—Morris hurried back down to the walk.

Waiting for the parade to assemble, two boys leaned against a hitching post in front of the Lyric Theater, practicing their drums. Their rolls and rimshots climbed the walls of the popular vaudeville venue, by the marquee reading *Al Jolson May 5* and *Alabama Minstrels Tonight,* moving like a prowler up the French grille balconies.

Most, this early, just wanted to converse about that bloody conflict he'd heard called "the Civil War" up North but here was "the War Between the States," or "the Cause." When this subject came up, anywhere in America, he kept his mouth shut. Fifty years had passed since the Yankees had come steaming into Mobile Bay and Admiral Farragut had cried, "Damn the torpedoes, full speed ahead," but it was as if the Jackal had appeared yesterday. Morris had learned, soon after stepping off the train here in 1907, that mention of "Grant" or "Sherman" started a fight. Even in school in Romania, he had heard of the great president named Lincoln, but to repeat his name here, except among the Negroes, was to risk a bloody nose.

Besides, with every holiday there were sales to be made. Fourth of July—bathing attire. Christmas—children's dresses. Last month had been the celebration called Mardi Gras. He had no evening dress to sell—not like Hammel's, run by German Jews, where blue-blooded city dwellers, whatever their origins, spent a pretty penny to outfit themselves elegantly for the occasion.

He watched Donnie McCall saunter in now, panama hat pushed back, red-faced and jowly. Beneath McCall's eyes were always deep circles, like his own Papa's. McCall, an Irishman he called himself, like Papa also had black-black eyes. A better customer there never was.

McCall nodded to his scuffed-up shoes. "Need a new pair, Mr. Morris. Something respectable for today's doings, not too fancy. The colored look up to a man with smart shoes."

Morris fetched two-tone lace-ups while McCall settled into a chair. Kneeling at his feet, Morris asked about the funeral insurance business as he shoehorned on the first pair.

"One thing folks got to do is die. And when they do, God rest their souls"—McCall stood, peering down—"they want to make sure their funeral's a send-off the likes of which"—he wriggled his toes—"has never been witnessed before. Too small." He sat.

"These better will fit."

McCall stood again, rocked back and forth. "Got my name on 'em, don't you think?"

"Right here." Morris patted the tips. "I can interest you in a new panama hat?"

"Could be tomorrow."

"I will put in the back one with your name just in case."

McCall paid for the shoes and said good-day. A tall man shambled in and plopped down in a chair.

"Got these suckers from you a while ago," the man said, tugging off his muddy boots. "Name's Jackson."

"A good price I remember, Mr. Jackson."

The clammy odor of Jackson's feet rose up. "Don't want 'em."

"Is not possible."

"You make it possible."

"How can I take back old shoes?"

"I paid $2.95 for these durn boots! They hurt my feet!"

Morris broke into a sweat. "Come, the wife she does not like when I do this, but"—he coaxed the man to the display case—"if she does not see." He handed him a bottle of 25¢ ointment.

The man turned it back and forth. "What's it say?"

"Dr. Zigorsky's Foot Elixir. A medicine, but for you a blessing. Worth many dollars."

"Cost me nothin'?"

Morris shook his head. "Hurry, before the wife, she sees."

"Got you a deal," said the man, who dragged his boots back on and hobbled out the store.

By eight o'clock the walks of Dauphin Street began to fill with people and Morris positioned Herman on a stool near the door to keep an eye out for passersby with sticky fingers. Some paused before the outdoor racks of M. Kleinman & Sons looking over the newest hats and boulevard ties.

A willowy, red-haired young woman turned into the store with easy gait, heading to the fancy ladies' section in the rear. Lillian came from the back office to greet her.

As they went down the rows, the woman selected a blue cotton dress and Lillian directed her to the dressing curtain which she drew around her. A moment later she rolled open the curtain and walked to the floor-length mirror.

"What do you think?" she asked Lillian.

"You look," Lillian surmised, "like a nice spring day."

"What an enterprising girl!" The young woman turned to Morris. "Now for a gentleman's opinion?"

He saw again the rich hair and pale eyes of the Romanian girl, Theodora Eminescu, turning to him in the window long ago. Her shoulders rose from her gown, the lantern glow bathing her skin.

"We call this, a *shayna klayde*. A pretty dress."

"But how do I look in it?"

"In this *shayna klayde* you are"—he hesitated, not wanting to sound fresh—"a *shayna madele*." He felt himself blush.

"By the look on your face, it must be good. Reckon I'll take it."

Morris quickly turned his attention to the register.

Before long the sidewalk was lined with Mobilians craning their necks for sight of the marchers, the Kleinman children among them. There were squeals and shouts as, far off, the full complement of drums sounded, buzzing along M. Kleinman & Sons' street-front panes. The tattoo of cornets charged the air. The first marchers arrived.

No matter their look—one man was rigid, another bent—or their size—one was tall like a youth, another once tall but shrunk in old age—the men carried themselves with the same tired, but defiant bearing. At ages sixty-five and seventy, seventy-five and eighty, they puffed their chests out against their gray jackets, feeble but cocksure.

"The *alter kockers*," Sam Lutchnik, a Polish Jew down the street, had said of the marchers, "the old men, still fighting their war."

It was a war that lived still from regiment to regiment, in the trudging boots, the gray coats buttoned tight around the sloping bellies of men who years before, lean and quick, thundered across the fields of Shiloh and Manassas, that town, Morris had heard, named for a Jew.

Two men passed, aided by young cadets—the first was missing his left leg, his stump wagging as he hopped on crutches, the second on crutches with no right foot. Behind them walked a veteran with a cane, tap-tapping on the street. With his free hand he waved at the crowd, his ruined eyes cocked toward the sky.

Some veteran groups had banners: the Raphael Semmes Division, honoring one man, Morris had been told, who stood at the helm of a big warship called Alabama and was buried at the old Catholic cemetery a few miles away, and the George E. Dixon Division, memorializing a poor boy from Mobile who had gone under the water in Charleston Harbor in a hand-cranked submarine called the Hunley to blast a hole in a Union ship, and was entombed in those waters.

The music rose, a tune called "Bonnie Blue Flag." It changed to a melody Morris knew well.

It was not a song that belonged to him like the Yiddish melodies he loved to hum from deep in his boyhood, or the religious songs like the soaring "Aveinu Malkeinu" of Rosh Hashanah, or the stirring "Kol Nidre" chanted at Yom Kippur. But these piccolos playing out the spirited melody gave him goosebumps. "Dixie," it was called. The song piped its sad merriment through the streets, where the onlookers clapped and stomped.

Behind the last division of men followed a crowd of marching ladies: A-frame dresses sweeping the street, silver hair up in buns or down in thin gray tresses reminiscent of the days they had waited for their young Johnny Rebs to return from the battlefields. Many had waited, and waited, their faces caught still in that moment fifty years ago when an emissary stepped onto the porch and announced, with deep consolation, that Jack Mayfield or Curtis Kellogg or Ira Glasser would never be returning, sweet Jesus be with you in this time of great need.

Among these women Morris saw Ira's widow, Dolores, who'd later married Joseph Levy, a German Jew who himself had died the year before. Today, though, Joseph was forgotten; Dolores walked mourning her bright, Confederate youth.

Young women now passed who smiled and waved in the modern way. These were the Daughters of the Confederacy: Spring Hill Chapter, Oakleigh Chapter, Saraland Chapter, Bay Minette Chapter. Girls no older than Ira must have been when the word came back that the young man's life had bled out of him at Chickamauga.

Behind a drum and fife corps filed the cadets of Mobile Military Academy, grave-faced adolescents restless for President Wilson to make a declaration of War, allowing them to jump into trenches alongside the Frenchmen and Brits, having at the dirty Huns. Some had already found action with General Pershing on the Mexican border, chasing the wily Pancho Villa back to his desert lair; the heroic tales they brought back had ignited their friends. The way they stamped their feet reminded Morris of Cossacks, rifles locked on their shoulders. Abe put two fingers to his lips and shrieked a whistle.

A towering lout bumped into Morris and veered into the store.
"I can help you, sir?" Morris asked, following behind.

The man wove toward the rack of hats, reached for a Stetson and knocked several hats to the floor. He stepped back, tottering.

The smell of corn whiskey soured the air.

Miriam looked in from the street. "*Shikker,*" Morris said to her.

"What did you say about me?" The man wove toward the counter, steadying himself on the cash register.

"I said you are drunk."

"Don't talk *Yid* talk."

"Out of the store, mister."

"I can do what I Goddamn please!"

"Do not curse the Lord God in here."

"*You're* telling *me* about . . . ?" The man gazed up blearily at the ceiling, then back down to Morris. "What business you people got hoopin' and hollerin' today?"

"Leave this store."

"This ain't your war."

Miriam had disappeared from the door; a band played a weary dirge.

"Passed by a woman here," said Morris, "Dolores Glasser, who lost a husband in this War. How old was he? Only a boy, fighting in Chickamauga, I have seen the place, such a sadness. Passed Molly Friedman, her brother today walks with two crutches and no legs, boom. Fighting for a Jew named Proskauer, I have seen his picture. A proud man from Mobile, too, with a fancy beard. He was not like you, not a horse's behind, not a *putz* making trouble in an honest man's store."

The man fell back from the cash register and glared at Morris. "You're a scrappy cuss, ain't you?" He took a step closer.

Morris picked up the crowbar.

Miriam came hurrying in with Officer Flynn, who gripped the troublemaker's collar and shook him. "You giving Mr. Morris trouble? I got a hole at the jail for a stinkin' mongrel to sleep in."

The man looked helplessly at Morris. Abe and Herman had appeared.

Morris shook his head. "No, he will not bother us again."

The man nodded dumbly as they went outside. When Flynn had gone his way, the man said, "You ain't such a bad Joe," and brought out a flask of whiskey.

Morris grasped it, took a swig, and, as the man stumbled away, spat it out behind him on the walk.

"*Ach,* my shoulder." Morris spoke to himself, sitting in the rocking chair near the door as a lull came in the procession. The sky had clouded over and rain threatened the day. Wearily he rubbed at his shoulder. Since the November night he'd first slept on those feed sacks in the Eminescu barn, he'd felt the Romanian cold haunting his body, like a sliver of ice deep in his wing. He ceased rubbing, wishing he had swallowed that hooligan's whiskey now, a nice elixir to ease his shoulder's ache.

Sheeted men with hoods over their faces trod silently by, on the shoulders of one a large, rugged cross. The Klan members were met with polite, steady, applause. Morris had learned it was prudent, when Klansmen passed, to look straight ahead, nodding, while revealing no emotion at all. What bone to pick anyway, could they have with him? Wilder enthusiasm greeted the wagonloads of farmers who waved Confederate battle flags and hollered and whistled back at the crowd.

At the same time as the children went cavorting down the street going *bang bang* at enemy soldiers there was the crack of real rifles from the direction of Magnolia Cemetery. The sharp report came again in salute to the Confederate dead, scattering swallows from the telegraph wires down Dauphin, igniting a spark in the feet of the children.

Morris rocked back, looking up at the pressed-tin ceiling of his store, seeing the brocade of ice on the window of his room as a boy with his brothers and sister close by, hearing the blast of rifles again in the frozen night. Under the blanket next to him stirred Chaim, who burrowed down deeper against the shattering noise. There was another volley of shots and, from the adjacent bed, Ben leapt up and came to join him at the window. Frantically they rubbed their palms across the thick, muted glass, trying to see. Golda began to cry in the next room.

Everywhere snow swirled through darkness, hiding the rattle of steel and the pounding of hooves, hiding the screams until it drew back like a veil revealing a man sunk down into the drifts and another alongside, tugging him up, and a horse, like a black ghost flying. Voices, shouts, villagers emerging from doorways running toward the figures in the snow. Another horse crowded the darkness, then another came thundering, and the door of Morris's own house opened as Papa, nightshirt flying, headed toward the courtyard, and Mama was at the door of their room holding Golda, putting her finger to her lips, exhorting, "*Sha shtil, kinder,* be quiet, children, do as Papa has asked and pray to the Almighty."

The night stilled a moment, then held sobbing, and angry, rising voices. Morris and his brothers rubbed busily at the window, wiping away their own curtains of breath, watching the men disperse, hearing the sobbing fall away and the voices receding into houses across the *shtetl* square.

Papa's face was long and dark when he came back in, and the next day when he went off to work at his distillery, and when he returned; and the next day and next, when sitting by the fire, prayer book open on his lap, he gazed off at the dancing flames. He said nothing until that night he came home, eyes sunk into deep moons, and told them the soldiers had visited him with swords and guns, with padlocks and chains, pronouncing his distillery closed: it was a law, they said, barring Jews from this business, as others had been barred from being doctors and men of the courts. Who knew, they said, what mischief Jews might perform on grains and yeast and water; on the magic liquor they sold to the good Christians of Piatra Neamt? How much money the Jews had accumulated, they complained, at the expense of the good people of the village! As Papa spoke his face darkened still, as though wanting to let loose tears like those that had come when they marched to the cemetery with his own father and tossed the dirt onto the casket and sat solemnly for days until the black veils were lifted from the chairs.

But he held back the tears, and sat one week, and then another, with prayer book open while gazing only at the fire. He called Morris to him and explained there was little money left for the family, and word had come throughout the region of Moldavia, from Dorohoi to Iasi, that others had businesses that were being closed down. He told Morris that he must leave school and go to work at a farmhouse on the edge of the Romanian plain; that he had contacted a grain farmer he knew through the distillery, Stefan Eminescu, a good Christian man with a son and two daughters, who could use a boy with good hands and a strong back.

Mama's hand rested on Morris's shoulder. "Azril," she said, "don't be so hard on him, tell him more gently," and he nodded and said her name, "Shayna Blema," pretty rose. "Pretty rose," Morris repeated, reaching up to touch her slender, soft hand. She started to walk away, but he held her hand firmly now; "*gai nisht,* Mama," he whispered, don't go, feeling the floor drop away.

"Morris?" Miriam's voice was exhorting him. Her hand jiggled his shoulder. "Chicken dreaming corn?"

He shook his head. "Not so good."

"The parade is over, and more customers will be coming soon." She moved away toward the cash register to go over the morning's receipts.

He stood from the rocking chair, the floor still dropping away, and stepped outdoors to steady himself, breathing in Mobile streets.

A Good Smoke

S moothing down his pencil-thin moustache and wiping at his heavy stubble, Pablo Pastor hoisted up his duffel stuffed with tobacco leaves and started trudging up Government Street from the docks. His sojourn on the cargo boat—from Havana to New Orleans to Mobile—had set the Gulf of Mexico deep in his bones. He had thought to disembark for good at New Orleans, but had heard the Spanish voices and seen the stalks of cut sugar cane bundled near the docks. *La caña* was what he had fled in Cuba—a life hacking endless fields of cane. There were other ways, surely, to earn one's keep in that grand Louisiana city, but he would take no chances. He had steamered on.

The seaport that bustled around him now—longshoremen loading timber onto tall-masted ships, roughnecks lugging green stalks from battered banana boats, gentlemen in top hats boarding the riverboat Nettie Quill—gave way to the commerce of the town. He passed vats of olives in front of the grocer Lignos Co., racks of coats before the general store I. Prince & Sons, a store with no name where a Chinese woman stood at a counter folding laundry. He glanced up to see the soaring statue of a naval officer with sword at his side—"Admiral Raphael Semmes, Confederate States Navy"— and figured this warrior was a protector of the town.

Following the flow of pedestrians, he turned from Government Street to Royal Street, then arrived at Dauphin, drawn toward the leafiness of Bienville Square. Beneath the town clock at the Square, he gazed at the men in pearly panamas ambling into the imposing stone building with its sign "First National Bank," and tilted his battered straw hat against the three o'clock sun. Once he had a bath and was shaved, had American dollars in his pocket and a fine *sombrero* like theirs and gentlemanly shoes, too—two-tones laced snugly against striped socks instead of sandals on barefeet—he'd become part of this town. The air was familiar with the damp drapery of Spanish moss and the pungence of the green bananas ripening to yellow, and—he sniffed the air and closed his eyes— ladies' sweet perfume.

Where, though, was this seaport's tobacco? In the first six blocks he walked, he counted fifty men, but only four lit cigars. He peered into the windows of drugstores with strange, Alabama names— Ortmann's, Megginson's, Molyneux & Demuoy—and saw but a few cigar boxes with pictures of a noble gentleman on the lids. In Havana, cigars had been everywhere. He had come to the right land.

Passing a drugstore called Ebbecke's, he looked in to see boys in short pants at the counter, and young mothers with tresses so thick and fair it made him blush and dream about their naked, bright skin like he dreamed about the naked, dark skin of his beautiful Marta back home in Havana who was waiting, full with their child. "Dear Jesus Lord," he said, "forgive my wicked thoughts."

The hunger he felt was in his belly, too, but he'd spent his last nickel at the port of New Orleans for a bottle of *cerveza* and *papas fritas* that he'd nursed like sea rations on the easterly voyage to Mobile. He could make out a few English words on the menu printed above the counter in Ebbecke's: "Sausage and beans, 4¢." He reached into his duffel and brought out a handful of cigars he'd rolled in New Orleans.

"*Cigarros*," he said, holding them out. "*Cuatro centavos* . . . four cents." A dozen men ignored him. "*Cigarros*," he said, "*three* cents."

A man in a black cap passed by. The man paused, turned back and studied the cigars, then Pastor. "*Bist du a Yid?*"

"*Hablo español, soy cubano.*"

"These cigars, you make them?"

"*Sí*, yes! For one cigar, five cents."

"For two cigars, eight cents."

"For two, nine."

"Ten cents for three."

"OK," Pastor said, then hesitated, realizing this offer was lower than the one before. The dime was held before him, though, and then it was in his own palm with the cigars exchanging hands.

"Morris Kleinman," the man introduced himself, biting off the end of the cigar and chomping down on the flavorful tobacco.

"Pablo Pas*tor*," he said, emphasizing the second syllable, so that it rhymed with "door."

Morris nodded. "Mr. Pa-store! This cigar, it is good business. *Shalom*," he added, heading on down the street.

"*Shalom*," Pastor repeated strangely, entering Ebbecke's, eating his sausage, then heading down the street to the Cathedral where he touched the holy water to his forehead, dropped his belongings, and kneeled before the glorious visage of Christ above the altar. He prayed for the well-being of his wife and unborn child, asking his Saviour and Protector to watch over him in this new land called Mobile. A priest appeared galumphing on one leg and listened to his confession, afterwards offering him a plate of rice and collards, a lavatory key, and a place to sleep under an eave alongside the church garden a few nights until he found his own lodging if he'd water the roses and other blooms.

Pastor kissed the priest's ring, thanked the Lord, and stuffed his tobacco-duffel for safekeeping in the rectory. With a straight razor and soap, he scraped off his rough whiskers leaving only the tiny sharp moustache Marta loved to trace with her finger.

Wiping the grime out of his hat, he donned it again and ventured out to explore the blocks near the Cathedral, hoping he might find a fellow *cubano* to tell him about this town. Down side streets he walked by a saloon where men in white suits bellied up to the bar, their panama hats hung on a rack, then a house where a stout woman with heavily painted face smiled alluringly from her porch. He turned by a butcher shop with a Star of David near strange script on the window and found himself again on Dauphin, sliding through the long shadows of the dusk.

"Old shoes" was what they called the prank—Abe's and Herman's favorite. Using the balcony as their private stage, they'd wait until the coast was clear—this evening Daddy was in the back of the store figuring inventory, and Mama was out paying a sick visit to Selma Gollub—then start their game.

First, Abe ran downstairs and foraged in the ruined-shoe bin. Then he came back upstairs with a pair of ragged boots and a cardboard box. They plunked the boots into the box and tied it with a red bow.

Next, Herman slipped down to the street and across to the other side, dropping the shoe box and racing back to join Abe upstairs.

Within minutes a slick-haired dandy came ambling along. He hesitated at the box, looked around, bumped it with the heel of his foot. He edged it with his toe into the shadows. He bent down and scooped it up and walked off swiftly with it tucked under his arm.

Herman jumped up and down, pointing. "He took 'em, he took 'em!"

Abe fell back with laughter until he sucked for breath.

"I know what y'all are doing," said Lillian, coming up behind, "and if Daddy finds out . . ."

"Tattletale, tattletale," Herman sang, "burn your britches, go to jail."

"He'll burn your britches is what he'll do."

"So you better not tell him."

"Any durn fool on the street can see y'all up here!"

"They want to watch me pin you?" said Abe.

"Come on, Mr. Weakling."

Abe fell to the balcony deck and put his elbow out, hand up

ready to arm wrestle. Lillian matched his movement and clasped his palm. He swiftly overpowered her, pushing her knuckles against the deck. "Say Uncle," he commanded.

"Uncle Benny." She smirked. "Happy?" She stomped off, went downstairs and returned with another shoe box. Inside was a broken-down pair of men's patent leathers, a gash down the heel of the left shoe. "Dare you," she said to Abe.

"Dare what?"

"Put these on the street."

"Daddy's outside now cranking down the awning!"

"Dare beats an arm wrestle."

"Oh, give 'em here," said Herman, who stole down and hid behind the rack of Stetsons until Daddy's back was turned, then leapt across Dauphin, dropping the box. Racing back in and up the stairs, he mugged a big victory smile for the others, but Lillian exclaimed, "Look!"

An angular man with a sharp little moustache and beat-up straw hat came shambling toward the box. He looked around furtively, then fell to the box, ripping off the ribbon and holding up the shoes to the light.

"Oooh, yech," Herman said. "Look!" The man was drawing the shoes to his lips. "He's kissing them!"

"Man kissy shoe," Hannah said.

"I hear Mama," Abe whispered.

"Man kissy shoe," Hannah repeated, skipping toward the steps. Abe lunged for her, dragging her back.

"Let me go!" she wailed.

"Look at this!" Herman produced a string of licorice from his pocket. She stretched out her fingers. "Won't tell?"

She shook her head.

"Promise?"

"Uh huh." She wadded the licorice into her mouth as Mama's footsteps creaked behind them. They stood like cadets as she looked them over.

"Where do I have eyes?" she asked.

"In the back of your head," they answered.

"Remember."

"Yes ma'am."

"*Shluf, mein kinder,*" she commanded. Get sleep, my children. She picked up Hannah and nodded to the others to come get ready. As they glanced over their shoulders at the street, the boys swallowed their laughter, but Lillian wiped back tears: the man knelt on the sidewalk, hands clasped together, looking to the heavens above M. Kleinman & Sons.

Across the kitchen floor tiles, Miriam ran her mop: by the pedestal sink where the milk dishes sat drying, by the gas stove where Lillian set a vase of lilacs on top of the meter box. She swabbed a second time before starting at the hallway. For one month the Cuban cigar maker had resided in the empty room at the end of the hall, having been sent to Morris by Father O'Connor—"He gave me your name," Pastor had explained—and the tobacco smell of him lingered in the corners and drifted through the foyer. She sprinkled out lemon oil and buffed the floorboards, chasing the ghost of the thin, Spanish man.

It was not so much a boarder that she minded—his fifty cents a week was a welcome addition to the cash register groaning, always, beneath too many bills to pay, too little *gelt* in its coffers—but that, as she told Selma Gollub, he was not one of their own. Just as she and Morris had roomed with *landsmen* Selma and Heshie their first days off the train, so they, in turn, had welcomed newcomers South once they had room above the store. Sammy Glucksman, from Romania, had boarded with them five weeks; Hank Green, formerly Heshie Gluchowsky, had lived in the empty room nearly two months awaiting his wife's arrival from Poland.

These men had kept their polite distance, using the washroom on the first floor and the back stairway from the street, and paying what they could neither in labor nor barter but in what the family needed most: hard cash. Come Sabbath dusk they joined the family in strolling to the Conti Street *shul* where the congregants davened and whispered about Finkle's new line of dungarees that were both way overpriced and miserably thin in the fanny, or Lucky Schwartz's girlfriend, so it was rumored, that he kept on the other side of Davis Avenue, the town's dividing line for colored and whites.

Miriam worked her mop closer to Pastor's room, listening for the rapid working of his fingers as he rolled cigars, or the sawing of his breath as he rested. To her annoyance, it was usually long after the cash register was first jangling that he rose and took his coffee with milk, and then, in the evening when the rest of the house was settling down that he sent the Aladdin lamp flaring in his room and spread his tobacco leaves on a table, rolling and cutting and touching hot paraffin to the tips.

To her relief there was now no sound at all.

When she came to his room he sat on the edge of his bed in his striped boxer shorts, holding a plump stogie in his stained fingers, looking right at her. "*Buenos días,*" he said.

"Good *afternoon,* Mr. Pastor."

"You are very well?" he asked. He grinned at her with uneven teeth. He gave off the smell of a man who ate pork.

"Yes, thank you," she said briskly.

His black eyes flicked over her.

She reached out and shut his door, closing him away.

While lying in bed, trying to sleep, Miriam heard voices floating up from the street below:

"The cigars in Lebanon," said Sahadi, "are magnificent. My people, they smoke the best. Like the wood of cedars it tastes, smooth, better than your shinny whiskey."

"Do you see Reiss today?" Lutchnik said. "He smokes the little cigars."

"The cigarette," said Morris.

"Very fancy Solly is," Mirsky said.

"Yes," Lutchnik said, "with his little finger out to here."

"Turkish cigarettes," Sahadi defended, "these are the best."

The voices rose and drifted, and Jake Kamil, joining them now, told Pastor how he made his own living: selling slop chests to sailing ships, how he packed the barrels with clean clothes for the sailors, took them back filthy, and supplied them again with clean apparel.

"It would be good," Pastor suggested, "to put in also cigars!"

"Ah," Morris said, "a man who will one day be rich."

Miriam flung the pillow off her head and leapt up. She leaned out, seeing the men beneath a billow of smoke. She reached to the bedside table and picked up one of Morris's butts and put it between her teeth.

Its papery texture, its old-glove taste: what a peculiar habit these men indulged in. She remembered sitting in the balcony of the synagogue in Iasi, hearing the rabbi explain that, as the sages told, because a woman was made from Adam's rib she was dry and odorous like a bone and needed perfume and emollients to sweeten her. What did the sages know of men's cigars!

Setting the butt back in its tray she went downstairs. In the office, open on the counter, was the ledger book. She opened it to the column, "Pablo Pastor, Rent." Only two weeks were marked, "*Paid*," the others scratched, "*Pastor's Golds.*" She heard the men departing and closed the book and hurried back upstairs.

In bed she feigned sleep. Morris slipped into his nightshirt, muttered his bedtime *shemu,* and slid in next to her.

"*Ziben* dollars," she said.

"*Vus zucks der?*"

"*Ziben,*" she repeated.

"So," he said, "seven dollars."

"With seven dollars how many days of chicken could we buy at Berson's?"

"*Ist krank Berson?*"

"*Er ist nisht krank.* I am not talking about Berson."

"You said, 'Berson is sick.'"

"*You* said Berson was sick."

"Do not raise your voice at me!"

"Morris," she whispered. "This man who is living in our house, who is he to you?"

"He is to me a man who is living in my house. What else must he be?"

"*Er ist nisht a gutte mensch.*"

"How not a good man? He pays."

"What you write in the ledgers, this is not the truth?"

"You are checking behind me!"

"It was open to a thousand eyes, saying he does not pay."

"He *pays*."

"With what? Cigars?"

Morris was silent a moment. "The money will soon come."

"The children cannot eat cigars."

"We have always paid with what people can eat?"

"This is different."

"Pressed shirts and mended pants?"

"This is different!"

"*Gunug!* Enough!"

"Morris!"

"*Ich gai shlufen, Miriam.*" He turned away to hunt his sleep.

Shirts and pants: they rose before her in a tall column on the table of the cleaning and pressing shop they'd opened their first years in Mobile. She remembered the feeling of the baby heavy inside her, wanting to come in the close summer air. In her arms little Abe fussed and squirmed. In the corner, near the furnace, Lillian played with her button-eyed doll; Miriam reached down and tugged her away. Morris had doused the rumpled shirt with water and laid it onto the board over the boiler, setting the long, heavy iron down on top. It made a high, sighing noise, like a woman clutching her sides, sending steam up around the shirt and coating his face with beads of water, like the water that formed on Miriam's face and ran down her neck and made her blouse wet where Abe nuzzled her bosom even as the baby inside kicked and turned.

She felt a squeezing at the back of her abdomen and uttered, "Oh, Morris!"

"It is time?" he asked, reaching to comfort her with one hand even as he held the pressing iron with the other. He touched her with both hands now, but quickly put one back to the presser. What would a ruined shirt cost them? Twenty cents? Half a dollar?

"No," she said as the squeezing subsided, "it is not time," and she breathed easily again; she urged him to continue working.

He finished and folded the shirt and set it on the stack. Just one more shirt and his duffel would be filled for the walk from Dauphin to Springhill Avenue to Ann Street and back down Old Shell. For every delivery he walked, a nickel they saved.

Four clean shirts garnered a week's bread from Smith's bakery; three, several gallons of milk from Berson's store; two, a payment on the bill they owed at Molyneux's for the elixir Lillian had needed, anxiously waking with a sore throat in the coolest March evening. This trade of cleaning and pressing that Morris had picked up in New York during his first years off the boat before heading South served better than all the others he'd learned: how much work might there be in Mobile for a man preparing corned beef and kugel? Or in buying and selling junk?

Miriam looked off through the front window, feeling another contraction come; she gritted her teeth, silent. It passed. As he pressed and folded one more shirt she said, "Go now."

"I cannot."

"You have time."

"You should not be alone."

"I am alone with all Dauphin outside our door?"

"I will take the trolley."

"And waste a whole nickel?"

"What is a nickel?"

"A sack of pole beans. A jar of molasses."

"But the baby!"

"Shhh!" she admonished, "Do not speak of what God has not yet given."

She watched him hurry out the door with his heavy knapsack of freshly pressed clothes: a slender dark youth in skullcap lost in the traffic of red-cheeked men in straw katies.

It felt like the world wanting to drop out of her now, and she was dropping too, into the chair they kept next to the window, setting Abe on the floor, who stood and tottered and fell and stood, as she placed her feet up on the ledge and whispered, "*Macht schnell, liebe.*" Hurry, love.

But the clock hands dragged and Lillian started weeping and Abe, struggling to stand again, bumped his head and wailed until she gathered them both in her arms, pressing them close so that they seemed for a moment to hold back the new child wanting to come. 5:10 said the wall clock as she prayed for the strength to make it the four blocks to Selma Gollub's. She prayed until 5:20, then 5:25, but she could not move.

"Lily," she said, "I need Aunt Selma." She clutched her belly. "At the *shul.*"

As she said these words she cursed her own foolishness and grabbed for Lillian's shoulder but her daughter was out the door. She picked up Abe and started to run after her but was felled into her chair by another contraction. "God be at my little girl's shoulder."

She saw a squat man in brown fedora pause near the window but could not bring herself to rap on the glass summoning a stranger who'd rake eyes over her puffed calves and swollen belly. 5:45. 5:50. She groped for a grape sucker in a canister on the shelf, and gave one to Abe who settled down into the corner in a delight of smacking.

Burnt cotton; sticky grape: the smells rose high into her nostrils, making her spin. She stripped off her undergarments and lay back just as she felt the baby splitting her in two.

As out of a cloud Morris appeared with Lillian bundled in his arms and Selma Gollub panting right behind. He frantically kissed her cheek and said something about Lillian and rain and trading pressed shirts for a trolley ride, even as he was turning away to let Selma lay firm hands on Miriam's legs and reach in deep to grasp the soaked and delicate head emerging. The turning, slipping, her body opening; glistening shoulders, hips, feet. The newborn was held up and slapped and pronounced a boy, their Herman.

Above Miriam the sounds of Selma and Morris and young Abe and baby Herman all blended and drifted away and the grandfather clock gonged five times returning her to this morning. She sat up, Morris next to her snoring, and announced, "I am again with child."

Morris opened his eyes.

Miriam stroked his brow and repeated her news.

Morris opened his arms and she lay down against him as the first light eased in from the Mobile streets. "We are blessed," he said, "even as I am a fool. This man you do not like, I will tell him this morning he must go."

But Miriam put her face in the crook of his neck and answered, "No, let him stay. He will soon make a home of his own."

Marta Pastor, by nature, was stout; at eight months pregnant— *embarazada,* she called it—she needed to turn sideways to manage the hallway from Miriam's room to Pablo's, where a second bed had been added and tobacco leaves, ready for rolling, were draped like carnival streamers on a clothesline out the door.

From where Morris stood near the dungarees in the store, he could chart her movements by the shake of floorboards overhead. The kitchen, the dining room, the front bedrooms—she lumbered from end to end of the apartment and back again. He imagined Marta pregnant to bursting, bosoms full and legs swollen. It was enough that he should watch his own wife guardedly as her belly bowed out in her sixth month. But another man's?

When he said to Miriam in bed that night, "I will ask Heshie if he knows of a place they can move, maybe the *shul,* a small room in the back," it was Miriam who countered, "What? Throw out a poor woman with child onto the street?"

Together, that next Friday morning, the women set out to the market, Miriam pointing out to Marta the butter beans and hominy, Marta to Miriam the ropes of chili peppers and plantains. "Here, we will buy one," Marta said of the stringy peppers and exchanged a penny for the curled red chili. "My Pablo, he loves his food *caliente,* very hot, like a Mexican."

They wove through the bins of sweet potatoes and mustard greens, the produce carts tended by ancient men with seamed faces and young daughters with apple cheeks and ratty hair. Barefoot black women, heads wrapped in kerchiefs, stood next to cauldrons slopping out creamed corn and pigs feet onto tin plates for seer-suckered white men who grinned and made faces at the shy urchins hiding behind their mamas' skirts, hair crimped around tissue.

Miriam told how she and Morris had met: Aunt Doris had arranged a "chance" meeting for them in the Flatbush delicatessen where he'd worked. Through Doris they arranged to meet again. And again. When Morris left the delicatessen to apprentice with a presser on the Lower East Side, they continued to meet in Manhattan, too, Doris always watching.

"Then news came," Miriam went on, "my step-mother, rest her soul, had died. God forgive me, but how I had hated her voice, like a scraping door, her finger shaking in my face. She was jealous because I looked like my Mama? Because Papa stroked my hair? I must go back to Iasi, I told Morris, and care for Papa."

The women left the market and made their way toward Berson's, where chickens, throats slit, strung up by their claws, dangled in the window.

"I was thinking, I will have the life again I had as a girl before the soldiers came, before Mama died," Miriam said. "But the letter came from Benny, my brother, 'Say *kaddish* for Papa. He died in the night.' In Romania, I had no home."

"It was God's plan," Marta concluded.

"Morris took me on a picnic to Prospect Park and said, 'Miriam, do you think I am a good prospect?'

"'Yes,' I told him, 'I think you are a good prospect.'"

After a last Sabbath smoke, Morris cranked down the awning on the street and brought Pablo with him to the table. Pablo wore shiny patent leather shoes and a sports coat and bow tie he'd bought for three cigars from Morris.

"I think," Marta said as they took their places at the table, "God will bless you with another girl. And me and Pablo with a boy."

"What is this you are saying?" Morris asked.

"Our boy, your girl."

"Lillian is making the 'shabbos' prayer."

Marta crossed herself and bowed her head. Lillian lit the candles, waved her hands three times over the flames, then covered her eyes and intoned the prayer.

"A beautiful language," said Pablo of the Hebrew.

Marta looked up. "Your girl, my son. A good match, no?"

"This is not possible," Morris said sternly, passing the boiled chicken while receiving the collards from Abe.

"If God makes a miracle is possible."

"Is not a miracle."

As Lillian poured iced tea, Marta reached into her pocket and brought out the pepper she bought in the market. She presented it to Miriam.

Even as the shudder began far back in her, Miriam bit off the tip of the pepper: it set a hot buzzing in her lower lip. She reached for the tea and gulped it down; the pepper's hot tingling spread to her tongue.

Reaching for the pitcher of iced tea Miriam knocked a spoon to the floor, and Herman squatted down under the table to retrieve it; he glanced at pants knees and dress hems and shoes. He gasped and tugged at Abe to come under too.

Abe bent down to look as Daddy fussed, "Sons, do not play!" but Herman was pointing to Pablo's feet: the cigar-maker's patent leather shoes bore the tell-tale gashes of the old shoes they'd set out on the street.

Amazed, the boys lingered beneath, the table rattling above them. Herman felt Daddy's hand reach down and clutch his shoulder, and he groaned, "I'll be whupped." But it was their mother's name they heard called out frantically and her own voice saying, "God help me, this is too soon!"

Marta was crying, "I am sorry," but Miriam was assuring her, "It is not the food you gave to me," and Morris was telling Herman to go run fetch Selma Gollub.

Up Dauphin, over to Conti Herman flew, by the dirge of the great Cathedral sounding its slumberous eight o'clock knell, past the junkyard behind Fowler's store where the flying-machine parts sat hulking in the grave Mobile shadows, toward *shul* where Heshie Gollub, the *shamas,* was opening the door.

"Aunt Selma!" he shouted, running up the steps to her apartment over the synagogue, starting to bang on the door, but stout and curled-over Selma Gollub was already on the landing, bag in hand, hurrying even ahead of Herman. Her feet left the ground by inches, flying—a magic woman, the other boys called her, half wizard and bird. Herman ran closer to look; the myth was true.

Without touching the ground, Aunt Selma rose up the stairs and to the bed where Miriam lay spread out now, her hands clutching the headboard, and when Miriam felt the woman's touch on her womb it was like a soft pale light flowing down her, helping her be still.

She felt Selma's strong hands along with Marta's holding her firm as wave followed wave of contraction and her body was opening to let the frail, curled torso come slipping out.

"God knows best, praised be His name, God knows what is best,"

Selma was repeating, and wrapped the limp form in a swaddling cloth and let Miriam hold him a moment before going to the door and telling Morris the news. And it was Abe rushing this time to fetch the rabbi, right into the middle of the Sabbath prayers, and hearing the news the men came out all at once to make a sad procession for the stilled child.

Miriam named her son David, and they laid their flesh and blood deep into the Alabama soil.

A Dream of Water

The days leading up to Easter, 1918, were busy for the store, with mothers buying union suits to pack for their boys going off to the Army, and farmhands from Toulminville or docks workers from Maysville coming in for a well-priced, church-going coat and tie.

Upstairs in the kitchen, Miriam and Lillian put away the dishes and brought out the Passover plateware, and the first and second night *seders* were festive and long. Morris, after closing the store early at the start of the holiday, resumed regular hours in time for their big sale weekend.

GOOD FRIDAY SPECIALS, Morris printed on a placard. He had refused to take the sign down even after being confronted by a lady from the Church of Christ Disciples who railed that the Jews, "having crucified Christ, should not now profit from His murder!" Pablo Pastor, clutching David's chubby hand, had stood between Morris and the woman, proclaiming that when Christ returned the Kleinmans would be among the twelve thousand souls from each of the twelve tribes marked with the seal of Heaven. "Thank you, Mr. Pastor," Morris said after the woman stomped away. "After this life, who knows? In this one we should at least make a good living."

Three months after David had been born, the Pastors had moved into a second-floor apartment at the back of Fosko Soda, across from the Cathedral. The men who sat before their stores in rockers became Pablo's customers; nightly, they puffed their worries into the damp Gulf Coast sky.

That the Pastors had chosen to name their boy after the infant that Miriam had lost seemed strange, at first. When they had asked Morris to be the godfather, he declined. The rabbi told him this was not allowed. Morris was relieved. Miriam's face had been long for many weeks after losing her own David. It was not until Mardi Gras day, with Hannah tangling herself up in a bright spool of serpentine thrown from a masked rider on a silver-plumed horse, that a smile had finally crossed her face.

But there was no sight even of the Pastors this Easter morning: the town was serene, ten thousand Mobilians tucked in churches, singing Hallelujahs to their risen Lord. By Pieme's Glass and Fowler's Watches shuttered in Easter quiet, by Bienville Square where the only motion was a sailor snoring on a bench, the Kleinmans made their way to the 10 A.M. ferry.

They reached the Bay Queen, finding it nearly empty for this first morning run. Abe and Herman hung over the dockhand who loosed the ferry from its moorings; topside, like an aristocrat, Miriam stretched out on a folding chair.

Morris pushed his face into the wind, watching the towns like glimmering threads on the opposite shore—Daphne, Montrose, and Fairhope. He closed his eyes as a steamship moved through the channel, its wake lifting the ferry in a gentle roll.

He had first felt this bay—rising and falling, rocking, gently rocking—in a dream. Could he have been only a few years older than Abe, his birthday son? He felt Shayna Blema's hand like the wind now touching him and flying away, impossible to hold. He'd hitched a ride that next morning on the back of a livestock wagon to the farm outside of Piatra Neamt where the tall gray man with one stray eye welcomed him with a nod to sacks in the corner.

Barley and oats: he smelled the grain bags, felt the great, lumpy bodies of them slung over his shoulder like Chaim captured in a game of chase and hoisted onto his back. In his hips, he retraced the path from the barn to the store with its cellar leading down to the stockpile of grain; down the steps past the bats' wings folded like black poppies, down to the hole where the sacks waited to be dragged up like dead bodies. After he lugged the sacks up they were picked over by Andru Antonescu who came in for feed for the horses who plowed his potato fields, or by his brother Alexandru who carted away grain for his distillery, working overtime to meet the demand now that Papa's was closed.

In the store Eminescu introduced him as "the Jew," and when one pig farmer threatened to thrash him for ripping a sack, Eminescu confronted the farmer, saying, "You gain nothing from our Lord by striking a poor Hebrew boy." When Morris started to thank him, Eminescu gazed back with one stray eye and nodded abruptly to the barn. "Go, eat, it is waiting."

With horses and goats making his *minyan,* he praised the Lord for deliverance and asked protection for Papa and Shayna Blema and said *hamotzi* and slopped his bread in the potato soup still simmering from the stove. It was delivered by the gypsy cook Olga who assured him she cooked his meals in a separate pot and cut the necks of the chickens just like the Jewish butcher; after all, she said to his astonishment, she'd once been married to a Jew. One fall morning, he was intoning the prayer after eating when the barn door creaked open and he looked up expecting to see Olga, but saw, instead, an angel come down from the churches of the Christian Lord.

Theodora was her name, Eminescu's elder daughter. Pale skin, red hair. Eyes like the air above Piatra Neamt on blue autumn mornings when the sparrows rose up over the Carpathian foothills writing their crazy script; air that would turn gray and wet before September was out and seep into the sacks that were Morris's bed. A sliver of cold had already lodged beneath his left shoulder blade.

On his feet, hurriedly wiping his mouth, he started to introduce himself but the girl said, "I know who you are. I've been at my aunt's house in Bucharest where Papa sent me after the soldiers came that terrible night. 'No place for a girl with all this,' Papa said."

"I did not know!"

"Know what?"

He could not say: that ugly old Eminescu with his roving eye and stone brow could have fathered such a creature. "I did not know that you were away."

"Oh?" She looked at him in puzzlement. Footsteps approached. Quickly she reached out and shook his hand, flashing a nervous smile, then fled.

The next night he watched the candle flare in her window and kept the picture of that candle in his eyes as he curled up on his sacks and closed his eyes. He slept his way into a far deep place, like a darkened room where a light like that candle suddenly shone; the light grew stronger, fanning out across water where cobbled houses glimmered against a sky the color of Theodora's face flushed bright from the cold when she came stamping in to see him. When he woke he believed that he'd glimpsed the Black Sea, where the Danube River emptied into the open waters, a place he'd heard the traveling merchants tell of, those lucky enough to have business in the towns along the shore.

He saw Theodora every morning now in the store, working alongside her father. With her hair tied up in a bun and bossing about her little sister Elena, she seemed older than in the barn, and far-away. But when Papa was not there, and Elena was out of earshot, she chattered away in a lilting Romanian. As he rose from the airless hole beneath the store, she told him about her favorite horse, a piebald named Smuts; about how tenderly Elena played the violin until mashing her hand in a well pulley; about the fever that beset her mother on Annunciation Day of 1886, and that took her body to the grave and her soul to Heaven by May 1 of that year; about her brother, Petru, who loved to ride the high white steed of the Romanian cavalry. Looking around to make sure no one was listening, she told him as well about how Petru pitied the army conscripts, especially the poor Jews who were treated like dogs and kept soldiering for fifteen years. They were signed up for the army as staunch youths, Petru had told her, but did not return home until they were old men with bent backs and haggard faces, answering not even to their boyhood names.

Come their celebration called Twelfth Night, with the candles flaring in all the windows, he watched Theodora's candle burning after all the others. She came before the window, hair illuminated by the flame. Her gown loosened, dropped: bare white shoulders. He turned away, hurrying into the depths of his barn, falling prostrate upon the sacks. "Oh Lord, forgive me," he whispered, but saw her in his mind's eye still. In sleep he again saw the candle too, flaring bright, illuminating the expanse of water that opened out beneath a canopy of branches.

On the eve of her sixteenth birthday, his twentieth month on the farm, he welcomed her into the barn where he gave her a wooden figure he'd whittled from a stick of ash. When she pressed her face to his he felt himself grow hot and his legs began to shake, but she whispered that Petru had said the soldiers would soon come; soon, she said, they'd ride through the night looking for the lone boy who lived in the Eminescu farm and rouse him up in the night with swords and bayonets, dragging him off to the army.

After gathering up his belongings he paused in the fields outside the house, looking up at Theodora's window. Darkness, a flickering of light: then darkness opening fully to light. Slipping out of her woolen dress with her back to the window, piling her hair on top of her head, she turned to the window. "Ah, God," he breathed, seeing her full, bare breasts where no husband had touched nor infant suckled; a place as pure and white as in the Song of Solomon. Then the lantern went down and she was gone and he was fleeing under the tabernacle of stars toward the looming Carpathians, running across fields like an endless sea rising and falling, rising again.

After the boat docked at Fairhope Pier and they ate a picnic Miriam had fixed of baked chicken and potato salad and matzoh, Morris and the boys changed into their bathing suits, wading into the grassy shallows while Miriam and the girls dangled their legs over the pier's edge, looking out to the sea. Morris wondered if Miriam's gaze fell on the crossroads of Iasi, her own village not a half-day, by buggy, from his own. She caught his eye and he waved, then looked back to Abe. Had she detected the naked girl he'd glimpsed across the Romanian fields of his own mind?

The Old Dixie Hotel was only a half-mile away. He had seen it from the Bay Queen time and again—the sweeping lawn with its wicker chairs and tables, the shrubs clipped with as much precision as "Red the Barber" used in close-cutting the hair of customers on Dauphin. The hotel was hardly a setting for even a fruit cup that might be kosher for *Pesach*, given the laws that prevented the mixing of meat and milk, and demanded a separate set of dishes altogether for the eight Passover days. But for just a taste of sweet confection on the shores of Mobile Bay, Morris puzzled, what could be so wrong?

"We will go to have Abe's birthday treat!" he announced.

"Morris," Miriam said in disbelief, "it's *Pesach*."

"Please, Mama," Lillian said.

"It's almost over," Abe added.

"We will go," Morris suggested, "and only look."

Miriam frowned.

They changed from their bathing suits into their street clothes and ambled the boardwalk to the hotel.

"Oh, Mama," Lillian said, as they arrived, "such pretty dresses!"

Little girls' frocks in lavender and rose; ladies' long dresses in snow-white and china-blue; and so many ribboned hats. At two o'clock the gentiles, done with church, had made holiday excursions to dine in outdoor elegance.

At the edge of the resort lawn the maitre d' nodded as they approached and gestured toward the tables.

"Thank you," said Morris.

Miriam was silent.

"Step this way," the man said and settled them at a table in the back.

"Near the water?" Morris asked.

He peered back over his shoulder. "As you wish, sir."

They were seated. "Ice cream, please."

"How many?"

Crystal vases held freshly cut lilies; lace napkins graced settings of delicately wrought silver.

"Three," Morris answered, worried now about the cost.

"We are five," Miriam relented.

"It may be . . ." Morris said quietly. "So much money . . ."

"Then we should not be here for two good reasons."

"It's Abe's *birthday*," Lillian implored.

"*Finif*," Morris said to the waiter as Miriam settled uncomfortably back down. "Five, yes, five."

Across the lawn, at a table festive with hats and orchids, he glimpsed a man from the First National Bank: Johnston Bouchard, who'd been helpful in arranging a loan for the store. Morris put up his hand and waved; others at the banker's table turned to look but Bouchard looked away.

"Who's that, Daddy?" Herman asked.

"Maybe is not the man I know."

The waiter appeared with a silver tray holding five sparkling bowls of vanilla ice cream, each with a cherry on top.

Lillian clapped her hands. "It's a party!"

Herman and Abe were already deeply into their desserts but Hannah's was the first spoon to clank. She became absorbed by the flock of children running across the lawn toting straw baskets, darting through privet hedges.

The sun dipped behind a stack of clouds, then burst forth again, making Morris squint as he watched her, little legs churning.

The waiter brought the check and set it down before Morris: 55¢. "*Not so bad*," he thought. "What other desserts do you have?" he asked boldly.

"Morris," Miriam warned. Her hard gaze spoke for itself: They had already strayed far enough.

"We have egg custard," said the waiter.

Morris smiled at his wife.

"Key lime, pecan pie, chocolate mousse." The waiter paused. "Shall I take back the check?"

Miriam asked to look at it first, exclaiming, "Morris!"

"I am only tasting with my ears," he said to her in Romanian.

"No fair," said Lillian. "At least speak Yiddish."

The waiter backed away.

"Did you see!" She handed it to Morris who examined the bill again. The numbers read $5.50.

"Hannah!" he called angrily. "We are leaving!"

Elegant hats at a dozen tables turned at his words; from underneath them gazed smooth, puzzled faces. They stayed fixed, staring, as the waiter walked up for the money.

Perspiring, Morris peeled off three two-dollar bills: all he had.

Hannah returned, breathing hard.

"We are going." By the tables of hats turning back around as he passed, by the men in two-tone shoes and children returning to tables with baskets heaped with bright eggs, he led his family.

"Look, Daddy!" Hannah reached into the pocket of her dress and produced a blue and red-striped egg. "Look what I found."

He stopped and lifted the egg from her hand. "We must leave this here," he said, setting it down. "It is nothing of ours."

As Hannah started to cry he swung her up on his shoulders, cantering a few yards with her on his back until this new game stopped her tears.

They caught the six o'clock ferry home, black clouds piling up like dark coats on a table, a wholesale order, unboxed, filling the sky. When the vessel docked at Dauphin the rain began to fall.

Hansom cabs with strapping piebalds and Model T Fords with poised drivers awaited some passengers; not the kinds of customers who frequented M. Kleinman & Sons. As the rain drove down harder, Morris and his family raced huddled together beneath a picnic blanket. He glanced up to see a swan-necked lady in a cab sniggering at the poor sight of them, like urchins in the storm.

They slept beneath the drumming of rain. It poured down the rooftops and storefronts with the words CEILING FANS or ICE-BOXES painted above windows. It aggravated insomniacs like the dentist, Asa Spicer, who lived and worked on a second-floor Dauphin Street address that he'd taken over from E.T. Belsaw, and was the rare black doctor, as Belsaw had been, sometimes sought out by white people in need; he tumbled to sleep so late he was not awake to receive patients until almost noon, no matter how they cried in abscessed dolor in his hall. It lulled to sleep the night attendant at Fosko Soda, who sank into a cot near the window that had been broken by a rock from Bennie Lubel's slingshot; water from the storm came spritzing through the cracks. To the boys at the Catholic Boys home, the rain was like God's great blessing; they had a baseball game scheduled against the Hebrew Athletic Club that was sure to be rained out. None of them could hit the tough fast ball of Lou Prince.

Monday it rained, Tuesday and Wednesday it rained, and by Thursday the wood-brick streets swelled up like loaves of Matranga's bread. Peter Dais's public dray banged down the warped street carrying coal and wood under heavy tarpaulin. Horses clopped tentatively down slippery slopes. On their way to Barton Academy, Lillian and Abe sloshed down the sidewalks, until it made more sense to walk barefoot, although Mama told them, time and again, bare feet were signs of the poor and the colored, and that there were old shoes enough in the storeroom to supply cast-off's to wear. At Yerby school Herman and Hannah played out back in a skiff that a fisherman used to haul his children.

By Friday morning the water soaked the sandbags laid before the entrance to the store. A slow tide, it lapped at the threshold of the door, rising over the edge, creeping into the showroom.

"On racks, *everything,* on racks," Morris said, "hurry!" With Abe and Herman and Miriam he boxed every last shoe and pair of socks and stuck them on shelves, and tripled up every shirt and jacket onto coat hangers and jammed them onto the racks that they elevated higher with concrete blocks.

Lying in bed that night he heard the noise: the water of his dream breaking loose, spilling through places he could neither hide nor seal. In nightshirt he hurried downstairs, feeling the water slither around his bare feet.

Rain streamed down the wall near the cash register, puddling near the boot stand and swirling beneath the dress racks. He fell against the wall and slapped his hands against the cracks. Chunks of plaster broke off in his fists. He spread his arms out to hold the water back. It gushed over his shoulders. Hair soaked, night clothes heavy with water, the taste of broken plaster and old gutter water in his mouth he prayed to God for salvation.

"Daddy," Lillian screamed behind him, "it bit me!" A rat wriggled frantically toward the door.

In fury Morris picked up a display rack and heaved it at the black shadow, but it was gone. The heavens suddenly quieted, the water soon slowing to a trickle in the house.

Early the next morning Hugh Mulherin came to visit Lillian, setting his black doctor bag down next to her bed and examining the rat bite. The rodent had left red puncture marks near her ankle. He felt her for fever, held a stethoscope to her chest, then washed the wound with hydrogen peroxide. "I think she'll be fine."

Morris, who'd sat up all night damp-eyed with worry, was finally able to get back to work, mopping up the store, setting his clothes racks out on the street to catch the returning sun. Lutchnik sauntered down the block and told him that, in Bialystok, Poland, he had also seen torrential rains. At their doorways, he recalled, the townspeople had stood watching the square turn to a wall of water, the bins of fruits and vegetables left to rot, the donkeys braying at the sheets of wind.

But never had he seen it as here in Mobile.

When the sun rose higher the day laborers from the Norwegian Seamen's Hall took up sledgehammers to pound out the water-logged streets. Lutchnik strolled back to his store. Five minutes later he dragged out a sign offering two-for-one coats: "After storm special," he called it.

Buster Rhodes retaliated with a 50¢ overalls sale. Morris added free Zigorsky's Foot Elixir with every purchase of boots.

Reiss jumped in the fray by offering $1.75 boots, and Lutchnik shot back with boots the same price and free peppermint swizzles, too.

"Pastor Gold," Morris scratched on his board, "with raincoat and galoshes."

The price war ran to Lower Dauphin where Hammel's discounted men's great coats by a third; on to Lower Government where Rips offered higher prices for watches and jewelry pawned.

While leafing through a copy of the *Mobile Register* Lutchnik hatched his second strategy. He tucked the paper under his arm and sauntered over to Morris's.

"The Lebanese, he is beating us. The Italian, he is beating us. Even the German he is making us look like Joe Shmo. You and me, we should kill each other so that they can win? Look." He leafed through the *Mobile Register* and offered Morris a plan.

By Sunday Morris's four-inch ad appeared: a muddy photo of panama hats and Palm Beach jackets under the promotion: "Morris Kleinman. The King of Cut Rate. High Quality and Lowest Prices In Town."

On the following page, though, in a six-inch ad, a portrait of Lutchnik himself looked back above fancy script: "Beat the heat and prices too. Lutchnik's will beat any price in town."

Lutchnik gloated when Morris walked across the street, rapped on his door and said only, "The first time you win, Sam. The next? Do not even dream."

Buster Smythe of Modern Furniture installed a fancy, electric light display in front of his store: a chair that, as light bulbs clicked on and off, rocked back and forth. "Very modern," the customers up and down the street agreed.

It was late that same night that Morris cranked down his awning, hollering, "Good night," to Sahadi, and "*Gutte nacht,*" to Mirsky, and "*Buenas noches*" to Pastor. German and Polish and Spanish voices called back from the street.

Lillian began to complain of feeling hot, and Miriam decided that a stroll through the night air would prove salubrious. With Morris and Hannah they headed to Bienville Square, leaving the boys behind.

Immediately Abe and Herman took up their positions on the store balcony and brought out the BB gun they'd won use of for two days in a marble game.

Abe sighted the water cistern on top of Modern and pinged the steps leading up to it. He waved the barrel at the light-bulb chair below. It rocked back and forth. "You're chicken," Herman goaded.

Abe pulled the trigger and the BB hit the side of the Modern building.

"Gimme," said Herman. He squeezed the trigger and one bulb of the rocker popped like a fire cracker and died. The rocker flickered back and forth, a wounded bird.

"Hooligans!" Buster Smythe cried from the street. "Your sons are hooligans!"

They squatted low on the balcony, then heard Daddy as he came strolling back from the square: "Do not speak of my sons like this!"

"They've tried to murder my beautiful electric rocker!"

"Your electric rocker stinks."

"It brings in more customers than you ever could."

"A fancy sign is not a man who runs a store, who knows a customer's name."

"Enough of your baloney, Kleinman!"

"My sons they have done nothing and you will not disgrace the Kleinmans on this street that is our home!"

Crouching low, they crept backwards into the apartment, hearing

Daddy: "Herman! Abraham!" He assured Smythe angrily, "They are asleep."

Into their beds they leapt, kicking off their shoes and pushing them onto the floor from under the sheets.

"I heard a shoe," Lillian's voice whispered, close on them now. "Did you do it?"

Abe set up a snore; Herman followed suit.

"Don't play possum with me!" Lillian warned. "I know it was y'all." She pinched Abe's ear.

They heard Daddy's voice in other rooms.

"Shh!"

But he was not coming in to scold. He and Mama had gone quietly into their room, and the boys heard the low, muffled sound of crying. Then they heard Mama leaving that room and going to Lillian's, but the crying continued low and deep, where only Daddy remained.

"Rat bite fever," Dr. Mulherin concluded the next morning, prescribing aspirin and bed rest. He said he had seen the sickness, usually occurring several days after a bite, in dock workers and sailors. He touched her ankle. The skin had grown red and puffy.

He produced a scalpel from his doctor bag, went into the kitchen and lit a gas burner, then passed the blade through the flame. "Ma'am," he said to Miriam, returning with the blade, "hold her tight."

Lillian began to cry.

The doctor gripped her shin. "Brave girl, now."

As he cut the skin and the pus drained out, Lillian writhed and wept, her howls flying up the walls and out the French doors and onto all Dauphin. Then she grew quiet, whimpering.

Miriam sent Morris out for chickens from Berson's and boiled them for Lillian to sip the broth. When Lillian's fever rose that night and she tried to throw off the covers, Miriam insisted she stay wrapped up. She swabbed her daughter's face with rubbing alcohol to help her feel cool.

In the aftermath of the rains the April air grew as hot and damp as summer, the humidity curling the pages of the accounts receivable book, the smell of fish vendors and banana boats at the docks drifting up from the waterfront. As if July had already arrived, Abe and Herman pulled the mattresses off their beds and dragged them to the balcony, sleeping beneath the coastal stars.

The following night there was a war rally at Bienville Square, and Lillian yearned to run there with the others. She closed her eyes and heard the throng denouncing the dastardly Kaiser and cheering for the American doughboys. She sang along quietly to a tune played on Daddy's Victrola:

> *Jimmy was a soldier brave and bold*
> *Katy was a maid with hair of gold,*
> *Like an act of fate,*
> *Kate was standing at the gate,*
> *Watching all the boys on dress parade.*
> *Jimmy with the girls was just a gawk,*
> *Stuttered every time he tried to talk . . .*

She smiled at the thought of the poor but earnest boy in a bright, spanking Army uniform, faraway in the fields of France, yearning sweetly for her.

> *K-K-K-Katy, beautiful Katy,*
> *You're the only g-g-g-girl that I adore;*
> *When the m-m-m-moon shines,*
> *Over the cowshed,*
> *I'll be waiting at the k-k-k-kitchen door.*

But her fever rose even higher, and her teeth clattered, and Morris hurried to the pharmacy where Paul Molyneux counted out more aspirin pills into a jar. As Morris fed another one to Lillian, he said a prayer to God, blessed be His name, to lay a gentle finger on her chest. "Let this sickness," he whispered, "not enter my precious child's heart."

The next night, wrapped in blankets, Lillian sat near the front window to catch the fresh air while Miriam cranked up the Victrola. As Morris and Pablo and Sahadi and Reiss and Spitzer sat in their chairs and smoked their cigars, they fell silent, wiping their eyes, listening to her gentle voice rising with the phonograph's:

> *Jimmy thought he'd like to take a chance,*
> *See if he could make the Kaiser dance,*
> *Stepping to a tune,*
> *All about the silv'ry moon,*
> *This is what they hear in far off France.*
> *K-K-K-Katy, beautiful Katy,*
> *You're the only g-g-g-girl that I adore;*
> *When the m-m-m-moon shines,*
> *Over the cowshed,*
> *I'll be waiting at the k-k-k-kitchen door.*

In the small hours, with the heavy air stacked in crates as high as Heaven, Morris and Miriam woke to her voice calling out: "Mama, Daddy!" Abe got there first, circling his sister in an embrace. Morris touched his cheek to his daughter's: it was damp and cool.

As Miriam threw her arms around them all they thanked God for this blessing, hearing the start, high above, of soft, calming rain.

Lonesome Whistle

Lillian returned to school the following Monday still feeling tired but did not complain, fearing she'd be sent back to the tedium of bed. By Wednesday, halfway to school with Abe, she told him to walk on, saying she wanted to linger in the sunshine. She leaned against a building and took a deep breath. Her throat was scratchy. At lunch she asked to be excused from the weekly session of calisthenics.

Dr. Mulherin said that Lillian, chaperoned by Miriam, might find her constitution strengthened by a visit to Citronelle, and that he would make sure Dr. Michaels of that village kept a special eye out for her well-being. At that health resort a half-hour's train ride north of Mobile, the salt breezes of the Gulf blending with the cool air of the piney hills were said to prove a salubrious clime. The mineral waters, full of iron, would put the pluck back into the sweet child's spirit. And for Miriam the Chatauqua entertainments—oratorical presentations and string quartets—would offer welcome diversion from worries over a sick child.

Morris agreed they should soon go.

That Sunday, still in Mobile, Lillian climbed on the carousel at Monroe Park to ride alongside little Hannah, Mama and Daddy looking on. On the painted horse she felt a hot pain in her right knee. Her brow was flushed.

"Lillian?" Miriam said, hurrying up to her.

"Just dizzy, Mama, from the ride."

After school the next day she could hardly make it back up the steps from the store, gripping the banister to pull herself along until Abe rushed up to help her. By morning, her throat aflame, she wished only to sit in a chair.

Dr. Mulherin came—the sight of him at the door with his gray eyes and black bag made Morris's own chest wrinkle inside—and this time held his stethoscope against Lillian's chest a long time. He peered down her throat, then shook his head. "Damnable strep," he whispered.

"My knees hurt," Lillian agonized. "And my . . ." She touched her elbow.

"Let's get you to bed, child. Miriam, fix up some of that famous broth of yours."

Out of earshot of Lillian, he told Morris and Miriam that the girl's resistance to strep had been weakened, most likely, by the episode of rat bite fever. He feared now a relapse of the fever that had coursed through her years earlier.

"Rheumatic fever," he said. "It licks the joints"—he paused— "and bites the heart. But she has a youthful hardiness. That, with prayers, will go a long way." By the next morning Lillian could not so much as climb out of the bed when Miriam tried to dress her.

Rheumatic fever. Morris knew too well the awful words. He repeated them aloud as he walked alone through the clothes racks. He passed the rip in the wall where the rat had leapt out and saw it, like a black demon, biting Lillian's heart.

He put his hands over his eyes and tried to press the picture away.

Through that night and the next, Miriam was up, hour to hour, keeping vigil, as Lillian turned into the pillows, rolled onto her back, reached out her hand and implored, "Mama, can't you do something?" Holding a damp cloth to her forehead, Miriam told her stories—anything at all to get her to settle down, to grow drowsy—speaking of her own girlhood in Iasi:

"My hair, Lily, how beautiful my mother used to fix my hair. In the mornings, when the sun was just coming up, Mama would brush my long brown hair, how long it was then, and roll it up over her left hand, like Daddy's *tfillin*, wound it tightly until it left its own mark of tresses across her skin, then unroll it and roll it up into a ball again. She'd fasten it up on top of my head with a pin Papa had brought from Odessa.

"I looked in the mirror, Lily, and saw myself change from a girl to a young woman. Ah, my mother's touch." Glancing in the mirror now Miriam saw herself, at thirty-seven, hair streaked gray, looking very much like her mother had looked the last year of her life.

"At night, Mama would let my hair back out long, brushing, and brushing. I can still feel ..."

"You weren't poor, like Daddy," Lillian said.

"We were not poor, we were not rich."

"Then Grandma Lilith died."

"Do not say it like that."

"But Mama?" Lillian sat up in the bed. "You told me she died, and that Papa Weiss married another woman who you hated, and she was so mean that you and Benny left for America."

"This is what happened, yes, but the truth, she is here before me, my Lillian, she is living here now." Miriam tapped her heart. "The sons, they say the *kaddish*, but the daughters, they keep the ones who leave living here until we are all in the world to come."

"But where *do* we go, Mama?" Lillian asked frantically. "Bubbe Lilith, where is she now?"

"In here, *mein shayna madele*, here." She took Lillian's hand and clasped it to her bosom, feeling her own heart pounding. "In here, brushing my hair, very softly, *mein shayna madele*." She stroked Lillian's hair. "Softly, when I stop to listen."

She tried to play dominoes with Abe and Herman, but sank back spent in the pillow. Her ankles throbbed, her knees and elbows.

To soothe the ache, Miriam bought a bottle of wintergreen oil and rubbed it gently on her arms and legs. The smell of mint brightened the room, as though the four walls held no sickbed at all.

Before long when Miriam changed the bed linens and laid fresh covers over her, Lillian cried out from the touch of the blankets on her feet. Morris went to Pafandakis's fruit market and returned with a small empty crate marked, "Satsumas," and set it at the end of the bed. Lillian rested her feet on a towel folded inside it, and Miriam draped the covers over the crate.

Dr. Mulherin prescribed a pill to strengthen the beat of her heart, Digitalis. When Morris raced to the pharmacy, he waited anxiously while Paul Molyneux ground up the Foxglove and rolled it into the Digitalis pills. After Lillian took doses for three days her heart beat with greater conviction, her breathing came more easily.

"Tell me more stories," she implored.

Herman swung his legs from the bedside and told about going to Monroe Park with Hannah, and how they held hands in the water below Tucker's Wharf.

"I love Tucker's Wharf."

"Daddy knows him, Mr. Tucker."

"He's fat, isn't he?"

"Fat and rich. Everybody pays a nickel, Abe and I figured, and you add up all the people who go there and it's a lot of nickels.

"So Hannah was with me down in front of the pier and I was teaching her how to grab hands and go under and pull together so we'd bump our *tuchases*. Hannah, she came up crying and laughing. 'You bumped my *tuchas*,' she said. I told her that's the name of the game, 'Bump your *tuchas*.'

"That's when Daddy, he was watching us, told us about Mr. Tucker, and this man with a big belly hanging out of his shirt who turned out to be Mr. Tucker waved at us and said, 'How y'all doin?'

"Hannah told him, 'We been playing Bump Your Tuckers!'

"Mr. Tucker smiled and said, 'Doin' what now, y'all say?'

"'Watch us, Mr. Tucker,' she said and she grabbed my hands and we went under and thumped our fannies together so hard I came up laughing and slapping at the water.

"'Bump your Tuckers,' Hannah said again. She climbed up onto the platform where the old man was watching us. 'Right here,' she said, pointing to her bottom, 'this is your Tucker.'"

Lillian leaned her head back on the pillow and laughed until she coughed.

Abe came to take Herman's place. "I wish we could go for a walk, big sister."

"I'm sure game."

"How about Farmer Laney's?"

"All the way out there?"

"We could have us one helluva melon bust."

"How about if I close my eyes and you take me there." She squeezed his fingers.

"We're heading down the road alongside Dog River," Abe began, "and just as we get to the curve that leads to the fishing hole where Pastor once took Daddy to show him how to hook a croaker, we turn the other way, beyond where all those churches are. Farmer Laney's is out beyond the hill, and seeing as how him and Daddy are friends from the time he came around with a load of watermelons, we can just walk right up to his front door.

"Nobody's at home, but I know he won't mind if we head off into his field. Farmer Laney can't read or write, but he knows better than any man alive how to grow himself some good eatin' melons.

"We walk up the rows where the vines are the thickest, and there's this beauty, all green and striped and fat like a sow. I drag it up and get it high on my shoulder, like this, and we walk on to the edge of the field where the stones make a fence. That's when I throw it down, and Lord when it busts is it good and red inside!"

"You taste it first," Lillian said.

"No, I want you."

Lillian was quiet, eyes still shut.

"Well?" Abe asked.

She wiped at her mouth. "It's good and wet and sweet."

Miriam came to the door. "Time for dinner. Let Lily rest."

"OK, Mama." He waited until she was gone from the door and leaned close to Lillian's face. "You'll be fine," he said, "you'll be swell," and listened, his own breath held still, for the sound and movement of hers. He bent and touched his lips to hers, stealing the sickness away.

The pain rises in her chest. She turns, moaning. "I'm drowning," she whispers, pushing at the pillows.

Dr. Mulherin returns and presses his stethoscope against her heart.

"Listen," he says to Morris, handing him the instrument. What Morris hears is a whooshing sound, like a sad wind on the shore.

"Do something, Hugh!"

Mulherin hands Morris a vial of codeine tablets, instructs him to give them as needed for pain, then looks down at the floor. When the doctor looks back up he says he is going to five o'clock Mass at the Cathedral and will return in an hour. "Be strong, Morris." He nods to Lillian. "For her."

"These will help, my Lillian," Morris says. "Oh, Lord God above . . ."

She takes a pill from her father, and though she feels her fever spiking, the pain subsides, like the water drawing back from the shore. She reaches out to touch Daddy's face. Her hand is quivering.

She begins to float.

The room revolves slowly as she hears Daddy's story about a trolley and rain and her small, pattering feet on the new cement walk of Dauphin Street as he grabs her up and hurries on to Selma Gollub's and then to the shop, finding Miriam already giving birth to Herman. She hears the words of the Passover prayer he sings softly to her, the memory of spring brightening the sultry air: *dayenu*. "It would be enough a blessing," he says, "to find your mother in time for the new baby. The Lord, blessed be His Name, was good to us on that day."

As he talks, the French doors leading outside seem to open right on her own room, and she sees the girls from Barton leaning in to see her, too. The crosses they wear on silver chains around their necks glimmer in the light, their flaxen hair shines. They reach out to her and she feels their flickering hands pulling her toward them and imagines her own hair golden, too. "*Dayenu,*" Daddy is singing gently, although it is May, but knowing that Passover is her favorite holiday. The song puts her in mind of the family gathered around the *seder* table, azaleas pushing up to the back windows in ragged profusion, the store scented with the tangle of wisteria finding its way over the fire escape, the Japanese magnolias in the empty lot behind Friedlander's store perfuming the night so that even the laborers, their bodies given to hot water and soap every two weeks, smell passably fragrant in the lotion of flowers deepening the *Pesach* air. "Christ's last supper," her girlfriends from Barton call it, and Daddy has told her that the Christians of the village where he was a boy, far-off and gray-dreary Piatra Neamt, believed Jews drank the blood of a Christian boy on that night and tore through the *shtetl* to revenge the savage act; but her own friends from Barton, she tells Daddy, they would not do such as this! They envy her long, curly hair!

"Piatra Neamt," he is telling her now, "I tell the man I am from a little place in Romania, very cold."

She has heard this story before but she loves it all the same: the wide city street with its Italian restaurants Daddy tells her about, the strange, Northern city where, knapsack on his shoulder, he walks into the big, red-brick, gloomy station where the thin, red-moustached man waits silently at the ticket booth. Morris Kleinman: twenty-five years old, five years out of Romania, his bride and infant daughter behind in the big city to the north, making his way alone to this Southern city where the train has terminated its run and he has first looked for work but decided to move on. It is March, and still cold, and the sea he has dreamed about is still all too far away.

Walking across the polished floor to the ticket master, the giant chandelier revolving above him in the drafty station, he reaches into his left pocket and takes out the first of his two money clips, this one for travel. With the change in his pockets there are eight dollars and sixteen cents here—all he saved from the New Jersey junk company—and he prays to God it is a number borne of majesty and good fortune as the *rebbe* told him all things in mankind have their numbers, good and bad.

He tells her all this again—Is it the same night, she wonders, or another? Has a day passed since Daddy began telling her the story, or a week? Why is his mouth twisted in agony as he looks down at her?—and the tale grows ever more vivid, as though she is at his side:

Morris reaches the window, places the money on the counter as the clerk counts out the last nickels and two-cent pieces and pennies and then he says, "One ticket, please, to a small town, very warm, my shoulder, I cannot live in the cold, in New York always so cold." The man is counting out the money. "I always want to swim, I dream of a sea, a warm sea." He is counting all the paper dollars and silver dollars, the buffalo nickels and Jefferson dimes. "A good place to work, a good place for a Jew." And the man at the window finishes his counting and concludes, "Eight sixteen," running one finger down a ticket guide and coming to stop on Atlanta, Montgomery, Demopolis, Jackson, Georgiana, Citronelle, Mobile.

"Mobile, Alabama," the ticket clerk says, sweeping up Morris's money into his cash register and handing back a bright orange ticket. "Next train to Mobile, two sharp, that's in ten minutes. Platform two."

And he is clutching the ticket and walking toward that platform, and the train is already there, the steam hissing and unfurling from under the black iron belly, and the conductor receives his ticket and he is stepping aboard as the whistle blows, and he is opening his arms to her.

And Mama and Abe and Herman and Hannah are there too, and

Pablo and Marta Pastor and little David, and the Lutchniks and Metzgers and Mutchniks and Friedlanders and Holbergs and Reisses and Hoffmans and Princes and the girls of Barton, and the stationmaster's voice saying, "She's going, God blessed be His Name, she's going," but she is saying, "Take me there," as the train starts into the darkness with other passengers' faces at the window, and Daddy's and Mama's arms closest of all.

The train to Mobile sounding, with howls and tears and arms pressed close, the conductor crying, "All aboard for Mobile."

For Mobile . . . Yisgadal, vyisgadash. . . . For Mobile . . . Oh Lily, don't go. Our beloved . . . sh'mah raboh . . .

Arms, faces, kisses. The dying voices, smaller, calling.

Darkness, and peace.

□

They covered the mirrors, walked about in their socks, sat mutely receiving the Pastors, and Father O'Connor, and Sahadi, and Matranga, and all the men and women of the synagogue.

Even when the clocks were set going again, chiming mournfully through the store, time stood still, the day of Lillian's passing stretching out to all days to come.

Morris and Miriam could not sleep but lay down sobbing in the pillows. Morris took to getting up again and going to his office, staring blankly at the ledgers, smoking down a cigar until he nodded off. When dawn came he leapt up, still in his clothes, grabbing his broom and attacking the walk.

He found himself talking aloud to Papa, telling him about the horrible tragedy that had befallen sweet Lillian. He tried to compose a letter to him at Golda's house in Bucharest: "Dear Papa, The beautiful child you never met, our dear Lillian, blessed is her memory," but unable to continue spoke the letter aloud. He finally walked to Western Union and telegraphed: "Beloved Lillian died in June. We are suffering. Morris."

An answer came from Golda. "We are in sorrow for Lillian. I must go to Poland. Papa will stay here with Uncle Shmuel."

"Soon," Morris whispered, counting in his head the little savings they kept in the First National, knowing it was far from the amount needed to sail the Atlantic and fetch Papa. Papa was not well enough to travel alone. "But I will come for you," he pledged. "When the war is done."

But the war raged right into Mobile.

Billy Spitzer came home from the Marne, having lost his right arm in a German artillery barrage; he sat before his family's furniture store, telling neighbors of freezing winds and bloodied trenches, while his German-born parents, Max and Inge, positioned an American flag proudly above their door. Kaiser Wilhelm II, said Max, should "only burn for all time in Hell, a bullet to his head is too good for such a criminal."

Lutchnik's nephew, who'd taught school in Biloxi, was hit at the Marne, too, in the belly, but never came home. Ebbecke's brother inhaled poison gas at St. Mihiel and lay in a London hospital, his lungs seared with chlorine poisoning. One of Morris's customers, Mr. Jonas, a farmer in Toulminville, had a son in the Meuse-Argonne Offensive who did return, but like a different son, suffering from what Jonas called "shell shock." Like a scarecrow the youth leaned against the fence outside Jonas's house, blinking, and mute.

When Miriam heard about tragedies that befell the sons of their friends, she walked to their homes, holding their hands silently, their grief, like salt water, deepening her own open wound.

For his part, Morris put a poster in the window of M. Kleinman & Sons—*Buy Liberty Bonds! Support Your Troops!*—and, when he swept the walk at daybreak, kept a keen eye on the debris. The Red Cross poster at Bienville Square had announced, *Do Your Bit, Save the Pit,* and urged citizens to bring date seeds and peach stones, prune pits and cherry pits, to Red Cross headquarters. *The carbon produced from these materials when placed in respirators,* the poster explained, *will save soldiers' lives.* Morris carried half a cupful to the Red Cross on the second day.

Then three children died up the Old Shell Road in Spring Hill of wracking fever and cramps, and two more with the same symptoms in the riverfront village of Plateau. The *Register* ran an account of the deaths with the headline: *Spanish Flu Takes Local Toll.*

When Morris tried to read aloud this awful news of the influenza that had circled the world to enter their town, Miriam said, "No, this too I cannot hear," and ran to Herman and Abe and commanded, "Do not leave this house."

"But Mama!" they cried in unison, and looked to Daddy who rocked and said gently, reassuringly, "They are strong," while saying his prayer for their safekeeping.

The boys rode their bikes to Monroe Park, perching on the fence near John Fowler's airplane and listening once again to how he alone had invented the airplane and first made flight. Showing off his newest invention—a seaplane meant to rise straight up from the water—Fowler railed that Orville and Wilbur Wright had traveled to Mobile at the turn of the century, copying down his wing strut design. He asked for donations to finance the completion of this newest machine.

He waved his hands in the air and continued, "See that German Fokker there?"

Abe and Herman peered upwards, imagining a monoplane bursting out of the sun, its machine gun spitting fire.

"Against my aeroplanes, the Huns wouldn't have a prayer!"

The onlookers cheered and flicked coins into Fowler's hat and took turns climbing into the cockpit.

"It's not your fault," one man cried, "the Yankees don't want us to claim having done something 'fore they have."

"Or get money for doing it!" another joined in.

When Herman took his position in the pilot's seat he aimed an invisible machine gun and rat-tatted the enemy craft. And when he took up his position on the store balcony that evening he looked out at cumulus clouds building. From those clouds floated German zeppelins, ready to drop their bombs on Mobile Bay.

Abe began to box. At the rackety YMCA, he wrapped his fists in tape and stuck them deep into gloves and banged at a punching bag, feeling Lillian touch his shoulder. When the Y was closed for a week out of fear of contagion from the Spanish flu, he took to walking by the somnolent square shadow-boxing the air, remembering the soft brush of her sisterly lips. "Dammit!" he cried, "why did this happen?"

As the flu receded like the summer's heat, and fall brought days packed with school, followed by Hebrew studies, then helping Daddy ready the early Thanksgiving sales, he raced to the Y after dinner, sparring with other boys.

When he saw the sign for the Sunday evening exhibition—*Knock out the Ukrainian Giant and Win Big, Nov. 10, four o'clock*—he grabbed Herman and they headed to the docks.

Among the stevedores and banana men and other eager schoolboys they watched in awe the Ukrainian Giant, a behemoth named Pavel Chemenko with red chin whiskers and a forehead that looked as though it had been flattened by a skillet. The Ukrainian lumbered about dopily, awaiting the next challenger, wiping the back of his hand across his skillet brow and flicking away greasy sweat.

From boys no taller than Herman, to weekend pugilists like Jake Ripps, Mobilians laid down a quarter to take turns battling the traveling boxer. Any fool who lasted three minutes on his feet kept his money; any hardhead enduring five doubled it.

Into the ring clambered a raw teen with barber bowl haircut and boxing gloves dangling at his side like loose sacks. When the referee sounded the bell he lit into Chemenko with lightning velocity. He delivered fists to the Ukrainian's ribs, sent a volley of jabs at his shoulder, punched at his chest.

All the while Chemenko rocked on the balls of his feet and

grinned with his snaggled teeth, deflecting the youth's gloves whenever they came toward his face, a bored champion swatting away flies. Tongue soon hanging out, panting and wheezing, the youth dropped his guard. Chemenko put his left hand up, glove big and round as a cannonball, and bonked the challenger's ear. The boy went down flat on his chest.

The crowd clapped and jeered.

Next came a broad-shouldered docks worker. He went at Chemenko with machine-like precision, arms pumping back and forth at his midriff, head down, working his way closer and closer to the champion's chin. His left hand cut upwards toward Chemenko; again, the Ukrainian merely batted away the blow at his head.

When Chemenko returned the left hook, his punch found its mark. On his knees, the bell gonging, the longshoreman shook his head woozily until the referee helped him up and out of the ring.

"Hey," Abe exclaimed, "look who's next."

Louis Flynn, the policeman's son, leapt to the ropes.

"C'mon, Loui*ee*!" Abe called.

Thirty seconds later Flynn was sent reeling against the corner. Rather than go back up against the monstrous boxer he dropped to one knee, leaning over and spitting blood.

Chip Calhoun appeared at Abe's side. "What's wrong, Abie Baby?" he taunted. "Why don't you get up there?"

Abe hurried into the ring, digging in his pockets for the pennies and nickels to make a wager.

The referee tied on his gloves. Abe looked over his shoulder and winked. The bell rang.

He set the crowd laughing, dancing in the corner out of range of Chemenko, waiting for the moment to strike. Peanut shells showered him from the crowd. Chemenko walked toward him. Abe danced back. Chemenko came closer.

The clock raced into the third minute.

"Now!" Herman cried and Abe, hearing Lillian's voice repeating his name, spun putting all his weight into a right hook that caught the smiling brute on the side of the skull. Chemenko stepped back and tottered. Abe felt Lillian next to him, wrapping her arms around him, celebrating his triumph.

He raised his hands heralding the cheers of the crowd, then dropped them to his side.

Chemenko reached out and popped him on the chin and he crumpled to the mat like a balloon figure whose air had whooshed out.

"Next challenger!" the referee shouted.

From the dock they staggered their way across the railroad tracks. A train whistle left a long, sad song in the air. They turned by the wall into the alley that led to the tracks. At the end of the alley appeared two figures like dark shadows. The figures stepped forward, blocking their way: Flynn and Calhoun.

"Hey, get out of our way," Herman warned.

"This your alley?" Flynn said.

"Damn right it is," Abe said.

"Do you see 'Christ killers' written on the sign?" Flynn asked.

"I don't see any 'Christ killers,'" answered Calhoun.

"We never killed anybody," Herman said.

"Baby brother gonna tell us what to do?" Flynn said.

"Move out of the way," Abe warned.

"What?" Calhoun prodded. "Jews own this here, too?"

Like a savage cat Herman leapt to Calhoun's neck, taking him down. Abe went at Flynn, the two becoming a tangle of arms and legs on the ground. Flynn managed to stand and start kicking at Abe's ribs, but this time Herman reached around and grabbed him and yanked hard, bringing him to the ground.

"Little horse butt," Flynn cried.

"Big horse butt," Herman shouted in his face, pinning Flynn's shoulder with his knees and pounding his chest.

A whistle shrieked from the other side of the wall.

"Holy Mother Mary," Flynn cried, "it's Pa!"

Herman leapt off. Flynn and Calhoun scrambled to their feet as they heard the voice shouting, "You kids, wait'll I catch you!"

Before Officer Flynn made it around the wall to spot them, they took off in a pack, rushing to the end of the alley, stumbling across the railroad tracks.

"Tell and we'll whip your hides!" Flynn said.

"We already whipped yours!" Herman shouted back.

"Shut up," Abe said to his brother. "Daddy finds what we were doin' *he'll* be whipping *us!*"

"But we did whip 'em, we did."

"Shut up," Abe repeated, wiping the blood from his nose. "You're a kid, what do you know?"

Morris heard the voice before daybreak. "War . . ." it seemed to call out. He sat up, went out onto the balcony. "Paris . . ." The words were deep and reverberant. He leaned over, looked down the street, past the Cathedral still dark, glimpsing the edges of Bienville Square, all quiet. He turned back into the bedroom and checked on Herman and Abe—both in bed, groaning, snoring.

The voice broke through the darkness again: "Germans . . ."

Morris slipped on his clothes—it was still too early to wrap *tfillin* and recite morning prayers—fished up a cigar stub and went downstairs. On the street he heard the sound again, and now recognized Gummy Fleurnoy's voice.

Why was the *Register* reporter, at this hour, calling out the news? He had heard Gummy, in previous times, shouting through his megaphone the baseball scores, and boxing matches, and sightings of hurricanes. Like a town crier he would stand at his second-floor window, updating the public on breaking events. While the telegraph clacked inside the office, he gave voice to the *dit-dah-dits,* bringing opera to victories and defeats.

To catch the words better, he walked two blocks downtown, past the Queen Theater where *The Beast of Berlin* was showing, past the

Crown Theater, where *Birth of a Nation* was opening that day. Gummy's voice bellowed out: "Eleven o'clock . . ."

"Eleven?" Morris said, looking up at the clock over the courthouse whose hands approached only five o'clock.

Suddenly a small figure in cap and knickers, his arms filled with papers, came hurrying toward Morris along the sidewalk, shouting, "Extry! Extry!"

Morris dug into his pocket for five pennies and exchanged them for a paper. The boy raced on, calling, "Extry! Extry!"—lights began to flick on in windows—"the War is over!"

Morris read aloud: "World War Is Ended. German Autocracy Conquered; Surrender Signed; Peace Reigns." The paper in his hands was shaking.

From the direction of M. Kleinman & Sons he heard a high-pitched banging. Catty-corner, in front of Spitzer's Furniture, he spied Max Spitzer, holding a cooking pot and clanging it with a spoon.

He turned his attention back to the newspaper: "The armistice was signed at five o'clock A.M. Paris time, and hostilities will cease at eleven o'clock this morning Paris time."

A *thunk-thunk* joined the clanging. Billy Spitzer, next to his father, used his lone left arm to beat a skillet against a window ledge.

"The var is over," Max shouted. "Vee beat the Satan!"

Marta Pastor, in her housecoat, came blearily onto the sidewalk. Pablo followed with little David right behind. Father O'Connor appeared and held his hands together in prayer and faced the top of the Cathedral, then hopped on his crutches.

"Extry! Extry!" the newsboy shouted again, running back down to the square.

Neighbors streamed onto Dauphin. Pots and pans and spoons and forks became instruments of an orchestra. The racket rose, a tintinnabulation waking every last sleeper.

"Oh," Morris exclaimed, "my beautiful Miriam!"

Since Lillian's passing, he had not seen her eyes brighten; now, she stood on the sidewalk and clapped her hands. Abe and Herman had dragged out their own pots and pans to join the kitchen parade. Miriam took up one of them.

A phonograph record blared from a window:

Oh the Prussians were crushing the Russians,
The Bulgars were bulging the Belgians,
You see,
But when the Yanks starting yanking
They yanked Kaiser Bill up the tree.

Everyone cheered.

As morning hours unfolded the streets became mobbed, auto horns honking, trolley bells ringing, "hallelujahs" and "whoo-ee's" soaring from down the block where band music played. As one band came closer—Pope's Excelsior Brass Band, with its timeless musicians, like ebony statues with drums and horns—Morris saw that the bass drummer had painted a picture of Kaiser Wilhelm on the skin of the drum. As the drummer twirled the sticks in the air, then brought them resoundingly against the long-bearded visage, more cheers soared from the crowd.

All down Dauphin, from the doorway of Fry's humble tailor shop, to Friedlander's new rug and shade store, to Strauss's elegant clothiers, Old Glories fluttered and shone.

With his sons' help Morris climbed on his ladder and affixed his Old Glory above the door. Its forty-eight stars shone like the firmament.

Milton Brown walked by and saluted.

"I wish we could win a war every day," Herman exulted.

"Thank you, sweet sister," Abe whispered over his shoulder to Lillian.

With the gift of a half-dollar each from Daddy, Abe and Herman wove through the jammed walks, slowing to greet Benny Lubel and Simon Miller, shaking hands with Eberhardt Karl selling penny sausages, shouting hello to Pastor, who walked the other side offering half-price cigars, smoke rising like wispy seraphs over men's heads.

They broke their fifty-cent pieces at the bakery, where Matranga had rolled out loaves of freshly baked twist bread. They spent money at Joe Bear's ice cream parlor, where the owner shouted, "Armistice ice cream. One free scoop."

"Hullo!" waved Asa Spicer, who sat on a bench beneath his dentist's office drinking warm beer, the foam smearing across his dark upper lip.

"Dr. Spicer!" they called, going up to him, asking for a sip of the beer.

"Come join us," Spicer was beckoning to Donnie McCall.

McCall shrugged and walked past, glancing down disdainfully at the dentist.

"I'll join you," piped Hannah, skipping up to Dr. Spicer. The dentist put his finger into the beer and held it out to Hannah, wiping her top lip with the suds. She licked her lips. "Yum."

"Let's go to the moving pictures," Herman said, as Hannah headed back to the store.

They passed by *The Beast of Berlin* at the Queen, deciding on the Crown's *Birth of a Nation,* and slapping down their coins. Already the theater was jammed with viewers on sudden holiday clapping to Goodman Smith's piano medley. They took seats near the back as the lights dropped.

Above the subtitle, *The Bringing of the African to America Planted the First Seed of Disunion,* slaves were shown being sold on a Southern street, white men making their bids, the Africans with their heads bent, wide-eyed and fearful, stepping down to join their masters. Abolitionists shook their fists.

"Durn Yankees!" someone from the audience called.

The screen showed lovely young white ladies now, hair in curls, lips like hearts. "That's Lillian Gish!" Abe said. "Purty purty!"

"A puppy!" said Herman, pointing to the screen where two pups frolicked with a kitten above the subtitle: *Hostilities.*

Laughter ran through the Crown Theater audience.

Slaves bent in serene cotton fields, broke to eat their meals, stood in the yard of their masters where they did buck-and-wing entertainments.

A new subtitle spelled out: *The Gathering Storm.* Images followed of dark-suited men standing around tables, conferring with grave faces.

Abe sat up, leaning forward in his chair at the sight of Abraham Lincoln, just as he'd seen him in pictures at school, stovepipe lean and sharply bearded. He was no hero to this crowd, who finger-whistled and hooted as though he were the long-bearded Kaiser, gravely signing the first call for military volunteers.

In one scene, a mulatto maid waved her arms and acted prissily as a fussy queen. The crowd tittered.

They sank down in their seats, watching the pictures unfurl: The South's victory at First Manassas. Night flares in the South Carolina streets. Couples waltzing at a mansion. The glorious Rebel Flag.

"The South shall rise again!" a man shouted.

"Yee hi!" called another.

Goodman Smith began a lively rendition of "Turkey in the Straw" as the screen showed the Confederate troops parading into battle, the Battle Flag held high by spirited boys trudging into the enemy's blast.

The subtitle bannered, *Conquer We Must for Our Cause Is Just: Victory or Death.*

The audience began to stomp their feet.

Goodman Smith plunked bass notes to provide backdrop for the renegade Union soldiers, Negro and white, who came sweeping into the South Carolina house, knocking over vases, chairs, cabinets of family heirlooms. The beautiful Southern sisters ran in terror from the Yankee marauders, hurrying to the basement, shutting the trapdoor, then clasping their hands.

When Goodman Smith began to play "Dixie," the audience cheered and wept. Across the movie screen hurried a band of Rebels racing to protect their loved ones, catching the criminals in blue in their violation of all that was sacred, beating them back.

A man on the row before them turned and spoke. "It gets better." It was Donnie McCall.

On the battlefield, under the swirl of banners and the clash of sabers, boys in gray fell by the hundreds and Atlanta burned. When Ulysses S. Grant appeared, a man jumped on the Crown stage and cried, "Death to von Hindenburg," but was cat-called by the crowd and dragged down by an usher.

By the moment white-bearded Lee surrendered at Appomattox to scowling Ulysses S. Grant, the crowd had grown quiet. Someone growled nearby, "Bastards!"

The appearance of white-hooded nightriders on the screen now, beating down sneering carpetbaggers, rescuing the fresh flowers of Southern womanhood from the hands of black-faced actors, set the crowd, downstairs, into a roar.

As Goodman Smith played, the audience began to sing:

> *In the beauty of the lilies*
> *Christ was born across the sea.*

Even the Klan horses were robed, their great equine eyes terrifying.

Abe heard someone at the door of the theater say something about a store, a window, and a rock being thrown. "Upper Dauphin," were the last words he heard before grabbing Herman's arm and leading the way out.

They climbed over the legs of men next to them who were busily stomping rhythm while Donnie McCall waved his arms and sheeted men thundered down from the screen, and the Negroes rushed over the cinematic roads to escape them.

Glory glory Hallejulah
His truth is marching on!

Exiting the theater they heard a crash up the street and a woman's howling. Why were Mama and Daddy in the middle of Dauphin, waving their arms? Had someone broken the windows of M. Kleinman & Sons? Abe's heart beat hot.

But Mama and Daddy, Abe saw, were not running from Kleinman's but toward Spitzer's. Against the shattered window panes Max and Inge Spitzer stood surrounded by a pack of boys. At their front was a raw youth with barber bowl haircut and loose arms dangling. "We've seen him," Herman said.

Inge, her face cupped in her hands, looked up crying, while Max stepped toward the pack, shaking his fist. "The Var is over, vee did nothing to hurt you. My only son gave even his arm! Vat did you give? Nuting! It is you who are the barbarians, it is you who are not fit to be Americans."

"Go back where's you come from!" the raw-faced leader shouted.

"Dis is vere vee come from!"

The flock scattered as Billy Spitzer appeared at the door, his stump arm waving frantically, his good arm holding a shotgun pointed at the crowd.

"Do not mind these hooligans," Morris said.

Miriam walked up to Inge and put a hand on her shoulder.

"Come," Morris said, "eat our food, drink our wine. Smoke Mr. Pastor's cigars. Our home, it is your home, too."

II

1925–1930

Family Portraits

Dear Theodora Eminescu,

I was the boy on the farm of your Papa, Stefan Eminescu, a kind man he was, I pray he is well in his old age and if the Lord G-d has taken him that he rests in peace. I pray this letter finds its way to you and that you are happy with children, a good husband, and much good fortune.

I am living in Mobile, Alabama, in America, where G-d gives me many gifts—a good wife, Miriam, and three healthy children who make for us much joy. Our child Lillian, of blessed memory, fell to a fever. Always we hear her sweet voice.

Life in Piatra Neamt was hard for many. My brother Ben died of a bad heart, Chaim of a fever too like my Lillian. My loving mother, Shayna Blema, died in sadness for her sons. May their memory be for blessings.

My Papa and my sister Golda are alive. Golda, her heart is breaking that he did not go with her to Poland. If you know anything about my Papa, his name is Azril, tell me soon. He went to live with his brother, Shmuel, but we hear nothing. I want to bring him to Mobile but I do not have the money to come for him in this year.

Theodora Eminescu, I pray that you are well and remember this boy who slept on the sacks in your Papa's barn. You were kind to me. Now I sleep many years on a bed over a store that is my own. Please write to me at the address of my store.

Sincerely,
Morris Kleinman

A long the cemetery rows, by the Japanese magnolia opening creamy blossoms beneath the cool-blue, Passover week sky, Morris made his way to Lillian's resting place. At the *seder* table, as always, he had felt her sitting with all the others; the holiday had been her favorite of the year.

"*Ziben yoren,*" he said, shaking his head in disbelief. Seven long years.

Reaching the plot he felt the mourner's prayer keening at his lips, "*El molai rachamin,*" and crying, muttered it. "O God, full of mercy." He reached down and found a pebble to set atop the stone. Nine other pebbles were atop the marker—the symbol of those who had recently visited the grave, who had kept their friend, sister, daughter alive in memory. He stepped back, gazed at the mute sky, looked back to Lillian, closed his eyes and saw her behind the counter of the store, in a checkered cotton dress, hair plaited long. When he opened his eyes he saw only her name chiseled in rock. He turned away.

He stepped toward the plot where Sam Lutchnik was a year and a half ago laid to rest. "Ah," he said sadly, laying his hand on the stone, "you, too."

It had been a chilly December morning that Sam had been leafing through a collection of *Mobile Registers* holding his ad; he had simply stopped, laying his head down on the page. Pearl had been brave at the funeral for her husband, receiving visitors with gracious reserve at their home above their store. Two months later, when she'd been coaxed out of solitude to go with Morris and

Miriam to a Mary Astor movie at Arlington Pier, she dissolved in tears watching advertisements for Mobile stores that preceded the movie. Outdoors, with the bay night closing over the park, the screen showed a portrait of Sam, eight feet tall, offering the best prices in town.

"What would you say to this?" Morris spoke aloud to the ghost of his competitor: "*Morris Kleinman, the King of Cut Rate. The Only King Left After the War. Yes?*"

Morris answered aloud his own foolish notion. "No, the Great War, who thinks about this now? These Southerners they are still fighting the first one."

Even as the ranks of gray-suited veterans had thinned, year by year, into a platoon of granite-faced warriors struggling down Dauphin with wheelchairs and crutches, the commemoration of the War Between the States still grew. The tube radio now played music in their home, the motor cars crowded Dauphin, and Morris's sons came up past his shoulder, but this old war endured in the stories Jackson Levy told about his grandfather Asher taking a cannonball in the right leg in Chattanooga; in the nicked and glistening swords from Vicksburg that Donnie McCall brought in to show off to Morris's customers.

Whether from defeat or death, Morris thought, the sense of loss never really went away. Like storm water on the backs of magnolia leaves it clung to the vanquished army trudging down the street, or to the father remembering his daughter's hand on his neck while facing only stone.

Morris bade farewell to Lutchnik, and made his way by headstones reading Glucksman and Steinfeld and Gross, the faithful born in villages like Piatra Neamt and Dorohoi and Iasi who'd stolen their way to ports like Hamburg and Liverpool to board tramp steamers that left them off, a dizzying six weeks later, in New York, Savannah or Charleston. In those Southern towns they'd stepped onto land as alien as Baltimore or New York, but hotter and smaller and slower in their manner, the baked streets leading to peddler warehouses where they loaded up with soaps and lotions, brushes and ribbons, umbrellas and slickers, and took off down roads to hamlets like Marks, Mississippi and Eutaw, Alabama and Jackson, Tennessee. In these towns, so often, the Jews already implanted there—third generation Southern boys and girls with German backgrounds and pedigreed names—looked down from their perches, curiously, at their crude brethren still bearing the *shtetl* in their beards and hats and voices.

He came to the end of a row and looked across the clipped privet between this Orthodox cemetery and the Reform one. Against the headstones chiseled not with Hebrew but with English—and names, like Rothschild, that sounded like Bavarian gentry—a young woman in blue dress with long, flowing hair moved with easy grace.

She caught his eye. "Hello," she said, waving. Her dress was ankle-length, made from cotton. He remembered a crate of these from Besser; he'd sold dozens in different hues until Bienville Square bloomed with their colors.

"Ma'am. Good afternoon."

"Mr. Morris, isn't it?" Familiar, pale eyes, strawberry hair.

"That dress, forgive me, I do not mean to offend. But that dress, I sell it in my store."

"It was your daughter showed it to me."

"My daughter, no"—he stepped back, reeling a moment—"my daughter, rest her soul."

"Oh, I'm so sorry, Mr. Morris. So very, very sorry. What a terrible loss!" She stepped closer to the privet. "I just figured you were here for somebody more, you know . . ."

"Like me?"

"Why, yes, somebody your own age. Somebody God would have taken more at the *right* time."

"Forty-four years of age, this is the right time?" He smiled. "I am not yet Methuselah." He looked down. "A fever."

"God rest her soul."

"*Baruch Hashem.*"

"At last she is free. To seek eternal salvation in Jesus Christ's arms."

"Ah," he answered quietly.

"My granddaddy was a Jew," she said brightly, "came here from Alsace, fought in the War, General Forrest's cavalry, only nineteen years old, was sent up to Selma."

"Mr.?"

"Solomon Green. Gruen, I think, originally. But he changed it. Didn't want to stick out too much. Oh, what's wrong with me?" She put out her arm over the top of the fence. "Hi, I'm Betty Green."

"Morris Kleinman," he said, reaching over to shake her hand, startled by the touch of a woman not in his family. He pulled back, feeling the two of them under the Japanese magnolias watched by a thousand souls.

"I will pay respects to your grandfather." He stepped to the end of the privet, through an opening and back down to where Betty was standing.

"I lived away from here a real long time," she said. "Over in Gulfport, my Daddy he was a shipbuilder, got work over there in the shipping business. Building shrimp boats and all. He got a fever, too, I swear it was a bug bit him, call it hepatitis, say it was in the water, but I'm fine."

"This lovely dress," he said, "it is from so many years ago."

"There was a big parade I remember, we were there 'cause of my grandaddy, remembering him and all. *Shayna*, you said, that's what you called the dress. *Shayna*, pretty. I remember, 'cause my grandaddy used that name for me when I was little." She grinned. "I used to think it was French."

"*My God*," he said to himself, "*what is it I am thinking?*" The girl from Romania rose up again, sixteen years old, her bare shoulders, naked breasts, in the window: a woman in her forties would she now be with tall daughters of her own.

"My grandaddy, he died leaving Granny Green to spend the rest of her life a sorrowful widow. Other than a few Old Testament prayers he used to say and allowing in his last will and testament how he wanted to be buried right here in the Hebrew cemetery, he didn't pass on his faith much. Granny Green said God was for them who couldn't make do on their own, but Mama got religion as a little girl and passed it on to me, like red hair and blue eyes."

Red hair and blue eyes. Yes, that's how she would look, still lovely and gentle in her middle years, with shy, willowy daughters.

"You don't believe in Jesus, do you? I mean, as God's only begotten son?"

"Miss Green, we are friends with all the people of Mobile."

"Did you think I was trying to pick a fight? Oh no, Mr. Morris, no sir. I was just asking about your faith."

"My faith is that you must work hard and do what is right and God, blessed be His Name, will do what is best."

"And you don't think God made a baby with Mother Mary?"

"I am not a learned rabbi to answer your questions, Miss Green. It is enough I try to be a good Jew."

"My Lord Jesus was a good Jew!"

Just as Morris noticed Saul and Sarah Shenkman at the cemetery gate bearing roses for their lost son, Betty Green leaned over quickly and pecked him on the cheek.

The cool spring air grew hot around him as the young woman headed off and the Shenkmans came up the path, cradling sad flowers.

In the sultry photographer's studio, this last day at Murphy High School, Abe stands surrounded by family, but he feels the empty space, like silent weeping, where Lillian should be.

Erik Overbey, a dapper Norwegian with piercing blue eyes, drapes the camera's black hood over his head, waits for the solemn, dignified expressions to take hold. Daddy in necktie; Mama in pearls; Herman in starched jacket; Hannah in pinafore. Abe's shirt is freshly pressed, his jacket buttoned down at the collar, diploma neatly rolled and tucked under his arm like a scepter.

"*Lily where are you, sweet sister?*"

Overbey squeezes the ball. The light bulb explodes.

Already over are the graduation ceremonies when Johnson Turnbull, III, stood at the podium and spoke of the "new day dawning when the opportunities for us here in Mobile, and all over the land, are better than ever before, to reach our many dreams." The final dance was announced for that evening at seven when Abe would escort Rosa Gerhardt, and Dan Berson would go with Molly Kahn. It was the one evening of the year when the gentile girls were there to dance with you, too—those strong, rangy farm girls with names like Janie Lyn and Sue Ann, and society belles named Christian and Elizabeth. But all that, tonight, was still to come.

Now in the hot, long angled studio light of the May afternoon, he hears Lillian's voice, softly singing, "K-K-K-Katy," on a spring night long ago.

After the photograph is finished he pronounces: "Mama, Papa. I've decided. Starting Monday now that school is over and my life of true, grown-up responsibility begins, I don't want to go to college at all." He watches Papa's face fill with worry, then spreading delight, as he continues, "If it's fine by you . . ."

"Yes, son?"

"I want to make my life . . ."

"Whatever is your wish, my Abraham, it is our joy."

"The store."

David Pastor was a rangy boy, his long arms able to reach as high as the hat boxes above the shelf in the storeroom. "Come, you will work three hours a day for my Abe," Morris had told the boy that next fall, as Pablo said the cigar business was good but not so good David should not learn to sell like the Jews.

As Abe's helper, David dragged and toted and stacked the ladies' wear, learning to put it quickly back in place after a farm wife from Spanish Fort had plowed through the cotton blouses, or a colored woman from Prichard had felt sixteen crinoline dresses before deciding silk would be better for her godchild's baptism.

"He smells like cigars, Mama," Hannah complained. "That's okay for Daddy, but he's just a kid!" Miriam shushed her, saying it was the smell, as she'd learned, "of a man who takes care of his own."

As David lugged and stacked and swabbed the shelves with a damp rag, he caught glimpses of Hannah. She was smart, he knew that much; and was a good badminton player at school. Her Daddy, Mr. Morris, fussed at her, telling her to "be gentle and do as our Lillian would have done, be a little lady and help the customers, too." To David, though, she seemed the gentlest of all.

At first Abe paid no mind to David's lingering near the cash register, even though Daddy's binding rule was "only family touches the register." Besides, he had more to worry about than a Cuban boy who was more trouble than he was worth. Since graduation Daddy had left it to him to rise at 5 A.M. and whisk the broom over the walk. On the fifth morning, when he snored obliviously past dawn, he'd waked with a start to find Daddy standing over him, broom in hand, saying, "It is done. To your prayers."

Abe became so worried about oversleeping that he hardly slept at all, tossing and turning and dreaming, half-awake, of cleaning the walk before heading down, half-asleep, to sweep it. And there were the impossible numbers: the 6 percent mark down, the two-for-one with the third item half-price. As if on an invisible chalk board, Morris could figure the sums in his head as quickly as any ninth-grade algebra teacher.

The afternoon young David laid his hand on the back of the register, Abe approached him, asking, "Don't you have a chore?"

"No sir."

"You know what the first rule of storekeeping is?"

David shrugged. "Open the front door in the morning? I see your Daddy doing that."

"Well, that, yes, of course, yes do *that*. You see *me* opening it, too, by the way. The first rule is, if you've finished your task, find another one. That's how you learn."

"Yes sir."

"Keep your eyes open."

"Yes sir."

He noticed the boy half-turned to the register, gazing up the wall. "David? Is something wrong?"

He shook his head, mumbling, "No sir."

"And remember, *only* family touches the cash register!"

The boy nodded sheepishly. "Are you gonna tell my Daddy I did something wrong?"

"Have you done anything wrong?"

"No *sir.*"

"Good, now clean up the packing material from the crates."

As Abe walked away David caught sight, again, of the arms and legs passing behind the upstairs wall over the register, the clear pink skin through the crack in the dry boards of the wall: a place where the plaster once fell in an endless rain that poured through the store.

"Hannah," David whispered that night, crawling into his own bed in the apartment behind Fosko Soda where his Daddy's tobacco leaves swept down the entrance foyer. He looked out the window to the top floor of M. Kleinman & Sons: a girl lit by a single white bulb paused in the window. The light went off. He crept out of bed and pressed his face to the pane, spying Hannah's silhouette.

He jumped, feeling his father's hand clenching his shoulder. "*Qué pasa aquí, hijo? Apúrate a la cama.*" Go back to bed.

"I didn't do anything wrong, Poppa."

"*Nada, por supuesto*, of course not. Why do you even say?" He eyed his son. "Enough in Mr. Morris's store. The Jews, they will break your heart."

Abe stooping beneath the cellar door to fetch the box with socks from Rabinowitz; Abe thumbing through the accounts receivable to find if Mrs. Pinkerson had made her promised July payment;

Abe taking his place in the rocker at the entrance to the store, leaping up as soon as he saw Daddy. All day long Morris watched his son.

Abe did not touch the clothes as he did, did not prize the blouses and slacks, understanding how the loan from First National had meant the difference between a low-profit cleaning business and high-markup, greet-the-customers-at-crack-of-day trade where, in a good month, Bienville Square bloomed with jackets and skirts from M. Kleinman & Sons. Selma Gollub had once spoken to Miriam of how she remembered the shapes of newborns in her palms. So it was, Morris soon realized, with each article of clothing he'd ever handled. Just rags, though, that's what they were to his Abraham.

This afternoon he was not even tending to clothes but was scolding David Pastor:

"I've caught you!"

"Sir?"

Abe pointed to the crack in the wall over the register. "Looking at the wall!"

"What are you *doing?*" Morris intervened.

"He's looking, Daddy!"

"Looking, what is looking? You are crazy?"

"It is not me who is crazy, it is the boy."

"What has he done to you?"

"Look!" Abe pointed to the wall. "There!" Through its cracks shone a line of light: the upstairs bulb in Hannah's room.

A storm long ago, Morris's body against the wall, water soaking his skin, plaster falling in his hands jagged as bones.

"Abraham, he is a child!"

"And my sister, she is a girl of eleven that this Spanish boy with his leering eyes should see?"

"Respect! Before your mother hears, and our precious Hannah. David?" He summoned the boy. "Go. Speak nothing of what this has been. You will go?"

"Yes sir."

"You will speak about this?"

"No sir. Daddy told me it was time to start learning cigars."

Morris nodded. "Cigars, yes, now go."

"You let him go, just like that?" Abe exploded. "Don't you see what he was doing?"

"What I see is that my son," Morris answered calmly, "needs something you cannot find in a store, in a school, in a rocking chair like an old man sitting on the street."

"What else is there, Daddy? Money? I'm learning how to make money, you just watch."

"What else is a woman, a good woman, at your side. Stop with this foolishness you are making. The answer to your question is a wife."

23 November, 1925

Dear Moritz,

 I am answering to you in English because my friend is a teacher he is writing to you what I am saying to him in Romanian. I received the letter you sent to my sister Theodora. I am sad to tell you that she is no more living here in this farm.

 She is staying in Bucharest with Elena, working in a factory of shoes. It makes five years now since my father dies. I am many years gone from the military where I am hit with one bullet for the King. So many years pass now, the war making our Romania different and our farm is very poor. No Jews are here still to work like you, a good Jew with a strong back. I have no sons and my sisters, they do not yet marry, so many men are killed in the wars. I am writing to a man in a town close to Bucharest to ask if he knows your Papa. He works in the clinic for men and women with sickness in their chests.

 Two years it makes that I do not see my sisters when they come to Piatra Neamt, under the hand of Jesus

Christ. I will give Theodora this letter and she will cry to hear your story.

I am happy you have money in USA. If you can send American dollars I will ask a special blessing.

Petru Eminescu

While reading the letter, Morris looked up to see David Pastor standing alongside him. "Mr. Morris?"

"Yes?" Morris answered from far away.

"Are you sad?"

"What can I do for you, David?"

"I come to tell you I'm sorry for making Mr. Abe mad."

"That's all right. You did your best." Morris reached out and took up David's hand. "What happened to you?"

The boy said nothing.

"Your hand . . ." He pushed up his sleeve. "Your wrist!"

The boy looked down.

"Someone hit you!"

"Whupped!" David said softly.

"Who *did* this to our David Pastor?"

In barely audible tones the boy answered, "My Daddy, for what I done."

Morris pulled the youngster to him with one hand, patting his shoulder, and with the other hand held up, to read slowly again, the words spiraling across Petru Eminescu's wrinkled page.

By arrangement between Morris and Saul Gerson, Abe escorted Saul's daughter Molly to the Purim Ball. The ball, coinciding with Valentine's Day this year, seemed to draw every Jew eligible from a hundred miles around. In the downtown dance hall the light glared on the slicked-down hair of fifty young men, some with dates, others standing at the stag line in the middle of the floor jiggling their change and looking at their pocket watches waiting for the band to begin.

Abe looked over the bounteous girls milling around the edges, hair plaited or brushed down long, bows bright on the tops of their fair heads. Some looked no older than fifteen, come from as far away as Pascagoula with maiden aunts who urged them out to meet resourceful boys; others were the age of Molly, one or two years out of high school and matched with dates, in the Old World way, by hopeful parents; some were women rising into the upper reaches of their twenties, seeking partners on their own; a few, judging by wearied looks, were surely thirty, though no one dare admit it.

Waiting for the music to start, Molly excused herself to go to the powder room.

Abe wove his way through the pleated dresses, the sashes and fragrances. Nearly every woman, it seemed, noted him as he passed. Who among them had not shopped, at least browsed, in M. Kleinman & Sons? Which one of these fancy garments had he not touched, at least as a bolt of cloth, before it was slipped onto a virginal arm and shoulder and back and waist?

He stopped and looked around, dazed. Where *was* Molly?

The four-piece band started into its first foxtrot and the stags were taking their pick of the available girls. Randy Plotnick, Charlie Salzberg, Aaron Grean—smoothly, deftly, they roved about the floor tapping shoulders, breaking in, swirling their partners away until the next intrusion.

Abe craned his neck looking for Molly; he approached Karen Fink, a redhead from Atmore who took his advance as an invitation.

"Why, Abe Kleinman, I'd love to."

"I'm not . . ." he started to protest, but the lanky redhead had him out on the floor pushing him back and forth to "Tea for Two."

He became vaguely aware of Molly's hot stare as he made cloddish box-steps around the floor, half-stumbling his way as the band changed to "Yes, We Have No Bananas," taking the hand of Doris Ackerman who was with him only moments before another man tapped him on the shoulder to cut in.

He faced another partner he'd never met. She had a long, slender neck and pale eyes. Although her hands were rough as a farm girl's when she placed them in his, her lively two-step was infectiously smooth and they quickly fell into rhythm, then broke apart, waving their hands in the air to the season's newest rage, "The Charleston."

By the time a slower tune started, a Tennessee waltz, Molly was standing in front of him. "Hi," she said. "Remember me?"

"I began to think you'd left town," he said.

"You really do know how to embarrass a girl."

"How can I embarrass you when I just learned to dance?"

"Every girl between here and Montgomery knows that by now."

"Daddy told me I'm a quick study. When I put my mind to it."

"Did he say you also got a swoll head?"

"Better than swoll feet."

After jerkily waltzing Molly across the floor, he was pleased to feel a gentle tap at his shoulder, a bullocky youth taking over as Molly's partner even as she whispered, "You don't *have* to let him cut!"

But as the band played up tempo with "Bye Bye Blackbird," he was already winging his way across the floor to take the slender palm of Iris Pollock, which he held only a minute before breaking away—tap on his shoulder—to give an insistent poke on the ribs to Chubby Levine, bringing him back to the sturdy redhead he'd danced with to start.

He became giddy with the swirl of girls before him now: the variety of hair cut short or bobbed or set into ringlets with curling irons, the eau de toilette splashed generously behind the ears, the lovely dresses so inert in the boxes from Besser's, alive here on the lithe bodies of Jewish belles.

He hurried after Molly as soon as he saw her exit the room. It was a block away that he caught up to her running down the street, the eyes and ears of all Dauphin beginning to observe:

"Why, I never!" she was exclaiming.

"Cutting in's what everybody was doing," he said.

"But why not cut *back* in. On *me?*"

"Well, oh, I didn't . . ."

"*Think* about it? Dance with the one who brung you is a lost cause on you, Abe Kleinman!"

"Shhh, do you want everybody to know it's *us?* Out here going on like this?"

She dropped her voice low down. "What would you rather be called, *Mr. Dreamboat?*"

"I'm sorry."

"You offended me in front of everybody who's anybody!"

"Please, *please,* Molly." He stopped and fell to his knee.

"What on earth? Now you're going to *propose?*"

In desperation he whispered, "Please don't tell your Daddy."

"You take me for a fool? Why, you're the fool," she said, then lifted her voice to the rooftops, "Abe Kleinman!"

Night Fires

T he Cathedral bell gongs three times slowly, lugubriously in the Mobile darkness and Herman wakes to see the bruise on the rim of the sky. He has seen that glow before, like a wound on the clouds, the fire beginning in the shanties of the south part of town and eating houses and stores. But there is only silence now, not like a decade earlier when alarm bells had rung and the men from the Creole Firehouse had rushed in their horse-drawn fire trucks to do David-like battle against the Goliath flames.

He props himself up on his elbow and watches the color against the far sky shift, deepen. Can he slip out without being noticed? Next to him Abe is snoring; in Lillian's old room is Hannah, sunk in dream; in the front, Mama and Daddy, unmoving. He rises, dresses, steals down the steps. Like a burglar he unlocks carefully, silently, the front door and steps outside, moving toward the sore sky.

He comes to the street Daddy has told him never to cross alone, even though he is a straight-A high school student, even though he knows plenty well what Abe is doing when he goes out late and returns with splotchy marks on his neck and curls up in his bed, moaning.

Reaching the curb he hesitates. On the other side, as though on the far bank of a treacherous river, loom the churches and meeting halls, the bars and nightspots, of colored Mobile. He sees faces moving past those corners that have surely walked into M. Kleinman

& Sons many a bright afternoon; but, except for Dr. Spicer, few residents of Dauphin cross the other way.

There is noise now: the crackle of fire eating through wood, through straw, and voices clamoring. Then comes a freakish crying, a frantic squealing, not a human's at all. An animal's.

He is on the other side of the street now, and a slender man leaning against a wall looks at him, warning, "What you doin' around here, you Mr. Morris's boy," but he keeps on, moving toward that crying, the man behind him calling out, "This ain't none of your business, fool."

He passes wood frame houses thick with wild camellias spilling over the steps, yard tables heaped with jars, clotheslines strung out from side porches where longjohns hang like lynched men. Toward him comes running a young black woman clutching the hands of her two small children. When they see him the children point and exclaim but she drags them faster. The sky, like a face, is flushed, bright with fever.

He arrives at a clearing where a barn sits atop a hill, flames climbing from its rafters. On the ground a black man is yanking at the barn door, even as it ripples into flames. He wrenches it open in time for two horses to bolt out, rearing and neighing. Inside the barn the squealing rises, the stench of charred flesh curling out. The yelp and screech of the animals is muffled, dies.

He steps forward thinking he is still over the store dreaming this giant cross he sees being erected by hooded men, the cross now bursting into flame, the night riders climbing onto their own horses, circling around it whooping and hollering.

Off to the side of the barn men and women are huddled, children at their feet pressing fists to their mouths. The hands of the women are clasped together but they are not facing the burning cross.

On their horses the hooded men turn toward them. The women are praying, the children are pushing up against their daddy's legs, the horses galloping faster.

As the first hooded rider approaches, one of the men on the

ground pulls a shovel from behind him, swinging it through the air, catching the rider in the jaw. The horse veers to the right, the rider's head bobbing as though he is no longer conscious of the horse beneath him. The women and children are scattering one way, the men another.

The other riders begin to chase the men, but one horse curves in the direction of a small figure whom Herman is startled to see standing at the edge of the field behind him, dark hat pulled low.

"This ain't no place for the likes of you!" the man on the horse is screaming at the figure, whose hat, tumbling away, reveals a thick fall of hair. Herman shakes his head; it is not a man at all.

Has the fire blasted his sight? He rubs at his lids. "Hannah!" he yells, running toward her. "What . . . ?"

"Just following behind you!" she cries in bewilderment, covering her face with her hands now as the horse roars by her, the hooded rider peering down. Herman grabs her hand and they start back how they came, the storm of horses and shouts and leaping flames growing smaller, Davis Avenue soon beneath their feet, the river of the city crossed, as they return to Dauphin where they belong.

It was not the first time Dr. Asa Spicer had been rattled from sleep by clunking at the door. Like babies, toothaches did not always choose the most restful times to come. Just as midwife Berenice McNulty Jones, on any given day, could see scores of children she had birthed with her hands, so Asa Spicer could observe jaws, gums, incisors, and cuspids he had set right. He had repaired the eloquent mouth of Pastor Douglas Pressler of AME Zion, and the outraged one of Hettie Masters, the cane-wielding teacher of the Rosenwald schoolhouse at Riverbend Road. At family requests he also serviced the deceased, providing cosmetic touches befitting the journey to Kingdom Come.

As howls now climbed the walls, he hurriedly laced his shoes, calling out, "Comin', comin', breathe deep, now!"

Only once in all his years had he neglected a desperate caller:

during the rains of 1918, sunk in exhausted sleep, he'd let a man languish outside his door. By the time he'd gone into the hallway, the sufferer—a white man, God help him—was writhing on the floor. With the poison of abscess forking through his body, the man soon died. No family member came to the coroner's to claim the body; no friend contacted the police. "He was a drifter," the final report speculated, "shown up at the Negro dentist's door."

How could he ever again hesitate to unbolt his door?

As soon as he'd done so he wished to shove the satanic spirits away. They were three men in white hoods with eyes blinking back from peepholes. Out of their pack stumbled a fourth, blood staining the hole of his mouth.

"Talk and we'll do you like you done that white man once fell dead here."

He nodded, but would not cower. He glanced to his dentist's chair where sharp, small implements glittered. He might lose his life, but not without first making sure these Kluxers rued the night they played with Asa Spicer.

Against the side of the stained hood the night rider lifted his smooth hand and cried like a banshee. Asa took his wrist and guided him to the chair.

"Fix him up, nigger."

Asa began to peel up the patient's hood. One of the men, the shortest, pressed a knife up against his throat.

"Let him do his job," barked the tallest. The knife was moved away.

"I am Doctor Asa Spicer," he said with high-wire calm. "I must remove this . . . *mask* . . . to help best I can."

The patient nodded, rolling up the cotton hood himself.

Asa drew back and said in astonishment: "Mr. Donnie McCall!"

McCall moaned and waved his hand at his swollen mouth.

"You've done been clobbered good," Spicer said.

Iron fingers gripped his shoulders behind.

McCall brokenly uttered: "Let . . . him . . . the fuck . . . be."

The hands let go.

Over leaping groans Asa examined McCall's lip, exhorted him to open wide and pushed aside his tongue, shining his operating light where a bicuspid has been fractured.

He motioned to the cabinet. "Fetch me whiskey."

"We don't fetch you nothin,'" the short man snarled. The tall one handed him the bottle.

As he gave McCall a long swig he reached for his forceps.

"Big 'ah,' now," Asa instructed.

As McCall's mouth opened to a fetid pit and his features contorted, Asa remembered another man, mouth wrenched open, eyes popping out like junebugs: Uncle Dugger Dabney, on the ground out back of the Pawcett Plantation, a night rider's boot at his throat. Eight years old again, watching the tyrant mash his uncle's windpipe, Asa picked up a rock and hurled it at the bully, but it sailed into the trees. The masked rider looked over at little Asa, removed his foot, laughed and walked away. Asa started to run after him, but Uncle Dugger, where he lay heaving and spitting, reached out and latched onto Asa's ankle. "Best," he gasped, "do nothin' at all."

Had the Lord sent these sheeted bullies into his office now for Asa to avenge Uncle Dabney's troubles? For forty years he'd played the scene again in his mind, each time leaping to the back of the night rider and choking him down.

He saw McCall in the dentist's chair now in his dozen, trickster poses: offering flim-flam funeral policies to fearful ladies grasping their Bibles on slatternly porches; shaking hands with ministers while promising heavenly, group discount sales.

Uncle Dugger's eyes implored him: time to make wrongs right.

He fixed the forceps around the shattered tooth. As McCall's yowls rocked the house, the other men put their hands over their eye holes, turning away.

"Hold tight," he advised, "and say your prayers." McCall's jaw in his grip was justice to be done.

But his medical hands stayed their course, wrenching out the tooth with a powerful twist, then packing the socket with gauze to stop the hemorrhaging.

After warning Asa never to speak of this night, the short man pulled the hood back over McCall and they helped their master out the door, rowdy boys again in the south Alabama night.

Asa walked to the ash can, only now beginning to lose his steady hand. He wrapped the bloody fang in yesterday's *Register* and pitched it in. A mouth was a mouth, he remembered, that was God's plan: pastor, teacher, Klansman, or corpse, teeth, in the end, were all the same.

Word about Donnie McCall started in the AME Zion church from Pastor Pressler. Lucy Davenport, one hundred and six years old, had been paying twenty-eight years to the white man only to garner a casket hammered from old doors and a few wild azaleas, a worry she'd expressed in her final moments: "Lord, don't let Mr. Donnie keep from me none of my due. I been waitin' for this journey a mighty long time."

No matter how Pastor Pressler complained, though, McCall just flipped to pages in a ledger book which made his point in hard facts: Lucy Davenport had gotten what was coming. She had beat the odds of an easy death, but not that of a sliding scale which favored those who died young. When Pastor Pressler appealed to McCall about the last rites of Simon Weatherly, who'd collapsed in the field at age nineteen, McCall explained the boy's family had not been paying in long enough to qualify for more than a threadbare burial suit two sizes too big.

Complaints about McCall were passed from Pastor Pressler to Deacon Smith, to Sister Clea Jackson, to Mancy Jackson, a tall man with rotted teeth who decided on his twenty-fifth birthday to get them replaced.

"Bad teeth can kill you," Asa told Mancy, beginning an endless procedure of gouging and yanking to make room for false teeth that made Mancy long for death to come on right away.

"But if I die they'll bury me like a pauper," he groaned. "That's the trick goin' round in insurance these days."

"Do you know who's schemin' all that?" Asa asked.

"Donnie McCall. Wears fancy shoes and robs folks blind."

"If I was you," Asa said, "I'd put the word out on that snake."

Pastor heard the story while selling Mancy Jackson cigars, and relayed it to Morris, who said, of Donnie McCall, this was not possible.

When McCall next came to the store, trying on wingtips, he looked down at Morris bent at his toes. "What you think?"

"What I think," Morris confided, "is some do not speak good of your name."

"Talk's cheap."

"A man's good name is his treasure."

"Am I here to be lectured or buy shoes?"

"Yes sir, of course. The shoes, they are. . . *goot?*"

"The word's *good.*"

"Good, yes, *goot* I sometimes say."

"God, you been in this town how many years and you still talk like a foreigner?"

"My shoes they are not"—he spoke the word carefully—"*good* enough for you?"

"You didn't sew 'em, you just hawk 'em."

Morris unlaced the shoes and slipped them off McCall's feet.

"Here." McCall peeled off a five dollar bill.

"These shoes they are not for sale."

"Then give me a pair that is."

"If you cannot show me your respect, then you cannot wear Morris Kleinman's shoes."

"Oh, a big shot! You people push a few rags and think you're taking over. Well, let me tell you something . . ." He jabbed his finger at Morris, who knocked it away.

McCall stiffened. "Let me tell you about respect. If you respected a good Christian like me you wouldn't be spreading poisonous lies about me cheatin' your precious *shvarzas*. So don't act like Moses on the mountaintop with me."

"I said anything about you cheating the colored?"

"I know that's the crap going round."

"I said to Mr. Pastor, 'This I did not believe.'"

"Hell damnation, do you have any idea what a favor I do those people? How do you think they'd have enough dough to be laid under in a shoe box much less a pine casket without me watching out for them? You think they know how to save? How to put it up for a god damn rainy day no matter how much rain's gonna fall? You know, they got brains the size of hard little nuts encased inside those big wooly heads." He leaned over. "Crack one open and you'll see."

Morris stood. "Then it is true what Pastor tells me?"

"Pastor shouldn't stick his nose in nobody's business but his own. You, too. Or y'all might not have much business left to mind."

"You are making a threat!"

McCall bent closer. "I've been good to you, damn good."

"One hundred pairs of shoes is not worth this shame."

McCall was not looking at him now but over his shoulder, nodding, "Howdy, Hannah."

"Hello," she muttered, coming up to her Daddy's side.

"Mighty fine day, isn't it?"

"Sir?"

"Fine day, I said."

"Out," Morris said. "Out!"

He reached down and took the shoes and handed the cash to the girl and whirled out the door.

The next night a fire started at Pablo Pastor's home over Fosko Soda. Two nights later one started in the office of Asa Spicer. Morris thought to point the finger at Donnie McCall, but he had no proof at all. Didn't the commandment proclaim, "Do not bear false witness against thy neighbor?"

The following midnight he sat outside in his rocker and thought of Petru Eminescu, not as a kind voice coaxing money from him in a letter, but as an arrogant youth riding into the barn on his stallion, looking down at him on the sacks of feed.

"What is a Jew doing here?" Petru asked Theodora.

"He is not just a Jew, he is our friend."

"Papa can be arrested for hiding one of them."

"He's not hiding. He's working."

"Jews don't work, they pray."

"Do you see those sacks of feed?" Theodora said. "Morris carried every one of them from the fields, stacked them, keeps account of them, gets them into the store cellar when the time comes."

"Who's standing over him with a whip?"

"Oh, Petru!" She went up to her brother and pretended to beat him on the chest with clenched fists.

"My nervous bird," he teased her, "covering for a lowly Jew."

Old man Eminescu appeared at the door: "He is doing the work my son should be doing. But you are gone high and mighty in your war."

"Papa," he said, "I wish only to make you proud."

"Morris is our Jew," the old man said.

Home for *yontif,* lying in bed next to Chaim, Morris heard about Moshe Plotnick who'd been taken off by the Romanian Army and put to work building fences on a mountainside. Lording over Moshe and a hundred other Jewish boys was a fierce watchman, Petru Eminescu.

In the bunk Chaim had buried closer in next to him, whispering, "They say he shot a boy, too, killed him with his musket for trying to run away. The boy had walked into a hive of bees and was only trying to run away from them. Petru knew about the bees but was happy for the chance to shoot a Jew."

Warily Morris had watched the military youth on his visits to the farm. The sound of his steed clopping over stones caused him to turn rapidly to hauling and stacking feed, keeping a pitchfork close in case he was singled out for drubbing. But Petru only nodded and went on.

One morning Petru approached Morris in the barn: "Do you claim association with the men who murdered Christ?"

"I know nothing about your Christ."

"Do you eat meat from the hogs that are sold to my father at his store?"

"Olga does not serve me meat of swine."

"Did the rabbis cut your foreskin when you were born?"

"I keep God's laws."

"Come here."

Morris did not move. Petru stepped toward him instead. "Let me look at your head." Petru pushed his fingers over Morris's scalp, explored the back of his skull. "Nothing," he said in astonishment.

By winter word came through Theodora that the army was coming for him; that it was time for the Jew to flee under cover of night.

Rising from his Dauphin Street rocker now Morris went upstairs and climbed in bed next to Miriam. Sensing her awake, he told her the story of Petru, then of Donnie McCall, and how each had looked at him with eyes that said, "You are our special Jew."

"This is not possible," Miriam said.

"Why is it not possible?"

"To them a Jew is a Jew."

"No one is burning a fire at our store!"

"Why will we not be next?"

"Because we are friends with those who might do so."

"And why friends?"

"Because we are hardworking. We make good business."

"And from this we will betray our own?"

"To keep our family safe, this is betrayal?" Morris turned into his pillow.

"Talk to me!" she demanded.

He twisted back toward her, sighing, "What choice do we have?"

"We can sell what we have and go away."

"Sell? Go away? Where!"

The rattling in the kitchen made them both jump. "Just me, Mama," called out Abe, returned from one of his sorties.

"You think that here our sons will find good Jewish brides?" she whispered fiercely. "All they will do is become like the common, drinking *goyim* with their common *shiksas*."

"Where will we *go?*" he persisted. "Where, New *York?*"

Miriam fell silent: the Brooklyn stoops climbed up in her mind, the fire escapes strung with clotheslines where blouses and BVD's flapped in the wind, the old women with their accents thick with Lithuania or Estonia yammering about the owner of the delicatessen who ran off with the cantor's daughter or the high price of *matzobrei* now that Pesach had come, or how the pretty girls with their starched dresses were too good for the common lot of boys who poured out of the *yeshivas* on Eastern Parkway, what with their swaggering, sudden American ways. They would not be too good for her Abe and Herman!

"Yes. Why not New York?"

"Who do we even know in New York anymore?"

"*Mein tyra brieder.*"

"Ah, Benny, your great brother, a gentleman, yes, but you have not even seen him in five long years."

"I wrote to him already."

"You *wrote.*" His voice rose, shaking.

"I cannot write my own brother?"

"You wrote about us, leaving here, going back to New York?"

"*Morris, shh, die kinder.*"

"*Nisht kinder*; they are *grown.* They can know what *mishigas* their Mama makes."

She slapped him quickly on the cheek.

He put his hand to his face and muttered, "Forgive me, God, for insulting my wife."

"You are forgiven, but still must listen."

"But we have made our lives *here*."

"We crossed an ocean to America, we cannot cross a country back to New York?"

The Brooklyn streets at dusk, the familiar voices in open windows speaking of the old countries in old country voices, the silverware clinking above plates of boiled chicken and red potatoes and *kugel,* the Sabbath candles flickering on table after table along bay windows of buildings with *mezuzzahs* on every doorway. Oh, the joyful freedom of *yiddishkeit,* she thought: Jews over you, beneath you, alongside you, out your back window.

"It is," Morris said appeasingly, "a thought."

He was not serious. She knew his voice, but it allowed her, without interruption, a long reverie on Brooklyn streets, far away now from this foreign Mobile.

At the kitchen sink Miriam reminisced about the Flatbush deli-catessen where she'd been introduced to Morris by Aunt Doris, and what a fine figure he'd made at the counter; at the dinner table she talked about the arches of the Brooklyn Bridge where they had walked beneath parasols to ward off the August sun, "so much nicer the sun than in this scorching Alabama"; walking near Bienville Square she asked her husband if he remembered the Prospect Park meadow where he'd proposed marriage.

Morris asked her if she remembered the cramped, one-room apartment over the cleaning and pressing shop where they first lived, and how the cats had screamed like banshees in their mating rituals all night, and how the boys from the Polish neighborhood ran through the Jewish blocks knocking skullcaps off the men.

"You would like more to have Alabama men threatening the lives of children," she asked, "than New York children playing pranks on grown men?"

"Ah," he sighed, thinking how wrong she'd been as he positioned a clothes rack on the street as a red-faced farmer waddled in, staring right at him like he was somebody he should know.

"Can I help you?"

The farmer faced him silently, stared hard, turned and walked away.

Next came a pasty-faced banker Morris recognized as a colleague of Hezekiah Ottinger.

"Good morning, sir. A friend of the First National is surely a friend of Morris Kleinman's."

The man looked around curiously, fixed Morris in his gaze, turned and walked away.

That morning the business was slower; in the afternoon it dwindled to nothing. Why did even the Negroes hurry by, afraid to look his way, like Riverly with his blue glass eye turned toward the store while his good one peered off the other way? Even the Johnson brothers slogged by with strings of bass over their shoulders, not stopping, as always before, to show him.

"You are happy now?" Miriam asked that night in bed. "The way they keep from our store?"

"You are making this story in your head."

The next night, after another day of customers avoiding the store like pox, she said again, "You are happy? Tell me I am right, Morris!"

"Yes, they are treating us differently. Like *drek*. You are happy now?"

"What will we do!"

"I will speak to Donnie McCall. I will tell him that we cannot be treated like this."

"Tell him that we are selling this store and are leaving."

Morris did not answer.

"That we are going back to where we are welcome, back to New York, back to Flatbush, back to where people like us belong."

"*Mobile ist mein shtetl. Du ist da mishpocah.*"

"It is not our *shtetl*. Not our home."

He found the side street off Government the next day, descending from the trolley, watching a Chinese man trudging on the walk with a heap of laundry on his back: a younger Morris from another world.

By the wooden porches of the Creole cottages with their palm fronds bowing over wicker chairs, by the railroad tracks running to colored town, by the dilapidated Queen Ann with its gray-haired crone peering down from a turret, Morris found his way.

Sitting on his front porch was McCall. He wore a straw katy pushed back on fiery skin and held a mug. "Why looky here!" He stood but tottered and plopped back down. "What you doing, Jew friend, drumming now?"

Morris caught the high, sharp smell of creekwater whiskey. "My Papa," Morris said, determined to make nice chat like a true man from Alabama, "in Romania, he made vodka."

"That right?" McCall licked cracked lips. "They make that from potatoes, y'all call it *bulbes*, don't you."

"*Bulbes*, yes, potatoes. How did you know this?"

"*Zuntik bulbes, montik bulbes, dinstik bulbes . . .*"

"Sunday potatoes, Monday potatoes, Tuesday potatoes. . ." Morris said in disbelief, translating into English the Yiddish children's song Donnie McCall was drunkenly repeating. "You hear my Herman singing this when he was a boy?"

"Vodka ain't like good ol' corn liquor," McCall wore on, as though he had not heard Morris's question. "Hell, you can make just about anything from corn but a baby, and the way your *shvarzas* turn 'em out they might could do just that." He hung his head then looked up, eyelids drooping.

"Mr. Donnie McCall," Morris said now, putting a foot on the bottom step, "for many years I make good business with you, I do nothing against you, I make no word against you and now you want to close my store with every bad word you make about me like the terrible men who closed my Papa's distillery in the old country." He moved up another step. "The business you make is your business, but do not make it my business, too."

McCall grinned and waved him forward. "A slug of shinny'd do you good, Jew friend." He held out the mug. "Prohibition Special."

Morris hesitated, then continued up the porch, reached out and took the mug. He sipped, started to spit it out but swallowed. The burning wash down his throat helped him go on.

McCall stood again, gripped the top of the rocker to steady himself, then motioned for Morris to follow him "We got us some indoor plumbing. Best make use of it."

"I do not want to make trouble for Mrs. McCall," Morris said. "I will wait outside."

"There is no Mrs. McCall. She upped and out o'here a year ago."

"I am sorry."

McCall laughed, guzzling the remainder of his mug, then wiping his face with his shirtsleeve. "Fuck her. It was March thirteenth. A Friday. Fuck Friday the thirteenth and don't walk under a ladder and all that other crap. *Drek.* That's the word you people use isn't it. *Drek* means shit. I sound like a damn rabbi, don't I!" He stumbled his way toward the bathroom, not bothering to close the door as he splashed his business into the bowl and yanked the chain to flush. "My daughter went with her. Bitches the lot."

"I am sorry."

"You sure are sorry a lot."

"What do you want from Morris Kleinman?"

McCall looked at him again with heavy-lidded eyes, eyes rung with dark circles like his own Papa's had been, not the eyes of a spirited Irishman but of a melancholy *landsman,* as though, strangely, Romanian villages haunted him deep inside.

Encrusted dishes were piled high in the sink. Soiled clothes spilled out of a laundry basket in a jumble. "Even the nigger cook left me. Guess she got the heebee jeebies doing my sheets!" He kicked at fouled bed coverings on the floor. "A fuckin' drink! Where'd her African ass hide it!"

McCall threw open one cabinet after another, banging them shut as he went along the kitchen wall. He came to a cluster of mason jars which he lifted out, awkwardly balancing them as though not sure which were filled. "God dammit," he slurred, dropping two empty ones with a crack into the sink. "Oh, here's the sumnabitch."

He put a knee on the counter, hoisting himself up to reach the highest shelf, cursing the cook who'd hid his bathtub gin in the farthest corner. His knee slipped and he was grabbing at another shelf that tilted, raining cups and saucers down on his head. With a *whomp* he fell on his back to the floor, blinking up stupidly at Morris who reached out to help him.

"Let me be! I feel like I'm on that damn"—he clutched the sides of his head—"ship. Fuck 'em all. Fuck 'em every one, bastards."

"*Ship?*"

"Get me off!"

"What is it you are saying?"

"I CAN'T STAND THE ROCKING, THE MOVEMENT, OH,"— he pressed his hands against his ears—"MY MISERABLE . . . OH, MY HEAD!"

Around McCall, cracked and shattered, lay the cups and saucers. One silver goblet rolled in a slow circle. Morris reached out and lifted it up. "*Oy, gevalt!*" he said in astonishment. Beneath its heavy tarnish he recognized the ancient lettering and hammered design: a *kiddush* cup. "*Baruch Hashem,*" he whispered.

"Praise to His name," McCall said, and Morris set down the cup and lifted the queerly Hebraic head with its fleshy neck and heavy jowls, the face with its large mouth and bloodshot eyes peering already from this chaotic kitchen floor of a grimy Mobile home to the rolling darkness of the World to Come.

What You Pay

onnie McCall's birth name, Heshie Gollub heard from Lucky Schwartz who got it from the grandmother of his girlfriend, had been Joshua Mendelsohn. Mendelsohn's father was a Bavarian Jew, his mother a German Lutheran. On the storm-tossed crossing to America sixty years earlier, Mendelsohn had changed his name to that of the first Irishman he'd met— "another luckless bunch," Lucky Schwartz had sneered, "the sons of Eire"—and took on the new religion, too, after landing in Charleston, then making his way to Mobile.

McCall or Mendelsohn—it was no matter to Miriam. She worried only that someone might accuse Morris of hastening the insurance-hawker's death.

Only she knew the truth of what had happened. Morris had run to a grocery and phoned the operator to say please send a doctor right away, maybe McCall was still breathing. Dr. Mulherin appeared, concluding that McCall had suffered a burst blood vessel in his head, most likely exploded as a result of his fall. To Officer Flynn arriving on the scene, Morris made the report that he'd come to visit McCall about a business dealing—the man, after all, had a closet full of shoes from M. Kleinman & Sons—and had heard a crash. "I opened the door thinking something is wrong," he explained, "and saw him there, on his floor."

That any yard man or society lady might have noticed Morris

going into the house with McCall filled Miriam with dread. Even though customers, colored and white, began to filter back to Kleinman's the day after McCall's funeral, Miriam waited for the man who might accuse her husband of the most heinous crime of all. "Like Asa Spicer," she fretted. "A man dies in his hallway so everybody asks, 'Is the man's soul on his hands?'"

"This," Morris assured, "could not happen."

Even as they heard tales of a black man convicted of violating a white woman on evidence that he'd whistled at her on the street; of a Lebanese merchant in Gulfport run out of town by a local fish-market owner; of a Jew at Sand Mountain north of Birmingham kidnapped by snake-handlers who demanded his submission to the Holy Ghost (they accepted a hundred dollars instead), Morris believed that just as God had given Jonah a gourd to protect his head against bad weather, so he had been given "the good people of Dauphin."

But Miriam saw specters of men rising against the storefront at night like those who had paused before her Iasi home, the Romanian guard searching out a Jew said to have bashed in the head of a peasant after a quarrel. At her father's window she saw the soldiers on their stallions wending through rows of houses, signaling *shtetl* dwellers they could be crushed given a commandant's nod.

She heard voices deep in the Gulf Coast night, shards of Romanian mixed with coarse drawls, so that when a window at the back of the store shattered after midnight's gong she leapt up and prayed for divine protection as Morris stole down the stairs wielding a cane. It was only Abe coming home late from courting, stumbling into the back door.

Falling back asleep she dreamed of a corner of green in Brooklyn, a bright stone bench where Morris kneeled and said, "Don't you think I'm a good prospect?" and she leaned to kiss him and tumbled into the grass like a radiant sea that flowed around her, and she came out dry and smartly dressed and strolling with a new hat and bag along Flatbush Avenue, greeting neighbors with a wave of the hand.

The next night she woke from the same dream and went to the window, imagining noisy Brooklyn stoops rising against lively brownstones instead of silent, dreary Alabama streets.

Who was there beneath the Modern Furniture awning, arms wrapped around a dusky girl? The man's back was to her. The girl's face she recognized through the shadows: Milagros, the niece of Marta Pastor's. The man kissed her and turned toward the store, jogging across the street.

"*Avraham!*"

The next day Miriam wept to Morris, "We must leave this place, this life here it is not good," but she did not tell him of Abe and the girl. To Marta Pastor she said only how, given the port's appeal to sailors and bohemians, she feared for impressionable girls living close by, particularly one as innocent as Milagros.

"*Es el tiempo para ella volver,*" Marta exclaimed. The time, yes, for her niece to return to Cuba for a husband like Pablo.

For their own children to find Jewish mates, Miriam repeated to Morris, it was time for them, too, to return to New York.

When the 3 A.M. pounding came at the door it was a fist against her chest and she did not wait for Morris to finish getting on his dungarees before saying, "They have come." She saw shadows of riders looming against Iasi windows becoming white-hooded men on Mobile streets setting torches to their door.

She was right behind him bounding downstairs, seeing the figures at the glass front wavering, rapping their fists and sticks and calling out, "Wake up, wake up, we have come!"

Morris wrenched open the door and flailed his arms as her heart felt another jolt. In spilled Benny Weiss, her frowsy and beloved brother, all the way from New York. Trailing right behind was his new wife, Fanny, who took one look around mopping her brow and sighed, "God damn."

"Oh, *mein brieder,*" Miriam cried, throwing her arms around Benny. "My brother, come from so far!"

"Far isn't half of it," Fanny said, who set up a stream of talking, like she'd known them all her life. "In the middle of the night we heard what we thought was Mobile so we jerked up and rushed to get off and by the time the *fashluganah* train was about to pull away we realized we were in Monroeville instead, and you think *this* is the sticks."

Herman appeared and grabbed up their trunk.

"Take it to Hannah's room," Morris said.

"By the time we got back up," Fanny went on, "some pig farmer had laid his dirty body across both our seats, snoring to high heaven and I said to Benny, *mishpocah* or no *mishpocah*, this is the backside of America so far's I can see."

"You are welcome here," Morris said.

"You got Coca-Cola way down here?" Fanny asked. "I could use a drink of *something*."

"Dr. Pepper, ginger beer, we have all. Hannah!" Morris called. "For Aunt Fanny, Co'-Cola."

"But is it true?" Tears welled up in Fanny's eyes.

"She's tired," Benny said. "Such a joy to be here," he said.

"Is it *true?*" she repeated stridently.

"Such a *simcha*," Benny exclaimed.

"That . . ." she talked over him.

"Fanny, not now!"

"That you have something"—she stammered the words—"some work. Here in this hotbox of a *shmatta* shop. That we can *do?*"

"Benny?" Miriam asked. "*Nu?*"

"Well, in New York, it's not that things are bad, it's just that"— he took a deep breath and slowly exhaled—"things have been better."

In the morning sun Benny gazed at the perfect, naked backside of his beloved wife. Against the green fleur-de-lis wallpaper—the room where Hannah slept but had given up for their stay—Fanny was an Odalisque, a black-haired, olive-skinned dream perspiring in sleep, like that painting at the big art museum on Fifth Avenue, the one with the pretty girl at the front desk who'd noticed him when he entered and seemed to follow him with longful gaze after he slyly winked.

He reached out and laid his palm on the small of Fanny's back, softly brushing downward until his hand rose back up the arc of her flesh. "Hmm," she moaned, and he wove a magic circle of touch on his ready, Flatbush doll.

Let the Orthodox have their child-making coitus with its formal rituals, its secret couplings in darkness, its obedience to the mandate to be fruitful and multiply. "Childless," the doctor proclaimed them. Sterile. Unyielding. Only words! What they had was nakedness, the carnal heat nowhere else, he sensed, in this house.

Nothing here but children: tall Abe half-minding the store; sullen Herman, heading off to college; regal Hannah, a gazelle like his sister had once been; and the ghost of poor Lillian, rest her soul, namesake of Mama, going to meet her in the World to Come, if such a place even existed, having never known this blessing of bodies in light.

All these lives had come streaming out of the body of his sister, but had Miriam herself ever felt, with her dependable but plodding Morris, what he and Fanny had felt? Always the smart, principled girl he remembered her; the obedient one who'd settle for a nice *landsman* like Morris and trek after him to the heat of Dixie. Just like Mama had been before she died, so genial and agreeable to Papa. Then that usurper had come wielding her stick like the Queen of Romania. But he had seen how Papa loved Margareta, draped his arm around her shoulder in the startling show of affection, even kissing her on the lips so that Margareta herself turned bright red the first time, but not the second. In front of all the children and Uncle Heshie, too, she'd kissed him back boldly, the neck of her dress pulling down to her shoulder, an image that lit a fire in Benny's legs like some forbidden French postcard.

Fanny opened her eyes and he felt that fire run down him as she watched him. In her flecked-green irisis was his own reflection, a tiny man turned upside down, a Brooklyn rake with droopy moustache and wavy hair, coming close with full lips to kiss her. She tasted sweet, like no other woman he'd kissed, not the girl at the museum with her thin Irish mouth or the Canadian dancer who'd come into his millinery shop the day before her cabaret left town and tried on two hats, both of which he'd given her as a gift, knowing he'd be married to lovely Fanny before the month was out. Only the Christian girls he'd touch outside of this union, that was his marital vow—the Italian grocer's second cousin from Palermo with her hands that trailed flour, the widowed Minnesotan who worked at the florist—but never a woman of his own kind, outside of Fanny.

And why should he, anyway, with these sweet kisses? On his cheeks, his neck, his shoulder she set her lips, scratching him softly between his shoulder blades until he groaned like a dog, then turning her attentions lower.

He, too, found the hidden parts of her, keeping his eye steady on her eyes, modern love-makers, not like these *shtetl* dwellers flung far into a shabby main street in a broiling, coastal town. Grasping her backside he brought her tightly against him, and as they joined together, giddily moaning and laughing, gently biting at each other's lips, flicking their tongues like bohemian lovers high in Parisian garrets, they began to rock.

Slowly, setting the small bed back and forth, slowly, drumming the wall. Faster, the metal frame clacking against the side table, even faster, the noise like a dance hall tapper.

"Oh, yes." Back and forth.

"Mmm, my." Side to side.

The tap dancer was going faster now, clickity-clack, clickity-clickity, Benny going to a limp heap in Fanny's arms as she squeezed him hard, her sweat a great pool on the sheets as she arched and said his name and shuddered her way back to easy silence.

Rising now, dressing, fanning each other cool with pages of the *Register*, they stumbled their way from the room.

"So what are you guys looking at?" Fanny said as they came

before Morris and Miriam and Abe and Herman and Hannah judgmental at the breakfast table. She fussed with her hair, then took one of the two empty chairs. "Don't they know the word *privacy* down here?"

"In famous New York," Morris said, "do they not know the word *lady*, and *gentleman?*"

"Morris!" Miriam warned. With her stern word in the sultry air they put their heads down and started to eat.

If it was not the horseflies, it was the mosquitoes; not the mosquitoes, it was the chiggers; not the chiggers, it was the fleas. Out of the very air where before had been only the heat laden with the smells of fried chicken and pine needles and rainstorms and *kugel*, Fanny conjured fifty assaults on her senses. As though giving credence to her complaints—about everything from bugs in her pillow to "hillbilly" music whining from the store radio—she was actually bitten by a spider one night, her right thigh going sore and red. At least, thought Morris, for the days she bellyached about the bite—"You think we allow spiders in Brooklyn?"—there was no banging and bumping of walls. Even as Miriam defended the love clatter to Morris as "my poor brother and sister-in-law's way of trying to fulfill God's commandment to make children," Morris passed it off casually to his children as "exercise," the wearisome calisthenics growing popular in all the schools.

But about this loud, bankrupt brother and his *kvetch* of a wife he was not truly casual at all.

"We are paying them one dollar each, every day," he told Miriam, lying next to her late, the house quiet, finally. "*Nu? Fur hake a chinick?*"

"They are not making a big noise for nothing!" Miriam fumed. "They are a new bride and groom!"

"*Drei yoren?*"

"Three years, it is hard to remember when we are married more than twenty."

"Remember? Who can forget the cleaning and pressing shop? The rags I must take from the cooks at the back door so that you can mend them for selling?"

"I am not talking about the store."

"Are you not talking about twenty years?"

"A store is not all we have made!"

"The children, yes," he said. "Of course, the children."

"And a marriage, too, dear Morris."

"As God intended."

"My brother is less with God because he acts this way with his wife?"

"Ideas! He has filled your head with these ideas!"

"There is something wrong if my brother is in love with his wife?"

"If he is so good at this love, he would go bankrupt in his store?"

"A store is not a marriage!"

"A marriage is not for the husband to lose all his money and turn like a *schnorer* to his family."

"My Benny is not a *schnorer*!"

"But he did lose all his money!"

"And what did Pablo Pastor have when he lived here with us?"

"It is not a crime to have nothing, but it is a crime to throw it away."

"Benny borrowed too much; he could not sell enough to pay back what he owed."

"He should not so have borrowed."

"He is here to make a new life."

"Far away from his creditors?"

"The Italians," she admitted. "He borrowed money from the Italians."

"Then he is a fool two times over."

"He is so much a fool he does not love his wife?"

"What has this New York brother filled your head with talk about love? A man who rises and sweeps his walk so his family can be proud of the place they are living and working, this is not love? A man who is honest with every customer, colored or white, so that he keeps a good name for his family, this is not love? A man who provides what he can so his children can go to school if this will make them wise and rich, this is not love?"

"A man who speaks of his wife's brother as you do? You call that love?"

"Better that I speak like this but do not refuse him money than I say he is divine as a king but turn my back on his need."

"Shh," she said, setting her hand over his eyes. He heard rustling, then felt her skin, shoulder to bosom, belly to knees, wholly naked against him for the first time in all their years. He reached down and unbuttoned the fly of his pajamas, but she tugged at his waistband, signaling him to strip bare.

Naked as the two first humans on earth before God, they pressed together making brief, delirious love, speaking nothing. The next night they came together again.

When Miriam's blood stopped its flow one month later, they knew it was not because the miracle of a child had been made, but because her body could no longer make a miracle. They found the pleasure of each other instead, so that the clack of Benny and Fanny's bed became an angel's footsteps walking rough new life into the house.

Packing off for college, Herman only pretended to smile; in truth his heart spiraled downwards at leaving the rooms where Fanny breathed. He'd watched her kiss Benny, slender arms slung over his shoulders; they held their embraces longer than any couple he'd ever seen. Hugging Fanny good-bye, he felt giddy from her perfume; the rose sweetness lingered on his neck as Daddy walked him to the Greyhound station to see him off.

When he arrived at Tuscaloosa and wandered lonesomely through the red-brick campus, he envisioned Fanny striding robustly next to him. Even as he started classes—spellbound by the

American history lectures of Professor Oaks, his hand cramping from the copious writing in Professor Atkins's composition class—Fanny was not far away.

He was invited to join a group of boisterous young men who lived in a Jewish fraternity house. They sprawled on beat-up couches, talking in comic, energetic ways that captivated Herman. Aaron Goff, from Brewton, admitted that when Professor Atkins warned about the hazards of dangling participles, he thought of his Polish mother saying, "Watch closely, the world it is a dangerous place!" Buddy Slutsky collapsed laughing. Randy Hyman said he wondered if Professor Oaks had "a dangling something" on his mind when he told the story of Hester Prynne to illustrate Puritan morality. Goff asked Slutsky if he had bosomy Sadie Berger on *his* mind. Slutsky rose and beat Goff over the head with a pillow.

Sadie's arms were soon around Herman, on the small path behind the tennis courts. He had felt only Mama's, Lillian's, and Hannah's correct kisses on his cheeks, never a strange girl's moist lips on his mouth. Twice more they met on the path, each time her touch raising his feet off the ground. He tried to remember Fanny but her face was a reflection on water shattering into pieces. It was Sadie who clung in his mind when he ambled moonily from class or plopped down on his frat-house bed. When he climbed back on the Greyhound for a long weekend trip to Mobile for Yom Kippur, it was Sadie, in his mind, who curled up on the bus seat next to him, laying her head on his shoulder.

But as soon as the upstate maples changed to south Alabama's dull pines, Fanny began to take her place. Herman imagined her fixing her hair right this very minute before a mirror, piling it on top of her head, her green-flecked eyes catching him in reflection. She winked; he lay his head against the bus window and sighed, watching the long-emptied resorts of old Citronelle pass his view, the same terrain Fanny would have watched from her midnight train window.

A back tire blow-out sent the bus veering onto the shoulder, and an hour was lost while the driver changed the tire. By the time the Greyhound pulled into the Mobile station, it was all Herman could do to race to the Conti Street synagogue in time for sunset, stomach already rumbling from hunger. He took his place next to Daddy, Abe and Benny, blowing a kiss to Mama and Hannah in the women's balcony. Next to Mama was Fanny.

The cantor began his Kol Nidre chant. Herman bowed his head. "*Dear God, forgive me for thinking in this way of my aunt.*" His thoughts changed to those of food: Mama's heaping plates of boiled chicken and potatoes. "*Dear God, forgive me on this fast day for thinking of food.*" He glanced back up at the balcony. Yes, Fanny's hair was piled high on her head.

In the morning they left the store early, walked back to *shul*, returned home to sit in silent contemplation, returned to *shul* once more. At three o'clock, with an eternity remaining until sunset, Abe whispered to Daddy and Morris nodded. "C'mon," Abe spoke in Herman's ear, "he said we could get some fresh air."

Up Dauphin they walked, past the Jewish stores respectfully shuttered, the rest of Dauphin buzzing with shoppers. As Herman related to Abe stories about his frat brothers, they turned in to Bienville Square. "There's something I've got to tell you," Abe said.

"So tell."

"Aunt Fanny."

Herman stopped, looking up. "What about her?"

"Well, you seem awfully interested."

"What is it, Abe?"

"Don't repeat this."

Herman crossed his heart.

"She's divorced."

"Fanny?"

"She was married to some guy from Long Island, he was big into horse racing."

"Okay, so?"

"*So?* Aunt Fanny, a divorcee! Don't you know what that means? Mama and Daddy don't even know it. I just heard Fanny talking to Benny about it, something about money the guy still owes her."

"Well then it's none of our business."

"Herman, she's got a *past!*"

"Everybody's got a past, Abe."

"Not that kind."

"Not *what* kind?"

"Hey?" Abe put his hand out and cupped Herman's chin, searching his face. "You're sweet on her, aren't you?"

"She's a nice lady."

"Say it, you got a big, wet crush on . . ."

He knocked Abe's hand away.

"That explains those bug eyes you keep showing at the balcony."

"Stop it, Abe."

"Look, little brother, don't tell me to stop it."

"Don't call me that. I'm off at college now, which is more than you've ever done."

"Don't think just 'cause you're spending fifty dollars of Daddy's blood money to learn ten-cent words that it puts you in charge."

"Are you saying I'm . . . *supercilious?*"

Abe shrugged.

"Answer me!"

"Who the hell cares."

"Don't know what it means, do you?"

"I know what you lusting after your own aunt like a dog with his tongue out is."

Herman shoved Abe just once before his big brother swung back at him, Abe's fist catching him under the eye. He turned, seeing red prick-points of light swirling before him. "You could have gone too," Herman said, feeling tears run down the cut. "You didn't have to stay home."

"Daddy needs me."

"Then why don't you goddamn help him!"

"Stop!" Abe cried, coming at Herman again, this time Herman shooting his fist out against the side of Abe's neck. They fell down grappling, the Holy Day earth, again plain Alabama dirt, dropping away beneath them.

Free and Clear

No longer did Benny lounge early mornings running his hand dreamily down Fanny's golden back. He leapt up heading to the street, seeking out a sleepy-eyed newsboy hawking the day's first papers. Like a famished man pulling at Matranga's bread, he yanked the *Register* apart for stories about the Wall Street crash.

When the first word of Black Monday had come, Morris had dismissed it, telling Benny he owned no stocks, New York was thousands of miles away, "and what is more, I am already making my second million."

"Your second million? What are you telling me, Morris?"

"The rich men always say, 'Oh, the first million, it is the hardest.' So why not start with the second?"

"Crack jokes all you want," Benny said ruefully. "You'll see."

As Morris swept the walk and Pastor came to sit and drink coffee, Benny read aloud terrifying New York stories: about a man losing thousands of dollars in steel who put a gun to his head on Park Avenue, and whose wife came home to find him hideously twisted on the floor; about a downtown tycoon who stood on the ledge outside his office window clutching motor company stock before jumping forty-five floors to the pavement.

Morris huffed, "When the army in Romania took my father's distillery, do you think he cut his own throat? He would not give to his enemies so much joy."

"A Catholic who kills himself, boom," Pastor said, "is doomed *en el Purgatorio.* His soul cannot be saved. God does not like a coward."

"A Jew who does this," Morris added, "he will bring on his family so much shame."

"These men have lost everything, *everything*," Benny said. "What do you expect?"

"That they act like *un macho*," Pastor said.

"A *mensch*," Morris translated.

But as weeks continued, and Benny's fistful of *Mobile Register* stories grew, Morris paused, leaning on his broom and listening, while Pablo bit at the edge of his coffee cup.

In grim detail Benny repeated stories that affected them most. Not the ones about millionaires reduced to selling off townhouses, but about men of modest means no longer able to pay their debts. Miriam and Abe joined them to hear about the Chicago boot manufacturer who, unable to meet his bank payments, turned plant ownership back over to the bank. They shook their heads at the sorrow of livestock owners watching their cattle and sheep loaded up for free and hauled away by the very men who'd financed them. Bank officers said they allowed three, five, eight missed payments before foreclosing on properties. What were banks, after all, to do with pigs, or boots, or bolts of cloth, but auction them for eighty cents on the dollar, sixty cents, forty cents, a quarter?

Stories came from closer to home, where the Panic took root in the smallest towns. Benny walked to the Battle House and brought back a *Collier's* with photographs of idle men standing in lines, hands jammed uselessly in their pockets. They waited turns at a window where men gaunt as the St. Francis Street undertaker slopped porridge into bowls.

"Look," Pastor said, "how many are smoking. Men will always buy cigars."

"Shoes," Morris said, "every man must still have shoes." The shoes on the sidewalk racks behind him grew dusty, though.

Benny heard Morris talking to Abe about deliveries coming in far behind schedule, and how it was harder to pay for earlier shipments without new goods available to sell. At Morris's suggestion Benny sat on a stool near the doorfront of M. Kleinman & Sons, soliciting customers. A man walked by turning empty pockets inside out. Another made a gesture like eating, saying, "First got to get my young 'uns some food."

In his room, alongside Fanny kissing him fervently on the neck and shoulders, he turned away, saying, "Not right now," and listened for voices through the wall: Morris and Miriam bickering about the dropping-off of sales, about the slowing activity of Dauphin from Hammel's to Mirsky's, about sending Herman extra cash for college and the funds needed for dental work for Hannah, even though Spicer offered to do it for barter.

"Benny," Fanny said, stroking his chest. "Where are you?"

"Right here," he said with annoyance.

When she fell asleep he counted in his mind the dollars they had saved together at the store, piling them up on one end of an imaginary scale, the other weighted heavily with I.O.U.'s. In a year and a half, at this rate, he would have enough to pay off the original loan to the Italians, but he would have to borrow even more to catch up with the interest on interest. He'd gone to Spitzer, explaining that he knew men in New York, Jewish bankers and financiers, who'd send Spitzer high returns if only he could make him a quick cash loan. Looking puzzled, Spitzer only said, "Why not your brother, or his good friend, the bank?"

Right now, he knew, the Italian men with their fluid smiles and fixed stares were circling the blocks near his Chrystie Street apartment, waiting for his return. When he looked out the window over Kleinman's, he saw the Lower East Side rooftops where the thin man paced, spying on him and Fanny, so that he kept the shades pulled all day. On the corner he imagined an identical man shadowing him, pushing up to the counter at the far end of the bar, keeping track of his movements. "They will never let you get away," his neighbor Max, a Chrystie Street tailor, had warned him. When the heavy snows fell, though, and the thin man on the opposite rooftop bundled himself back indoors, it was their time to flee. "Tell them," Benny told Max, "we are honorable people. We are going to see relatives who'll make good on what we owe." As the train had pulled out of Pennsylvania Station, Benny glanced out seeing the dark rail of the man rising against the station wall.

In the train bunk as soon as they departed Benny had wrapped his arms around Fanny, floating his hand down the contours of her shoulders to the small of her back. Through Washington, Virginia, the Carolinas, Georgia, he'd made love to her a dozen times, each time clinging to her as they drifted to sleep, dreaming of Coney Island and the float he'd wrap his arms around to stay buoyed in the sea. Over Morris's store he reached out now to enfold her in his embrace, and when she woke she began to kiss him feverishly. He closed his eyes, drifting, floating.

"What's wrong?" she whispered.

He stood, covering his limp penis with the pillow. "I have things on my mind," he said.

"Another woman," she said.

"Doll, you know there's no one but you."

The night next, and the next, when she failed to arouse him, she said, "Times have been tough before. But we'll come back."

He received the weekly pay from Morris that next afternoon, but, turning to go up the stairs, heard his sister say to her husband, "It is the decent thing to do!"

"What is decent is not what we can now afford!"

"*Morris, sha shtil. Macht nisht kein gavide.*"

Benny understood. "*Be quiet, Morris. Don't make such a fuss. Benny will hear.*"

He finished climbing the steps and tucked the two dollars into an envelope he kept in a hatbox beneath the bed.

When Fanny merely kissed him on the forehead and said, "Goodnight, my love," he lay awake thinking how he might get the money necessary to repay the loan and return, on the first train leaving, to New York. He saw himself stealing down the steps, into the office, easing open the register. Before he completed this scenario he dug the fingers of his right hand into his left wrist and excoriated himself, "*What kind of man is this who thinks to steal from his own sister?*" He draped his throbbing arm over his eyes and did not open them until it was morning and he heard Morris downstairs yelling:

"Who stole the money from the cash register? Who stole the money!"

Benny raced downstairs to find Morris standing over the open register like a toothless maw.

"I open the register and where is the money? Only family touches the cash register. Only *family.*"

Why was Morris looking at him? In the middle of the night, rising from bed, tip-toeing down to the office . . . no, hadn't it been only a devil's fantasy? Benny looked down at his wrist, his finger marks visible. Had he sleepwalked his way to easy salvation, reaching for the key Morris kept hidden to all the world but that Benny knew lay behind the bin of cast-off shoes?

The front door jangled and Miriam came in toting sacks of vegetables and melons and two whole chickens from Berson's, and when she heard Morris shouting, she said, "I took the money, Morris. Because we are not selling does not mean we cannot eat."

"You took the money?" Morris was quaking.

"Oh, Morris." She dropped the groceries and put her hands over her eyes, tears running down as she shook.

"The register," he repeated, voice dropping, slowly pushing the drawer closed.

"What was I . . . to . . . *do?*"

He walked over and put his arms around her. "Always, food on the table. Before all else, food on the table. Yes, you were right, it is what the money is for."

When the sun is high in the Mobile heavens, Benny gets up from the edge of the bed and feels himself walking downstairs onto the street. His feet tread the pavement by Fowler's Watch Repair where a bearded man gazes out from a window of dead coils; by Eberhardt Karl's where silence lingers above empty cafe tables; by Pafandakis's market where green bananas rot to brown, and green beans wither in bins. At the Norwegian Seamen's Hall the men from the magazine photograph tumble out of the pages and stand in a rattlesnake line that wraps the corner of Joachim; their eyes follow him like the slits of snakes, like the man still stalking him on Lower East Side rooftops.

A block further another line begins, this one dissolving into a crowd pushing to get in the doors of the bank at the corner of Royal. Their jaws are working, voices yammering: the din of people, rising, like water. "*Money*," he hears, "*money.*"

Near Bienville Square he sees truant children running to passersby, tugging on their hip pockets and asking for money. At the corner of the Battle House a stout lady in a ribboned hat waddles up the steps, trailing help behind. The eyes of her attendants—a Creole maid in white uniform, a black manservant lugging a trunk—lock on the ground. The lady reaches into her handbag, crossing the threshold, pulling out money.

He sees the L&N tracks coming close and hears the sound of the train whistle. He thinks of Morris bending at the feet of a buyer trying on shoes, telling the customer his name is already on them. He thinks of a seat on the train where his name is written—third car back, ample and cushioned—waiting for the trip to New York. The train whistle blares. He crosses over the tracks, heads to the docks, the iron horse clamoring at his back.

At the foot of Dauphin, where pilings sit like stumps of soldiers, boys and ancients hold cane poles, lines slack, corks motionless. Gulls, loud as cats, screech near pails of worms.

He feels his right foot go up over the railing and his left swinging up too and hears the protests of the men as he watches the surface coming closer and gasps as he hits the water, dropping under the black bay. Legs churning, he bobs up like one of the corks of the fishermen yelling and waving their arms, and he raises his hand to beckon but feels the bay's vast hand yanking him down and dragging him out to where the Bay Queen steams the channel.

His arms beating the water send up a flurry of spray and he sees the arc of Fanny's shoulders in the turbulent light. He reaches for her but misses, reaches again. Thrashing and coughing, he lunges at her golden back, the bay clogging his nose and mouth. Wildly he swings, beseeching, "Fanny, help me, *doll*, help me," but it is the bay alone that repays his ardor, crashing down into his lungs.

The money from the life insurance company came to Fanny two months later, a check with more digits than the number of cus tomers who made purchases in the store some long, weary hours: one thousand dollars which she cashed and kept in tens and twen ties in her mattress, handing one to Hannah for a new *shul* dress, another to Herman for his trip back to Tuscaloosa. (He folded and placed it next to his heart.)

While the family was sitting shiva, Morris had draped with black cloth not only the mirrors of their apartment, but also those in the store dressing rooms. As when Lillian had passed away, the whole building seemed to sink to its knees in mourning.

The creaking Morris had once heard from Fanny and Benny's room now became the sound of his sister-in-law alone, heaving with tears; from behind the door of his room, which Miriam kept shut the long afternoon, came crying and gasping.

He busied himself dusting clothes only to go back, dusting them again. Abe wanted to put everything on sale, marked down to half, or two-thirds off, but when everything was for sale, as Morris told him, this was bad business.

"But what is the difference," Abe complained, "when nothing is already worth nothing?"

At least Pastor's business was steady, cigars the single escape of men at evening with nothing more to do but send curls of smoke, like drifting dollar signs, into the heavy spring air. Or leap like Benny into the unforgiving bay.

Fanny knew that, without Morris's help, Benny would have been proclaimed a suicide and laid face down in the *shul* cemetery, disgraced from now until the Messiah appeared. Leaning on his broom chatting with anyone who'd listen, Morris fabricated the story about how Benny had once swum across the great East River, from New York to Brooklyn. Benny "got this big idea," he explained, to swim from the foot of Dauphin out to Blakeley Island. But the channel had sucked him under and wouldn't let go.

Only Fanny knew that the closest Benny had ever gotten to immersion by choice was going to the Tenth Street baths in lower Manhattan. On their visit to Coney Island he had waded into the surf only as deep as his knees, making a hectic retreat back to the sand if she so much as splashed him. When they'd ventured in deeper, together, he'd latched onto her shoulders until she feared she might go under too. They had gone to a concession and bought an inflatable raft.

But Fanny did not dispute Morris's story about her husband, the swimmer. She only thanked him for "letting the truth be known." Morris told the story so many times for fear rumors would start about Benny—and that Miriam would suffer shame—that he began to wonder if it were not actually true. On occasion he walked to the end of Dauphin and looked out over the bay, seeing shining waters that nurtured life, and where, on an Easter Sunday long ago, he'd ridden atop a ferry, sweet Lillian at his side. Invariably a shout came—probably a boy far down the docks who'd hooked a fish—and he heard Benny's desperate voice, joining sweet Lillian's, in the wind.

When Herman came home for summer break, Morris made this same walk at end of day with him, telling his son that he should go to the YMCA pool every day and learn better to swim. As they crossed the railroad tracks they heard frantic yelling, fishermen throwing down their poles to lean over, grabbing at somebody slipping over the railing. Fanny's hair was the last of her to disappear.

Herman was already kicking off his shoes and leaping to the rail to dive into the water but he hesitated, pointing. Morris came huffing alongside, looking down to see Fanny, on her back frog-kicking toward the piers, her hand hitched inside the locks of a mewling and spluttering businessman. Morris recognized him: a young colleague of Hezekiah Ottinger. As Herman made a motion to jump in now, Fanny shouted, "God, no," and pulled her free arm powerfully through the water, dragging the banker behind.

Herman and a fisherman bent down to haul up the shivering man, while Fanny came climbing back up on her own, face flushed red, hair tumbling down in wet ropes. As she came over the railing, and a crowd of onlookers began to cheer, her blouse, torn down one side, opened.

Morris looked. Her breast was shapely and white, the dark skin around her nipple puckered from cold. She did not seem to notice. Herman walked up and covered her and kissed her dreamily on the brow.

That night Fanny said she had now saved a life in exchange for the one she could not save, and that it was time to go home.

She handed Morris and Miriam an envelope jammed with bills that were half Benny's dying gift to her. As Morris thanked her but tried to give it back, she shook her head, saying, "Take, *take*. Use this in memory of my Benny. He was your Benny, too. And I will take the rest and go back where I belong, because though I love you and your children, my Dixie *mishpocah*, this place where you live, to me, is nothing but *tsouris,* headache and misery. It killed my Benny, but I'll be damned if it'll kill me."

"It flows like water," a college professor had told Herman of money. *" 'This is a joke,' I told my son. What do I know?"* As Morris paid Hannah's dental bill, Herman's tuition, and grocery bills with

Benny's money, he felt like a man carrying a watering can through a drought-stricken town.

He thought long and hard about where to pour this money that had been made out of the very depths of the bay. When Hannah said she wanted a new necklace for the school dance, when Abe asked for extra funds for a trip to Panama City to visit a friend, Morris declined, saying, "This money is for bread, not cake." Though others warned him that the bank might close its doors on customers, freezing their deposits, he trusted more the First National than a shoebox under the bed; he deposited the bulk in the bank.

When the rabbi suggested a special gift for the synagogue, Morris made one, asking that Lillian, little David, Shayna Blema, his brother Ben, and Benny be remembered in names on a bronze plaque beneath the tree of life.

Sitting outside in rocking chairs at night, smoking with Pastor, joined by fellow shopkeepers, he felt the sheaf of bills he retained in his vest pocket like Benny's hand against his chest.

"Spitzer," Sahadi said, "the poor son of a bitch."

"What has happened to Spitzer?" Morris asked.

"He doesn't have long to go."

"*Spitzer?* Ah, it is his belly. Yes, he was holding his belly. Mulherin, he can help maybe."

"Where he is sick no doctor can fix," Sahadi said, patting his pocket, "unless he can give him a shot full of money."

"But so many people," Morris said, "in and out of his store all day."

"They sit," Reiss said. "They shmooze. They go."

"But something he must sell, *something!* The furniture it goes out, I see it go out."

"It is what he is using to pay others," Sahadi explained.

"A bed to the drugstore," Reiss said. "His boy Billy, his aching stump of an arm, so much medicine he needs."

"A rocker I saw him take to Pafandakis for vegetables," Sahadi said.

"He owes the bank," Mirsky said.

"The bank does not need another chair," Sahadi added.

"Maybe," Morris said, "he can sell the store. Pay what he owes, take the rest and . . ."

"What?" Reiss asked. "Make schnitzel? The window of Eberhardt Karl's is already filled with dead meat feeding the flies."

"So who will waste good money eating at a restaurant?" Sahadi said.

"A vulture," Mirsky put in, "can eat there without paying money at all."

"What vulture?" Morris said.

"The vulture whose name is Mr. *Foreclosure,*" Reiss answered.

"When I come to America," Mirsky said, "I learn the word *clean,* and I learn the word *dirty. Shmutzig.* Mr. Foreclosure, this is *shmutzig.* He comes into my store and I will give him"—he socked the air—"only my fist."

"You will punch at Mr. Foreclosure," Morris said wearily, "and you will punch at Mr. Foreclosure, but in the last round he will knock you in the teeth."

Pastor leaned forward. "When the bank has its hands around your *cojones,* your balls, what can you do?"

"I will first go swimming with New York Benny," Reiss said.

Morris stiffened.

"A bad joke," Reiss conceded.

Morris waved his hand in the air. "What joke can we make about this that is not bad?"

"*Shh,*" Pastor whispered. "He is coming."

Arms folded over his barrel chest, Max Spitzer trod toward them, stocky frame rocking, work boots kicking dust. Morris felt Benny's money, a secret in his vest pocket; it burrowed deeper, hiding, as Spitzer's eyes roved across them.

Pastor held out a cigar. "For you, Max."

"You have ever seen me put a stinking cigar into these lips?" Spitzer touched his mouth, then held both arms out to them like a candidate seeking votes. "You *know* vat is the problem. Vhy do I have to tell you vat you already know?" The *V*'s, like wedges, cut deeply into his words; beer smelled rank on his shirt.

"You men, you can help me!"

"What we can do," Morris consoled, "we will do. Your Inge, your brave Billy, tell them we are here, your friends."

"I need a loan. From each of you."

"Loan of what?" Sahadi asked.

"The bank," Mirsky urged, "try the bank. They will understand."

"Borrow from them? To pay them vat I already owe?"

Morris sank back. "How much do you need?"

"One, maybe two, thousand dollars."

"A big difference this one, maybe two," Pastor said.

"This is funny to you?"

"*Cuidado, amigo.*"

"Speekee English," Spitzer snapped.

"'Careful, friend,' that is what I am warning to you."

"You have no idea vat real overhead is!"

"You are saying, *to me,* I do not *work?*"

"A few rooms, some cheap tobacco leaves, you are in business. This, *amigo,* is not overhead."

"Now we speak Spanish. Good. You are *un hijo de puta.* I will translate. A bastard."

"Stop it, stop it!" cried Sahadi, while Morris waited in silent calculation, Benny's dollars pressing his heart.

"Vee have come from all the corners of the world to make Upper Dauphin our home," Spitzer cried, "and now all of you vill turn against me?"

"What do you want us to do?" fumed Pastor, who stood and thrust his chest out.

"Help your brother. Like the Christian Bible says."

"My brother," Pastor said, "does not hate me for what I do not have."

"You are saying I am trying to rob you?"

"I did not say this."

"No," Spitzer said, "*all* of you are robbing me!"

Pastor's hand flicked to his back pocket and brought out the long, curved blade he used to slice tobacco leaves. "*Pendejo, te mato, no me hables así!*"

"Stop it!" Mirsky yelled, coming between them. "We are becoming like wolves fighting over a dry bone."

"How can you say we are robbing you!" Pastor went on, pushing Mirsky aside.

In Morris's mind turned the sheaf of bills like the magic bird that had once turned and banked through his rooms, disappearing into the blue, Alabama sky.

"Vee know who the bankers are," Spitzer came back at him. "No, Pablo, you are not one of them. Forgive me"—Pastor lowered his knife—"but others here are."

"So much schnitzel has made you crazy," Mirsky huffed.

"Shut up! Vat do you know about the food I eat or the beer I drink or the God I pray to."

"Spitzer?" Morris said in astonishment. "This is whiskey talking?"

Spitzer turned and faced him. "The bankers," he implored, "talk to them for me, Morris. Not the ones here"—he shook his hand in the direction of the First National—"*ach,* they are nobody."

"*What* bankers?"

"The ones up in New York, I know that you know them."

"Who am I to know bankers in New York?"

"Benny told me."

"Benny was pulling at your leg."

"Rothschild, Warburg, what names are these? 'Oh, Max,' Benny said to me, 'if you need help, these are my people.' Now I am asking you, *help me!*"

"How can I . . ."

"Don't think I haven't seen the money you have. Hidden. Secret.

Your poor wife she suffers to make soup from only beans and water, but you keep enough in your pocket to . . ." He pointed at Morris's vest. "Don't hold out on me, Kleinman!"

Silence. Up and down Dauphin the sound, echoing, of a motorcar.

"This," Morris finally said, "is how you ask your friends for a loan?"

"You know vat a puppet is?" Spitzer started back in. "The legs and arms they go like this?" He crouched, arms flailing, eyes bulging like a man jerked by the neck. "Do you know who is pulling the strings on us all?"

"When they broke your window we took you into our home," Morris answered.

"You *do* know, don't you?"

"Your window, when they broke your *window*."

"I do not need now a vindow. Soon I will need only a casket."

"You will hold your own life up against us? There is no honor in this."

"There is honor in your people ven they turn up their nose at the meat of the swine but still act like one?"

Silence fell again on the street, this time turning hard and edged as Pastor's tobacco blade. Mirsky picked up his chair, turned his back on Spitzer and walked away. Sahadi and Reiss went in their separate directions. Pastor kept looking at Spitzer, his hand twitching near his pocket, until he spat on the ground near the German's shoes and whirled to go.

Morris faced him. "I thought they said to me you were dying. Now, I know, it is true."

"You must help me!" Spitzer called to no one, standing alone after Morris went back to his store.

In the dark, in their room, Miriam heard Morris stripping down to his BVD's, and felt him sink down next to her on the bed. Through the odor of cigars she smelled the heavy sweat of his body.

"All of you, you have been fighting," she said. "I can smell this, like the way Señor Pastor smells to me of pork. I hear Spitzer, what does he want?"

"To shame us. That we should give him money."

"Inge, she will hang her head in sorrow that he so brings shame on them."

"Your brother's money," Morris began.

"Benny's soul, it watches over *our* children."

Ten days later the First National Bank took possession of Spitzer Furniture: the storefront against which he'd heavily borrowed as collateral, and the five rooms of cast iron beds and wing chairs and footstools and pie safes and étagères, the lot of peeling, warping furniture he had not already sold off at prices only one nickel over what he paid to acquire them, some as long ago as when Confederate veterans paraded gallantly down Dauphin.

With four hundred dollars of Benny's money and two hundred of M. Kleinman & Sons still in the bank, Morris met with Johnston Bouchard, who showed him a bright, involving smile at first mention of the word "loan," approving one based on Morris's cash and collateral for five thousand dollars, enough to make what had been Spitzer's Furniture now his own.

That same night, not telling even Miriam what he had done, he took the key in his possession, went across the street, opened the door and entered.

Pulling away cobwebs that wove across flaking bed posts and cabinets, attempting to flick on an overhead light only to remember electricity had been shut off, pausing in front of a dresser mirror, its silver backing mottling the glass like age spots on an elder's face, he looked at the man who had brought him here: Morris Kleinman, nearly a half-century old, eyes cupped by dark half-moons like his father's the day he'd looked up from his prayerbook and told him he must go.

He clenched his fist to strike at the splotched reflection, but it made him think of the prayer straps wrapped around his knuckles at dawn and the muttered prayers going up to God, who surely by now had taken His reproachful gaze elsewhere, watching over others not foolish enough to throw themselves, like Benny, into unknowable waters, or, like Morris, unfathomable debt.

He sank into a damp easy chair, the smell of mold crinkling his nose. With a burning at the top of his stomach he put his head in his hands, whispering, "Lord, Blessed be Thy Name, what in Hell have I gone and done?"

III

1931–1936

Easy Terms

June 16th, 1931

Dear Moritz,

The angels took away your Papa.

I found out from Yosef Krakov about a nurse at the sanitarium. I wrote to the nurse who said that Azril had left that place and that I could send her money to find out what happened to him. So many troubles Azril had, what can a poor man so old do? She took the money and wrote back that your Papa, rest his soul, had gone to Heaven. I know that he was made a good burial and other Jews have died at this hospital and a rabbi came from your church, I have faith in God for this.

Theodora and Elena they are in good health and ask about you. Moritz, God has given you a blessing in Alabama, and if you can send American dollars He will bless you again and again.

Sincerely,
Petru Eminescu

Morris folded the letter back up. "Papa," he whispered.

Stepping over the soil thrown up by gravediggers for the final resting place of Boots Schwarzbaum, going by the headstone propped against the fence waiting to be set into the ground for

Subie Shenkman's unveiling, making his way by the men and women he knew who'd ambled atop the Mobile earth but now lay beneath it, Morris made his way slowly. "*Dreysten yoren*," he said. Thirteen long years.

As Lillian had begun to slip away he'd held his hands behind her head, weaving his fingers through her tangle of hair, trying to keep her from dropping into darkness. He thought of Fanny grabbing the locks of a drowning man, pulling him to safety. He had been powerless to rescue sweet Lillian.

He looked at his palms where her head had rested. On his left hand was the gold ring engraved with K, the first purchase, after food and lodging, that he'd made in America.

He kissed it and laid his hand on the top of Lillian's stone, where five pebbles lay. He reached down and added one more, whispering his mourner's prayer. Still, the world remembered his beautiful daughter.

He uttered the anguished words for Papa, too, fell silent, gazed off at the sky. He shuddered at the picture of Azril Kleinman taken out like refuse, buried by strangers in a grave where no fitting prayer was said. He made himself cleave to the image Petru had given: a rabbi, black-hatted, reverent, bowing and chanting prayers for a fellow Jew.

Where he looked in the direction of Washington Square a flicker of red in the window of a distant building caught his attention. The color flashed again, like a flag waving. Was it in the window of Wilmer Hall, the orphanage, where pallid children peered out at bright families strolling to town? When he saw the red glint at the window this time, he thought: balloons, a party, a boy without Mama and Daddy celebrating with bunk-mates, digging into cake sent from a mess hall. He could go there offering a gift, a baseball mitt or model airplane. The color flashed again. A flag of distress, a cry for help?

Was it a sign that he was now one of them too? Could a fifty year old man, suddenly without mother or father, be called "orphan"?

God's sky stretched from Wilmer Hall to Mobile Bay to the villages of Romania, an assemblage of lives as varied as the hodge-podge of junk beneath the tarpaulin of Peter Dais's public dray. Nowhere did that sky touch down now where anyone called him "son." Although he had not seen Papa for over thirty years, he felt him gone, abruptly, like Lillian slipping from his arms.

He sighted the red again. Was he being taunted? Ridiculed?

He spoke to himself: "Morris Kleinman, the blessings you have"—he paced by the earth opened wide for Boots Schwarzbaum—"you will every day count."

"Amen," a voice said.

He looked across to the Reform plots to see Betty Green. She had not aged a day.

"Ah, the *shayna madele,*" he said.

"Not so *madele* anymore," she said. "More like what my Grandaddy called a *'Bubbe,'* I think."

"It is you who find me an old man talking to air."

"And making more sense than most folks half your age!"

Was it right to feel his heart lighten from this woman's voice, not even kin, as they stood on ground soaked with mourners' tears?

"God must have his plan," she said, "us meeting here like this. Maybe it has to do with me being witness."

"You have seen a crime?"

"I didn't mean it like *that.*" She smiled. "I been out in Texas for the *longest* while, staying with my sister."

He joined her to pay respects to her Grandfather, and caught her up to date: that Herman, finishing college, would soon be joining Abe at the store; that Hannah still had not been spoken for; that Abe was doing his best, "but furniture, it is not the same."

"What happened to all those pretty dresses?"

"Our store now is furniture."

"Is that good?"

"We are patient."

"First folks I know needing table and chairs, I'll head them in your direction, Mr. Morris."

"You are very kind." He looked down.

"What you got balled up in your hand so? The Lord sent me here the same time as you, so He must want me to ask."

Impulsively he smoothed the letter out and handed it to her.

Her lips moved slowly as she read, until she handed it back to him and grieved, "Lord have mercy on him, your poor Daddy. Alone like that."

"Yes, thank you."

"And all these years not even your brother or sister could find him to help out?"

"Romania, it is a hard country. You leave, you cannot go back. Papa, he says to my sister, 'Go, I am an old man and do not want to leave my home. Make a good life for your children in a place faraway. Never, *never* come back.'"

"Seems like there are more sad stories in this world than people sometimes." Betty pulled a handkerchief from her pocket and reached over to pat his forehead. "You're just a sweatin' and tremblin'."

"I must sit."

"Nerves," she said, as they found their way to a bench. "Losing your Daddy'll do that. It sure happened to me, and when I lost my Mama, too. I was getting on past thirty but could have been eight years old I wailed so. And you know I hadn't even seen her in two years when it happened, 'cause I was in St. Louis married for a while to this son of a gun who raised his fist at me until I was out the door. I'd just moved out on my husband when the Western Union man came to me with the news about Mama. I hadn't seen her in two long years, and missed her every day, but it was different all of a sudden. I guess I always knew that if I just got on a train, and walked down the road, she'd be there for me to cry my eyes out if I needed. She'd brush out my hair until I felt like me again."

"Miriam brushed my Lillian's hair."

"But the Lord helps us through our sorrow, Morris. He sent His only begotten Son."

"A son can also give pain."

"God's Son died for us."

"This is pain."

"Pain to give us joy, Mr. Morris."

"Better that the father should suffer."

"I'd have rather me break a leg than my Daddy when he was with us."

He turned and looked at her. "My Papa, I let him die alone. What is an ocean to cross when a father is old and dying?"

She reached out and dabbed his brow again. "He was not alone. He had the Lord."

"He did not have his son."

"He had the Lord's son, and you'll be with Him one day and your Daddy, too, I'll pray for you. And you know what else I'm going to do? I'm going to pray for your new store. I'm going to place my hands together like this and ask Jesus Christ to shower Mr. Morris's new furniture store with blessings."

"You are very kind, but . . ."

"No prayer is too small for the Lord Jesus to hear. Even the one your poor old Daddy whispered far away."

"What prayers you make in your religion," he said, "I will accept. And I will say a '*brucha*,' for you. That is . . ."

"You mean like, '*Boruch ata* . . . ?'"

"This blessing you know?"

"Grandaddy Green's voice right inside my head. I don't know what it means exactly, but I figure if it was good enough for Moses, it's good enough for a simple Alabama girl like me."

"You are very kind."

She reached out to smooth his hair; he stiffened his back.

"Oh, I didn't mean to *offend* you. I was just thinking about Mama brushing my troubled heart quiet."

After glancing around quickly, he reached out and, in fatherly gesture, patted the back of her head.

She leaned over and draped her arms around him. He felt himself tremble but did not pull away.

"Watch over him Jesus," Betty Green whispered, standing, kissing him on the patch of skin on his balding head, leaving him alone with squabbling jays and a thousand silent souls.

When Morris received the long distance phone call he knew right away the hectoring voice: Besser, in New Orleans.

"We no longer have general mercantile," Morris said, explaining how he had tried to manage two stores for a while, then sold off Spitzer's storefront, liquidated his clothing line, and crowded the furniture into M. Kleinman & Sons. He had just acquired an empty floor space next to the store to take the overflow of furniture.

"I know, I *know*," Besser said. "From Shiransky in Biloxi who tells to Nachamson on Canal, I know. Not that you tell me such news. Dead you could be in the gutter of the hick town you are living and still I would be sending you crates with dresses."

"I owe you money?"

"Money, no, a visit, yes. I am told you are starving like a dog."

"We are eating well."

"I am not sending bread but a train ticket."

"We have a furniture store," Morris said, "We are not bums on the street."

"Where were you born, Morris?"

"Piatra Neamt."

"Where was I born?"

"Dorohoi."

"Come, I will scratch your back, you will scratch mine."

"I am teaching my oldest the store."

"So you will get two tickets. Who can complain?"

As Morris set the phone back on its cradle in Mobile, Besser hung up on his end in New Orleans. The Dryades Street clothing merchant stood and scratched his belly and passed through his factory, looking over the bent backs and hurrying fingers of two dozen women cutting, stitching, and sewing. A fetching Cajun girl just moved from Mamou glanced up as he passed. He winked and smoothed back his hair. A raise soon, perhaps, for her. She grinned and turned back to her needles.

"Foolish Morris," he thought, still hanging on in that hick, coastal town.

How many young men Besser had known who, drumming their way as far as a crossroads in Alabama or Mississippi, had paused to rest their weary legs only to end up breaking glass under a *chupa* next to the sole daughter of Sam Abramowitz or Louie Hershkovitz. By the time they were weighted down by six children and payments due on property and a middle-age paunch from Bubbe's mashed potatoes they realized they had fallen short of their golden destinations. Why did any of them stay put? Pure laziness, he figured. So it was with Morris hanging on in backwater Mobile where night-riders lit crosses for their Saturday night amusement, and the Baptist-this and Church of God–that meant you had to lick your dry lips all day long without a lick of good Dixieland to go along, not like in New Orleans where speakeasies were on every corner and the clarinets were jumping, making old country *klezmer* sound like a dry whistle while your mouth felt like one too.

Pinkerson, a Dauphin Street music shop owner with ties to New Orleans, had relayed to Besser that the business Morris had gotten into was calamitous, at best: clunky old armoires and moribund couches, ottomans like poisonous mushrooms sitting squat in the showroom and highboys like barrel-chested lunks blocking your way at every musty turn.

Believing at first he'd taken a calculable risk in buying a bank-rupt store, Morris now suspected that Spitzer, along with Ottinger at the bank, had been aware of greater hazards than first known: faulty plumbing; an electrical system that blew its fuses at the switching on of only two lamps; termites gnawing their way through floorboards. Morris had practically given the storefront away just to keep from being sunk by it, carting the furniture, with the help of Peter Dais's dray wagon, to M. Kleinman & Sons.

It was more than Besser could bear that a trick like this should be pulled on one of his own—not only a Jew and merchant, but another Gulf Coaster who slept with the Carpathian Mountains and Moldavian cold worrying his dreams.

Although it had been many years since they'd talked, face to face, Besser knew right away the man in fedora and bow tie coming down the block: the paunch belly, the full lips, the dark, alert eyes. Next to him strode Abe, lanky and dreamy, shiny pompadour sagging down his forehead. With a backslap he welcomed them.

As they entered the factory, Abe pulled out a comb and pushed up his curl. The women at the cutting tables gazed up at him; the Cajun girl giggled.

"You didn't tell me you were bringing Valentino," Besser said.

"Better he should be good with a broom."

"For this he has a wife."

"You think this one has yet to choose?" Morris turned to Abe. "Besser, he had a wife, but he sent her back to New Jersey."

"I wanted children," Besser explained. "She was not able. Another I will soon find. A man who has much to offer"—he gestured to the clothing plant—"has choices."

Morris reached out and patted Besser's belly. "And who can offer such a watermelon?"

Besser nodded to Morris's expanding midriff. "You too are a generous man."

"Thank you for the train tickets. Here is the money . . ."

"No, *no*. I have called you here because, in business, you are too generous."

"What do I have to be so generous?"

"A store of furniture."

Morris shook his head and turned to Abe. "He wants that he should be like Rebbe Yacov. In Piatra Neamt, Rebbe Yacov taught me in *cheder*. In riddles he spoke until I got headaches."

"If you are not giving away, why then are you taking?" Besser asked.

"Taking what? From who?"

"Money. From the family. That could bring for Abe a nice wife, for your daughter a good husband."

"We have not traveled all day to New Orleans to hear foolishness from a man who sends me a bird in a box."

"Ah, Morris, I close my eyes, I listen to your words, and who do I hear? My Papa. Everything must be done in the old way, he would say. The wife, the children. The business."

They came to a room filled with the rattle of sewing machines, a dozen women, feet rocking the treadles, stitching threads back and forth across the scissored patterns. A nervous laughter trilled down the line as all eyes glanced up at Abe.

"You buy, you pay. You pay, you take," Besser said. "What is this?"

"Making good business."

"With dresses this is good business. With shoes this is good business. With furniture? Lousy."

"Mr. Besser's got a point, Daddy."

"A *mensch* and a *tzadik*," Besser exclaimed. "The young people are not yet old enough to be wise. But they are also not yet old enough to act stupid."

They came to a back room loaded with racks of dresses on one side and half-assembled crates on the other.

"What is the worst thing over your head?" Besser asked.

"A roof with holes."

"Debt," Besser explained.

"I come here for you to tell me this?"

"The people who buy from you, why should not they be the ones in debt?"

"If they are in debt how can they buy?"

"Do you know what is time?"

"About two o'clock," Abe said.

"*Time* is not what you find on a man's watch but in his purse! You *sell* on time. You take a little money up front, and take the rest a little at a time."

"Lay-away."

"No, they pay a dollar and take the chair, and they carry on *their* head four dollars debt, a little interest. You make the financing."

"And if they do not make good payments with the other four dollars?"

"What did the bank do to the German?"

"Took his store."

"You are like the bank. You take back the chair."

"And what if they don't want to give it back?" Abe asked.

Morris shook his head. "Who would live with the shame of keeping a chair that he did not pay for?"

"Some people," Besser answered, "if they can buy a chair for one dollar, it is worth the shame."

"These kind of people I do not need."

"What you *do* need is to clear your debts."

"But I must do what is good."

"Good, such a word. You would rather be the *schlemiel* and lose money? Of course it is good."

Morris saw the New Jersey landscape rise up around him again: the scrap iron and bicycle spokes, the claw foot tubs and busted pie safes, the rakes with slats missing like gap-toothed old men. It was a graveyard of worn-out, cast-off junk, carted on the backs and in the wheelbarrows of men desperate to make pennies on the refuse of their lives, and picked over by those willing to pay slightly more for the privilege of using it. All alone he'd been left in charge there the third week of January, the new century successfully unfolding when the Newark policeman, nightstick wagging, had come hurrying down the muddy road asking to see the bill of sale on a lot of kitchen implements Morris had just purchased: skillet, iron, furnace poker, bellows.

"You've bought stolen goods," the cop said.

"I should know is stolen, is not stolen?"

"Did you buy this merchandise?"

"Yes, I bought."

"Then you've broken the law."

"But I am a good man!"

"Tell that to the judge."

And he'd found himself standing before a rumpled justice of the peace who'd stared over the bridge of his nose and said, "Morris Kleinman, this time I'm going to let you go, but let me issue a stern warning. This is America, not"—the man waved his hand—"over there. The next time you're caught selling stolen goods, you'll be convicted like the very men who steal those goods because in the eyes of the law, you are the same."

"But I am a *good* man," Morris had protested, even as the judge was banging his gavel and calling up the next defendant.

"I am a good man," he repeated now, looking over at Besser who shrugged, advising, "So be a good man. Sell on time. Finance what you sell. Make a killing. Who are you hurting if you let them keep what they do not pay for?"

"It's just hurtin' *us*, Daddy," Abe answered. "Just us."

Besser held out his hands and clapped them together. "It is not enough he should be handsome? Also so wise?"

When Besser, that evening, arranged a visit for Morris to the wise men of Dryades—Shmuel the chair-maker, Shiransky the upholsterer, Gluchowsky the sofa king—Abe begged off for time alone. Feeling restless with the old men's jawboning, and giddy from the hungry looks of the women, he set off to explore the town. By the time Daddy was his age he'd seen Bucharest and Budapest and Cracow and Paris and New York. But where had *he* explored? Citronelle, Alabama; Biloxi, Mississippi; Pensacola, Florida.

Dodging the rumbling trolley on Canal Street, he found himself at the edges of the French Quarter. Heading a block down Royal he paused to watch canopied cabs stopping before the portals of a columned hotel. Ladies in sequined dresses and men in top hats ascended steps to a chandeliered rotunda where dancers swirled to champagne music.

A few blocks farther down doors swung open and a dwarf wearing a black beret and variegated ascot leaned out and beckoned him. "Exotic dancers," the man croaked. "Ladies from France, ladies from Africa."

Abe peered in but saw only dusky figures leaning against tables with shadows crisscrossing the room. He glimpsed the sparkled brassiere of a dancer; her tassles flashed in the light, then disappeared in the darkness. He had over eight dollars in his pocket— what Daddy had once plunked down at a Richmond station window for a ticket to Mobile—but for Daddy there had been no sweet temptations along the way. He patted his pocket, headed on.

A hammering of drums drew him a block deeper, to a corner of Bourbon where two boys tap-danced on the walk to music from behind walls. Their shoes clickity-clicked with the fury of a Western Union operator; hands out, teeth flashing, they bobbed and weaved. Abe imagined the Cajun girl from the factory at his side, laughing and applauding. He'd throw his arm around her; kiss her languidly on the mouth.

When the door to this corner nightspot opened, he heard the drums soften and a clarinet's licorice coils drawing him in. A black torch singer was draped over a piano where a stick-man, gangly arms swinging, said the next song was from his buddy Roosevelt Sykes and plunked his hands against the keys. The singer moaned:

> *You got that dress way up above your thigh.*
> *It's enough to make a man wink his eye.*

On one side of the singer was a plump trombonist with red bandana; on the other a banjo player with silver-capped teeth.

> *Now there's too many hands in your persimmon pie*
> *When one hand is my desire.*

Never had Abe seen so many coloreds and whites together in one close room. Some danced, black with black, others black with white;

some, complexion barely visible through the smoky light, pressed tight talking, spooning, falling away to raise bottles and guzzle brew. One girl reminded him of Milagros; her young man like himself. How far they were, though, from the confines of a street like Dauphin. They began to dance to the music, cheeks together, hips grinding. This was like no place in Mobile.

A trumpet player stepped forward, dark cheeks ballooning, the horn climbing toward high *C* as the music shifted to a raucous tempo. Abe pushed through the dancers and guzzlers and spooners and found himself two feet from the band, the bell of the trumpet wrapping around his head. The singer unfolded herself from the piano top and walked right at Abe, belting,

> *Lover man you better treat me right*
> *Or I'm goin' with another lover man tonight.*

Her slack titties shook inside the low-cut number she wore, a slinky red party dress like nothing he'd ever handled at the mercantile store. He could imagine the slick fabric in his hand, the velvet feel of her skin just the other side.

She flared back her lips and through horse teeth scatted and moaned, the trumpet player pointing his horn at the ceiling and blasting down heaven.

Behind the small stage a door was opening and closing leading party-lovers deeper into the back rooms of the club. Next to it was a powerfully built man who bent toward revelers as they tried to enter, catching words they yelled in his ear, waving them through. Abe went closer. Between swings of the door he glimpsed the unbelievable sight of a siren on a tabletop, naked to the waist, big bosoms lolling. She pranced back and forth toward men and women who crimped bills under the strap of her G-string. One youth, baggy-shirted and nappy-chinned, attempted to climb up on the table and grab her; a hand reached up from the crowd and yanked him back and he was pitched, stumbling, toward the door.

Abe started to enter but the bouncer laid a fat paw against his chest. "Private club."

"I'm in town visiting."

"Members only."

"I got money."

The man leaned down and shouted, "Two dollars," in Abe's ear.

Keeping his eyes trained on the swinging bosom of the dancer, Abe nodded, fished out the bills and entered.

Heavy smoke swirled through the room, more pungent and intoxicating than Daddy's cigars. Here were no bowed and weary men sucking at stogies, but angular couples inhaling lithe French cigarettes, pinkie fingers to the air.

When he felt a tap at his shoulder at first he figured he was being asked to step aside; he inched forward, but felt the poke again. "Don't run away from me now."

She was skinny, orange-haired, bangs cut straight across her brow. Her small eyes popped out at him: blue orbs joggling in bloodshot sockets. She wore a shiny blue dress and was considerably younger than the singer, maybe nineteen or twenty. Even through the smoke he whiffed her rose water and talc.

"Lookin' for a date?" she asked.

He looked around.

She dug her knuckle into his shoulder. "Funny man, I'm talking to *you*."

"Me?" he said, suddenly bashful, "I'm only in town tonight."

She snorted. "I think that's long enough."

"I think you've got me confused with somebody else."

"You don't *like* me?" She looked at him with big, bug eyes.

He felt his throat go dry; she rested her chin on his shoulder. "I like you just fine."

"Then you *do* want a date?"

"Well"—he glanced around, worried that somehow Daddy and his cohorts were watching—"OK, sure. Where do you want to go?"

She had grasped his hand and was already leading him through the crowd, out a side door and down a narrow hallway.

"I don't even know your name," he said, following her toward the room.

"What do you think it is?"

"No idea."

"C'mon, guess."

"Uh, Suzy?"

"You smart boy, you!"

She turned at the doorway, barring his entrance. "You got ten dollars?"

"I think maybe . . ." he said with genial puzzlement, "I've got . . ." He fished in his pocket and came out with six he had left. "I had more, but the man out front . . ."

"It'll do," she snapped, whisking the bills from his hand, turning into the room, and, in a single, fluid motion, slipping her dress up over her head and flinging it onto a chair. Her buttocks were firm and white.

"Oh, my god," he gulped, "I didn't mean to . . . I can step out if you need to change."

"We do get some strange ones in here!" she muttered, turning around to face him: bony, winged shoulders, taut pink nipples, low-slung, narrow hips, thatch of black hair at the secret place he had only dreamed about on the other side of countless articles of ladies' apparel.

He closed his eyes and started across the floor, dizzyingly holding out his arms to hold and kiss her.

"Un unh," she warned. "I only kiss with my boyfriend. Now take off your clothes. Six dollars don't last long. Open your eyes, cowboy." She pointed to his feet. "I don't allow shoes on my bed."

"Sorry." He stopped, turned to the side and slipped off his shirt. Without untying his shoes he pried them off, then slid down his pants, leaving on his boxer shorts.

"C'mon now," she urged, "we don't got all day. Mickey."

Through the walls rose a groaning, lost in the sudden, muted blaring of the band.

"OK," he said sheepishly, still turned away.

"Let me guess. This is your first time. Mickey."

"Why're you calling me Mickey?"

"Because I like the name Mickey. It's *sweet.*"

"Well," he answered nervously, "*thanks.*" He sidled toward the bed and flopped onto his back. "Ready."

"You think I'm gonna play the man? For six lousy bucks you do the work."

Rolling over he felt the naked length of her beneath him—damp skin, sharp ribs—and closed his eyes whispering, "Suzy, oh, Suzy," into her neck. Like Milagros on a dusky Dauphin corner she smelled now: talcum powder covering the hard, raw scent of sweat.

"Don't you know nothing?" She reached down and tugged at the waist of his undershorts. "Take these damn things off."

He jumped at feeling her small hand grip the bone of his penis, guiding him firmly into her patch of wet, springy hair.

"Jesus!" he whispered, slipping into her.

"Pray over it, Mickey."

"Oh, Jesus!" He slid back and forth, unable to get enough of the delicious feeling.

"Lover boy," she laughed.

"Oh, Suzy," he said, breathing rapidly, skin tingling, pillows and bedsheets and orange hair turning around him as he bucked hard and shook, spewing deeply into her.

"You are one beautiful lady," he whispered.

"Sure I am," she said.

"Oh, baby, I love you." He clutched her shoulders, nuzzling into her neck.

"Yeh, I love you too, now get off."

He shrank like a prune. "Let me hold you."

"C'mon, dreamboat." She shoved him off. When he rolled onto

his back she twisted around and pushed at him with her foot; he clambered out, standing woozily.

She leapt up on the other side, wiping herself desultorily with a rag she then pitched into the corner, and threw back on her shift. She stepped over to his clothes, picked them up and hurled them at him. "Hurry up."

Abe held out his hand to her. "One beautiful lady," he repeated. "See ya', Mickey."

"I just want you to know," he began, "that whatever I spent here tonight was worth it. No, it was a hundred times worth it!"

"*Worth it*, you son of a bitch? You think discounts are my usual terms? For you it was a fuckin' bargain!" She yanked him by the wrist toward the door where he stumbled into the hallway, holding his balled up clothes in his arms. Out the next door came a girl who looked right through him on her way to the water closet. He heard a howl, a trumpet, another door open and slam. He slipped on his clothes and jammed on his shoes.

Making his way back through the strip club and into the roar of the speakeasy, he slapped his leg, crying, "Gosh damn!" He burst back onto the street, a maverick let loose from his stall, drinking up the perfumed New Orleans air.

That the visit to New Orleans put new life into Abe's zest for the store was not lost on Morris. The excitement of the trip there and the new terms for selling furniture—three dollars down, two dollars a week for up to twenty months—was evident to Miriam and Hannah, too.

"Maybe he's got a girl in New Orleans," Hannah surmised to her mother as they made Sabbath stew: a rich mixture of boiled beef and potatoes and okra and corn, enough to last them the long Saturday when they still obeyed the injunctions not to light a stove (Marta Pastor did that for them), and only walked to *shul*, waving off offers by their gentile friends for a lift in a motor car.

"A girl?" said Miriam. "God help us."

"That wouldn't be so bad, Mama. Milagros went there."

"Marta's niece?"

"Yes'm. And she wrote me and said it's a grand place. I'd like very much to go there. I wish Daddy'd take *me.*"

"I thought the Pastor girl went back to Cuba!"

"She was supposed to, but just before she was about to ship out from New Orleans she got offered a job."

"What kind of job that she could not do back where she belongs?"

"Some kind of restaurant work down in the French Quarter. It's supposed to be very exciting there."

"What does she know of this."

"I'm sure she can learn. I *like* Milagros. A lot."

"Marta Pastor, I think she does not know about her niece in this bad city."

"New Orleans isn't a *bad* city."

"It is a place where men do horrible things to women, and some women let them do these things. In Budapest, I heard of this. The Hungarians."

"Oh, Mama, there probably aren't even any Hungarians in New Orleans. Besides, what kind of things could men do that are so horrible if women let them?"

"Let strangers touch them."

"Mama!"

She nodded. "Hand me the collard greens," she said, receiving with sadness the head of greens and juking these into boiling water.

"Anyway," Hannah said, "Milagros isn't like that."

"You do not know what is like a girl who is not one of us."

"Aunt Fanny . . ."

"In *marriage,* no matter how was Aunt Fanny," Miriam returned sharply, "it was with God's blessing."

"Mama, you're blushing!"

"Hush! These are not things to talk about anyway. And certainly not now, making the *shabbos* table." She held up her hand. "Shhh."

On the street below she heard Abe loudly proclaiming to a customer the good value of a dining room suite.

"Go, find out what secret your brother is keeping."

"You just told me it wasn't right to talk about these things."

"You think I am asking you to talk about something you should not? If there is a secret in Abe's heart that we should know, then it is not a bad thing you should find out."

"I am not Lily, Mama."

She stopped her ministrations over the table and looked up at her daughter. "What do you mean by saying this? I am blind?"

"It's just that Abe, he would tell Lily but not me."

"God keep the soul of your sister. You must do what she would do."

"It doesn't matter she's dead. Abe still talks to her and not me!"

"Hannala, the memory of your sister!"

"Lily this and Lily that, who can forget?"

"Don't be this way," Miriam cried, her hand snapping across Hannah's cheek, its dull imprint rising like a splotchy ghost across the pure skin.

Hannah's lips puckered and eyes crinkled, but she did not shed one single tear. She picked up the brush next to the table and, staring back defiantly, began slowly to pull it through her hair. "I miss Lillian, too," she said. "But I'm me."

Miriam saw neither Hannah nor Lillian before her at the table; no, it was her own mother, dark hair, strong brow, brown eyes facing her down. She reached out but felt the young woman pulling away, like her mother had pulled away, declaring with silence, "You cannot keep me for your own."

French Quarter Blues

Since the depths of that night when Asa Spicer had been snapped awake by hooded men pushing their way into his office, the dentist had found himself often, in 3 A.M. dread, sitting up with a start. The racing of mice behind the wall, the fussing of pigeons on the eave, a boom of thunder—every stray noise yanked him awake.

The banging at his hallway entrance was a nightmare returned. He picked up a hammer and approached the door.

"Dr. Spicer!"

"Who's there?" he called back.

"Dr. Spicer," the voice implored. "It's me. *Abe!*"

"Kleinman's boy?" He inched the door open and saw the young man standing there, eyes wide, a scared boy looking for help. "Well, I'll be. Come on now."

"Dr. Spicer," Abe said, shuffling in, looking down at the floor, "I figured I could come talk to you seeing as how you're a doctor and all. I know it's late, but I didn't want Daddy or Mama or Hannah or anybody to know."

"Is this a pain that you been feeling for a while, or something that's come on all of a sudden?"

"Sudden like," Abe said, sinking down into the chair.

There was no visible swelling in his jaw. "Let's take a look. Lean your head back now." He reached over for his dental mirror.

"No sir," Abe said, "it's not there."

Spicer nodded. "Problem with your neck?"

"No sir."

"Headaches, then?"

"Well, no sir."

The doctor waited patiently.

Abe gestured toward his head. "It's not up that way at all."

"But I'm a dentist, you know."

"It's just," Abe blurted out, "I've heard people say that you can fix anyplace. Maybe it's 'cause the tooth nerves run all through you, they say."

"True, the teeth do affect the whole body. Abe, what hurts?"

"It's not *what.*"

"OK, where?"

"It's more like *when.*"

"OK. When?"

"When I pee."

If Abe had been black he would have chuckled aloud at a youth come to agonize about his groin with someone whose specialty was gums, but you never knew how a white man might take that ribbing; maybe he'd even go up and down Dauphin, the agitated state he was in, complaining Dr. Spicer didn't respect a man's concerns over a pained prick.

Solemnly he returned: "I 'preciate you being real honest with me. Now I need you to keep on being honest."

"Don't tell my Daddy!"

Asa put his hand over his heart and nodded. "Have you had recent knowledge of a young woman?"

"God doesn't punish men for doing it."

"I'm not preaching at you, son!"

Abe looked down. "Yes sir, I have."

"You know this girl pretty good?"

"It's not her fault!"

"Just trying to get some facts, Abe."

"Yes sir."

"Any sores?"

"No sir."

"Thank the Good Lord for that. Five minutes with Venus, five years with mercury, if you got the syph."

"It's like somebody sticking a match up me!"

"You got the clap, boy. You gotta go to the hospital and pee into a jar and let them take a look."

"Can't *you* do something for me?"

"I can't cure you if that's what you mean."

"Can you at least go with me to the hospital?"

"A colored doctor taking a white patient into a white hospital? What country you live in?"

"Then take me to the colored hospital with you."

"You got to tell your Daddy before I'd do that."

"He'll say I've done something wrong."

"He's a man, ain't he? How you think he got you?"

"Can't tell him."

"You're sick in the peter, got to tell him. You know your Daddy's proud of you! You should be hearing the way he talks about you gonna make him and all you a million dollars the way you running that store—and with nobody having money to spend as it is!"

"He never tells me that."

"The time you run out at night over to that cross burning and your baby sister followed you, but you brought her safe home. Shoot, he loves to tell that. 'Without my boy there,' he tells me and Pastor chewing on his big cigar, 'Hannah might a never come back alive.'"

Abe was silent.

"That was you he was braggin' on, I know."

Abe was still quiet.

"Never figured it was Herman, was it?"

"No. No!"

"So, you don't have to be playing secrets with me. The hill yonder side of Davis Avenue, where y'all come across them Kluxers burning out Juby Blake for lettin' a white woman and colored man stay together in his barn. There was a baby up there, too, kind of mysterious. I know too much about them, come up here one night put a knife right against me"—he touched his throat—"near 'bout the last time I saw God's good earth."

"Maybe you're right," Abe said. "Maybe I should tell my Daddy."

"Us men we get ourselves in a heap of trouble pokin' around where we shouldn't oughta."

"Thank you, Doctor," Abe said.

"We'll get you fixed up good as new."

Abe scrambled up and was out the door. Spicer set down his dentist's tools and climbed into the patient's chair, put his feet up and gazed out the window. He prayed for the young Jew, asked that the Good Lord heal the worry in his man's parts. At least, for a while, he'd given him peace of mind; made him understand, like most hardheaded sons had trouble doing, that his daddy was a man, too.

What white doctor in all Mobile, he wondered, could handle his challenges so well? Who among them would religiously endure an over-the-store practice that earned less than a barber's? The indignity of working four blocks from a gleaming new hospital with life-saving machines, only to be told "Do not enter" because of the color of his skin?

Pavel Chemenko, the Ukrainian giant, now punch-drunk and paunchy, could lift one of Morris's sofas with one hand. In Kiev, legend had it, he'd done a strong man act for a tent show in the evening, picking up a calf every night for three months, soon hoisting a whole cow. During the day he'd worked loading barrels onto train cars until he accused another man, the son of a military officer, of trying to steal his purse. In a fistfight arranged for after work Chemenko easily felled the man, who'd gotten up onto his knees but collapsed and died. The work captain said that if Chemenko wished ever to close his eyes peacefully in sleep again, he'd flee town. Making his way to the Black Sea, and taking work as a deckhand bound for America, he'd come to port in New Orleans where he wandered into a Magazine Street gym and soon was traveling the Gulf Coast boxing circuit.

After winning two-bit wagers by local contenders from Corpus Christi to Atchafalaya—Abe's chin, Morris learned, among those crumpled—the Ukrainian had finally succumbed to a decade of punches. Although not once had he been knocked off his feet, his eyes registered, all at once, a thousand aftershocks. When he'd started lumbering about the ring losing money for his promoters in a New Orleans bout on Tchoupitoulas, he'd been let go, finding himself back where he started: looking for work up and down Magazine.

Pinsky from Cracow, who ran a second-hand furniture business, hired him for a month to help him lift old, heavy furniture into vats of lye that would eat away the peeling claw feet and spindled legs, cleaning away their former lives to prepare them for resurrection in the new. When Pinsky's full-time man returned to work, he recommended the Ukrainian travel to Mobile and look up Morris Kleinman, a friend of Besser's who'd been to visit.

That Chemenko could hoist a rocker with one hand while affixing thick straps with the other and setting it down into the lye, was good fortune for Morris. When he explained to the punchy bear that he might need help as well with "taking back furniture customers do not pay for," Chemenko smiled and said, "I good at breaking in door."

"We do not *steal* the furniture," Morris said, shaking his head at the brutishness of the man: the kind of dutiful peasant he remembered from his boyhood, as dependable as a mule for hauling and shouldering and just as thick in the head.

"Pinsky, he tell to me, if they do not give, you take. One door in New Orleans, for Pinsky I knock down."

"Kleinman is not Pinsky. Mobile is not New Orleans. Here you ask, they give."

Chemenko put his right arm out and cocked a muscle. "In Kiev, I lift one cow."

"Good, when I want to take back a cow you will know what to do."

Chemenko grinned a big, skewed smile, setting a bed frame down into a pool of lye set up out back of the store. Morris looked over the edge at the white compound burning clear the rusted metal frame. One day earlier it had sat in the ballroom of a pig farmer at the edge of Toulminville, the place where a good man slept and dreamed and prayed but did not make his promised payments.

"Mr. Jonas," he'd said, arriving at the farm with Chemenko at his side, "I try to make good business too, and you pay me only two dollars, but I need now the other ten."

"I just don't got it, Mr. Morris," he'd said. "You just go on and take it back, 'cause I done already slept my two dollars' worth out of it."

"Thank you, Mr. Jonas."

"Thank you, Mr. Morris."

Chemenko had simply lifted it with both hands, loaded it onto the back of a truck, and they'd rattled their way home.

But all that night Morris had not slept, envisioning Jonas, weathered and crick-backed, stretched prone on the floor: unjust punishment, surely, for a hard-working man who could not afford to pay for a bed because half his pigs had contracted swine fever and died. He heard Jonas's voice again saying, like a gentleman, "I done slept my two dollars' worth," and saw him waving good-bye at the door like he was sending a beloved child off to school.

When the bed was cleaned up, repainted, and ready to be sold from the "used and repossessed" showroom, Morris set his hand on the headboard and said to Abe, "I think I will make a gift of this to the farmer, Mr. Jonas. He is a good man."

"The same bed you just took back from him?" Abe spoke with annoyance, sunk down in his favorite chair.

"No, not the same bed, a *better* bed."

"What did farmer Jonas ever do for you?"

"Show to me his respect. Mr. Jonas is poor, but he is a good man."

"Am I a good man, Daddy?"

"You are my flesh and blood."

"That's not what I asked."

"You are my son."

"Suppose you didn't know me, though?"

"Suppose this, suppose that, you are talking like your mother. Maybe this, maybe that, it is not a way to be for a man."

"Then I am not a good man."

"Yes, son, you are a good man."

"I have . . ." Abe scrunched down further in his chair. "There's this . . . woman! Me and her . . ."

"Ah, *mazel tov!*" Morris clapped his hands together. "You have chosen a bride! Of course, why didn't I think of this! Long face and moaning. The daughter of . . . ?"

Abe shook his head. "No, Daddy, not the daughter of . . ."

"Well, it is good, still very good. This is not the old country with its matchmaker foolishness. In America we choose. Who is the girl so lucky to have my Abraham?"

He shook his head again. "That is not what I'm trying to tell you."

"I am only ears."

"It's the other part. You know, about a man. A woman. Together."

"Yes," Morris said, voice fading, "go on."

"We had sexual relations, Daddy. I met her . . ."

"Enough!"

"But . . ."

"First, do not tell this to your mother. Second, you will marry. I have nothing more to say."

"But there's something else *I* have to say."

"God help us, she is with child."

"No. I think I caught something. Like a disease or something, when I pee."

"*Oy vays mier,*" Morris cried. "First to the *doctor. Then* to the rabbi. What poor Papa has this disgrace for a daughter! In private I must talk to him. Oh, the heartbreak of a man, but we will arrange. What is his name?"

"I cannot say."

"This is not suppose this, suppose that, my foolish son. This must be done. *Now.*"

"I don't *know* her father's name."

"The girl, she is not a Jew?"

"I don't know, not exactly . . . I don't think so."

"What is her name?"

"Suzy."

"Suzy? This is all?"

"Just Suzy. I . . . I don't know her last name."

"Then that is all I have to say. Come, we will talk to Heshie and Selma Gollub. They know about such things."

"I'm in love with her."

"This Mobile, I should listen to your mother, it is not a place for a Jewish son."

"To hell with Mobile, she's over in New Orleans. I met her in this club, a really nice place, very fancy."

Morris sighed. "A wind in the night."

"You mean, you're not *mad?*"

"What is there to be mad? You will go to the doctor, then you will get married. End of talk."

"How can it be the end of talk?"

"It is over. It did not happen."

"But I haven't yet asked her to marry me!"

"Not this *shiksa* with no last name!" Morris boomed. "You will marry the daughter of Schwartz. I will see him tonight. We will talk."

"I'm not marrying anybody but Suzy!"

"Go to your room."

"Go to my room? *What* room?"

"The room where is the bed of a little boy who does not know better than to put Mr. Shmuck into a New Orleans whore."

Abe stood and faced his daddy. "She's not a whore."

"You have made her a whore."

"She only takes money to pay for food and rent."

"You spent the money made by this store to buy a sickness in the peter from a *shiksa* trash with no last name? No, I am not mad. I am crying. That my son could be such a *dumbkopf,* such a poor, turned around *schlimazel.* My *son!*"

"Then I am not a good man."

"Would a good man do such a thing as this?"

"You mean, would Herman? Herman the hero you're always going on about? Y'all don't tell me a damn thing that goes on around here, it's just you and him praising each other to high Heaven and me working my tail off."

Morris reached out and cupped Abe's chin in his hand, peering into his eyes. Was there a fever run into his son's brain? "You do not know what you are saying," he lamented. "My poor boy, you are sick."

"I went to Dr. Spicer."

"Ah, God, blessed by Thy name, forgive me for not seeing this until now. Like Lily out of her sweet mind with fever." He grabbed up Abe's hand.

Abe jerked away. "Don't you preach to me about Lily!"

"My son, you are sick!"

"You know what Daddy, I've never felt so *un*sick in all my life," and he turned and ran out the front door. Morris closed his eyes and put his hand to his chest, feeling the burning twinge, and, to calm his hurtling blood, whispered, "Miriam, Miriam."

The Hummingbird Line pulled into the New Orleans station at 8 P.M. that evening and Abe, having stood on the platform between the cars since Bay St. Louis, was the first one off the train.

By the market vendors jabbering their bastard French, by the macaws and parrots asking for crackers and plaintains in disembodied voices, by the rag-headed fortune teller with feline eyes staring toward the milky Cabildo, he made his way along the streets.

Back on Dauphin, he'd had trouble conjuring the exact lines of Suzy's shoulders and belly and hips. But here, hurrying across Bourbon cobblestones, he felt at his fingertips the delicate collar-bone, the small bud titties, the cool white stretch of her lower belly that made him ache to stretch across it. "Mickey," she'd called him, a name he ached to hear her say, that even now, when he listened for it in the French Quarter air, made his cock thump inside his dungarees. He'd barely uttered "Abe" in her presence, but she said Yankee names sounded ugly.

He passed a corner cafe where, through an open window, a big, sweaty man raked a spatula across a grill. Steam billowed up, the aroma of pork sausages pouring into the air, the pungent odor making Abe's nostrils flare. Abe stepped to the portal, watched the fat cook scrambling bell peppers and onions and long casings of the forbidden meat. The cook scraped the grill onto a plate and handed it off to a waiter who whirled it away. He was drawn now by another smell down the block: freshly baked bread.

Remembering he had not eaten since leaving Mobile, he entered the bakery, purchased kaiser rolls and doughnuts, continued to a delicatessen where he entered, bought salami, swiss cheese and a dill pickle, then headed back out to roost on the curb, fashioning a bulky sandwich.

Only three blocks remained between himself and his chosen. While replenishing his strength, he lost himself in reverie of her mouth: he asked her to marry him, she held out her arms, he pressed his lips languidly against hers.

Two men and a boy passed by wearing yarmulkes, and he remembered it was Friday night: Erev Shabbos. They were walking from *shul*. The men almost stepped on him as they passed. Here in this city he was wonderfully anonymous, giddily invisible.

His attention was caught by a young woman in a second-floor window across the street. Through planters holding hibiscus and elephant ears he glimpsed her bare shoulders, saw her, behind a veil of carnival beads, stripping off her skirt and dancing, arms weaving, to unheard music. Had she seen him sitting here? Was she performing just for him? He felt the tension down his back set there by fighting with Daddy now drop away, sloughed off like last year's skin.

The thrill of being a new person, a roué, he laughed, named Mickey, made him jump up from the curb and go back in. This new, debonair beast inside him was ravenous for sustenance. Down the deli counter he went choosing foods with dramatic tastes—liverwurst, goat cheese, sour cream, onions—foods that celebrated his new-found strength, his decision to make a sexy lady his own.

Drunk with love in his heart, food in his belly, and flavors on his tongue, he continued as far as Toulouse pausing only once more, to buy flowers. A few doors down from the jazz club he saw the busy tap-dancers, heard the pounding drums, listened to the torch-singer belting out "St. Louis Woman," the words pouring through him as he pushed through the grinding, necking couples and faced the bouncer at the back, handing him a couple of bucks, and entering, unphased, past the woman wearing nothing but a thong and red pasties who lumbered over the tops of crammed tables.

Around him brawny men and angular women pushed close, heads thrown back in easy horse laughter, mouths free and easy coming together like drunks finding the lips of a bottle.

These were his people; not the dull, tired men of the Conti Street synagogue with their unsurprised faces locked over sleepy prayer books, or the heirs to Dauphin Street rag and stick shops with their first generation Papas preaching the gospel of bargain and time. No, it was here, on a far-flung corner of Bourbon Street with "Basin Street Blues" beating outside the door, where he belonged.

He found his way into the back hallway and down to her room. He had only been there once, but had gone down it so many times in his mind he knew it without looking. He reached her door, placed his ear against it, heard the tunneling of his own breath; or was it someone else's, heavy and rasping, inside the room?

He eased open the door, peered in. Through the gloom he could make out jumbled bedsheets, Suzy's head against the pillows like a pallid moon, bangs splayed across her forehead.

The breathing rose; a moaning, like he'd first heard from Benny's and Fanny's room.

"Suzy," he whispered.

Was she snoring?

"*Suzy!*"

She bolted up. "What the hell!"

Shadows moved, stopped.

In a stupor she lay there. "Oh, baby, is that you?" She shielded her eyes from the slice of light from the hallway bulb. "Shut that door."

"Yes, it's me! Mickey."

"Oh, Mickey," she said woozily.

"I brought you flowers."

"You got some money, too?"

"You know I do."

"Such a sweet man." She reached out her hand.

"I love you," he said.

"How much?"

"As much as you'll ever want."

"How much moola?"

"Enough for a lifetime."

"It's what makes my world go round, baby."

"Let me kiss you."

"C'mere."

Abe kicked off his shoes and moved to her through the dim light, setting his mouth down upon hers, shocked to feel the wet muscle of her tongue pushing out at him.

She jerked her head back as if punched in the face and she opened her bulbous eyes, big as marbles. "You taste like fucking Sicily!"

"It's me, baby," Abe exclaimed.

"You stinky *Eye*-talian. It's *not* you."

"It's *Mickey*. I want you to come away with me."

Her fingers against his face became a cat's claws and the shadows in the room were shifting and turning and moving toward Abe as he gasped, "My Suzy!"

"My asshole!" she cried, and the shadow became another man's bald head and naked shoulders butting against Abe, ramming him out the door.

"And don't never come back," she yelled as he stumbled down the hallway, her wild harangue bursting inside his heart as he found his way back to the cobblestone labyrinth of New Orleans streets.

Georgia Sun

A
t Erik Overbey's studio on Dauphin Street, as the photographer instructs the Kleinmans where to stand for the graduation portrait, Herman waits for the moment to tell his family what is heavy as a volume of Alabama history on his heart. Before him, flush with pride, Mama takes up her position sitting erectly on a chair. Next to her on one side is Hannah, her hair a majesty of brown curls, on the other the empty place where Lillian should be. Behind them, standing, Daddy is already staring at the camera, eyes bright with satisfaction: a college graduate, his son.

Abe sidles up, saying nothing.

Herman knows the story—Hannah has whispered it to him on the store balcony that morning—about Abe's visits to a New Orleans woman of the night, how he'd lost his head and professed love for her, how he'd soon headed with Daddy and Asa Spicer to City Hospital to return with a look, hard to mistake, of relief.

Herman, diploma in hand, takes his position next to Daddy. Erik Overbey studies the composition, walks over to his camera.

Herman knows what he must say, even as they are radiating with joy—*kvelling* is the word in Yiddish, he has explained to David Pastor—for being the first Kleinman in all the generations of Kleinmans to graduate from college. Just two days ago, with Daddy having taken the Greyhound to Tuscaloosa to be with him, he had stood with the two hundred and sixty-three other young men of the Tuscaloosa university who would surely assume their places among the leaders of the state, helping guide it out of the depths of the grinding Panic and into the glories that Alabama was destined to achieve.

After the ceremony there had been a party where Aaron Goff, Randy Hyman, and Buddy Slutsky had announced their intentions to return home and help their Papas, applying what they had learned in history and mathematics and economics to carrying shipments of bowties and boaters and galluses and poplin dresses on into the next generation.

Through countless late nights his friends had debated over back-hills shinny the shaky future awaiting them among aisles of pants and shirts and rockers and highboys, especially when dollars in a customer's pocket were scarcer than starlings on a stormy morning. But faced with fathers who braved cossacks, border guards, turbulent seas, Ellis Island physical exams, and broiling Dixie roads to make this day possible, each had vowed, "I want to make my life, too, the store."

Herman had said he would wait, though, to be with Mama and Abe and Hannah to make his decision known. When back in Mobile, he told Daddy, he would make the claim on what his future would be.

As Overbey ducks under the black cloth and one bulb explodes, then a second, and the Norwegian emerges to say he is done, Herman, trembling inside, turns to the others and robs the joyous light right from his father's eyes: "I want to try making a living elsewhere, Daddy, to start over. Like you."

He took off to Atlanta, Georgia on a train the following week, a basket packed with Mama's fried chicken on his lap, the addresses tucked into his shirt pocket of two students with whom he'd gone to Alabama. At the *shul*, he'd gotten the names of some *mishpocah* of Mobile families, people who might be looking for an ambitious young man eager to make his fortune in the burgeoning Georgia city. But when he arrived, finding himself a room at a boarding-house on his own, he stamped through the streets, looking for work as a stranger. Daddy had done as much, he figured, without much schooling or English.

He got a job selling shoes until lack of customers forced the owner to lay him off; he took a job cutting deli meats, but the deli owner was struck down by a heart attack and his widow closed the deli's doors for good. He found work in a bookstore, recommending to customers the books of F. Scott Fitzgerald, but he watched the Fitzgerald volumes gather dust as the rube Georgians spent their lax hours with noses pressed to the scandals reported in the *Atlanta Constitution.*

Indeed, it was only President Roosevelt who seemed to be able to keep anyone employed, his job programs sucking out, from the snaking unemployment lines, the able-bodied, down-at-the-heel men, book sense or no sense, and putting a pickaxe or shovel into their hands to dig a hole from here to nowhere, but all the same, giving them work.

When a neighbor down the hall in his rooming house suggested to Herman that he "go on the dole" like so many others, Herman answered, "I'd rather pick up a shovel."

It was at a project of the new CCC—the Civilian Conservation Corps—that he did soon find himself, shovel in hand. "We are," he wrote Buddy Slutsky, "digging up a swampy area near the river at the edge of town to rid it of mosquitoes, everybody's so worried about malaria." To Mobile he only wrote, "Mama and Daddy, I am doing well in Atlanta. There is so much work here for a young college man . . ."

"So what could hurt using a shovel?" he asked aloud to no one, thinking of Daddy. His father had worked in a dry cleaners, sliced bologna, and sold junk before making his way to a life of *entrepreneurship.*

He repeated that word again as he stood on the spongy land alongside dozens of other young men, some digging into the muck to hurl another shovelful of rank earth onto a wagon, others bringing down axes onto stumps, others working saws. Their charge was to clear out and drain the land for a new neighborhood within one week. Many of the workers lived on a camp site in a clearing nearby.

Entrepreneurship—it seemed of a different language now, a promise on the other side of an ocean. Perhaps if he'd crossed the Atlantic like Daddy he'd be able to endure the bending and digging, the slopping through mosquito-laden bog until he figured out how to become a Vanderbilt, Rockefeller, or Rothschild. He wanted to believe the letters he'd written home with their sweet air of success, that Atlanta was the city of the future and he was the young man of Atlanta.

As he dreamed of Dauphin, seeing the long rows of chairs and tables, the repossessed and restored four-poster beds, the upstairs bedrooms where Mama and Daddy looked back at him, he heard them lament, "This is the life we have worked our fingers down to the bones to provide for you?"

He jammed the shovel deeper, faster, sensing a life someplace far from Dauphin, farther even than Atlanta or Charleston or Savannah, all the way to New York. He'd called an end to his romance with Sadie Berger, thinking one night, heady with her kisses, that he might propose, but deciding he was not ready. He'd made his ritual trip with frat brothers to a Tuscaloosa whorehouse, finding not a dangerous vixen like Abe had found but a tired matron laboring to accumulate dollars.

He pictured himself in Benny's millinery, Fanny, in curved hat, bussing him sadly on the lips. He saw them together, arm-in-arm, on a newsreel Fifth Avenue, Fanny shaking off her widow's gloom as they strolled by miraculous window displays.

As the heat lifted in waves off the wet land, and Herman saw rows of men, backs glistening, heads covered with smashed hats and torn bandanas, he envisioned a far cooler place Fanny had told him about: the verandah of a sea resort at Cape May, New Jersey, the two of them in rockers sipping iced drinks, conversing about the dreary South before turning their attentions back to the invigorating shore.

Now he heard a cry, and saw a man throwing his hands up in the air, ax flying from him, and falling to a heap in the mud.

Shovel at his side, Herman fell in behind others hurrying to where the man lay doubled up, hand clutching at his shinbone. He was as old as Daddy, face dark as night.

A foreman barreled through, shoving onlookers out of the way. The foreman stooped next to the victim, spoke roughly, reached into a satchel and brought out a roll of gauze and wrapped it around his leg. Blood soaked the old man's sock and shoe.

The foreman stepped back. "You good for the rest of the day?"

"Yes sir," the man said, standing with the help of a young man half his age.

The foreman started away, glancing over his shoulder at the pack of onlookers. "Back to work, bums."

As the workers split off to return to their places, the old man brought his ax high in the air but yelped, twisted and crumpled down. He quickly got onto all fours, and, with the young man tugging his arm, stood again, wavering and bringing high his tool.

When he fell this time and tried to stand yet again, tilting his head back and moaning to heaven, struggling to bring his ax up, Herman shouted, "Stop! You'll hurt yourself worse!"

"I gots to work!" the man shot back.

"How in God's name can you work?"

"Gotta eat, boy." He tottered as he spoke. "No work, no pay."

"Hey, foreman!" Herman shouted. The foreman stopped and turned to him. "Tell this poor man that's not true!"

"What other way you go to figurin' it? College boy?"

"At least pay him the day and let him go home so's he can heal up and come back tomorrow."

The foreman walked back toward Herman. "He's too old to be here anyways. Besides, we got a hundred blockheads ready to take his place. Yours too if you don't shut the hell up."

"You really been to college?" another man with a shovel said at his side. "What you doin' out here when you got *college?*"

"Out here working," Herman said, "like the rest of you."

"Well," the foreman bridled, coming close, "those men can't afford to lose their jobs and they've lost fifteen cents worth of pay already standing around jawboning."

Herman recognized the clenched teeth, the jutting chin: Louie Flynn blocking his path at the docks alleyway.

"You don't scare me," Herman said.

"What the hell do I care? As of right now"—he snapped his fingers—"you ain't workin' here no ways."

"Then I've got even less to fear, don't I?" He pointed to the man. "Pay him for the day and let him go home."

"You don't even work here no more *and* you're trying to run my business?" The foreman reached down and wrapped his hand around the handle of a stray shovel.

"What's fair is fair!" Herman clutched the handle of his own.

"Go on, curly boy, git!"

Herman waited. *Don't make the first move,* he said to himself, his body vibrating with a rush of blood. The foreman held his ground. *Steady.* Blood rocked his temples.

A hand shoved him squarely between the shoulders, throwing him forward where he was met by the broad side of the shovel against his head.

Down he went into the sludge, the snarling mouth of the foreman blocking the sky, muddy boots of other workers tromping away. He went to grab the foreman's leg like he'd grabbed Louie Flynn's, shouting, "I'm gonna get my brother Abe and we'll come back and get you, redneck sonuvabitch," but the bully was disappearing into the sharp sun.

"What . . . ," he moaned, "who . . . ?", feeling someone grab him beneath the arms and hoist him up. A truck rolled toward him and stopped alongside while two strangers climbed out and helped him into the back. He lay down, watching the aching blue sky revolve away; the truck bucked and kicked its way to the edge of town where he was told to "get out, go on, and don't ever come back."

Finding a bus stop he made his way into the city, keeping his broken head atop his shoulders as far as the rooming house where he trudged up six flights, managed to get his key in the door, and crashed onto his cot, pillows receiving him like great, soft hands.

When the door to his room creaked open and footsteps whispered toward him, he gave himself up to what they brought.

He started when the fingers touched his lips, sensing he must rise and knock away the intruder, but fell back to dreams of burning hills and bellowing animals and hardscrabble fields that worked grit into his skin. On his back in pale dawn, feeling a cool rag swab his forehead, he blinked awake, staring into almond eyes.

"Fanny?" he said from his stupor.

He lifted himself up on his elbows, headache resuming, but she was rising from his bedside. Walking to the doorway, stepping into the hallway gloom, she turned, waved and was gone.

How had Fanny found him? Why had she vanished? Worried he might miss her if she returned, Herman spent the day close to his room. Had she really been there at all? He went as far as the hospital two blocks away, got his head bandaged and took pain pills the doctor administered, and wove his way back to his room where the medication knocked out his lights.

When she reappeared in the depths of night he woke alert. She touched her fingers to his lips, stroked his brow.

She'd found out where he was staying from Abe, she explained, and since she was in Atlanta anyway she'd gone by his lodging and got the name of his work project. She'd gone to the CCC camp only to be met by men knocking off for the day who spoke with reverence about "a gall durn fool college boy getting slapped up side the head taking up for some colored."

Herman laughed at Fanny's yakkity, nasal Brooklyn voice imitating a cracker's slow drawl.

"They must have thought I was your Mama."

"No," he said, "I don't think so." He reached out and touched her thick black tresses.

"You've got to rest," she said, removing his hand. She looked over at the tattered curtains, the rickety table and chair. "What in God's name are you doing in this hole?"

"How'd you get in, anyway?"

"The man at the front desk is a friend of mine."

"You tipped him?"

"You're worth a quarter."

"But what are you doing in Atlanta? Christ, Fanny."

"Hey, it's me who's asking *you*."

"I'm on my own is what."

"Good Lord, Herman, a million books inside that head and you should be a *goy* laborer scratching in the dirt?"

"I'll get where I'm going before long."

"You sound like Benny. Benny, he used to talk like that."

"It's just that, I'm not sure what I'm after. But I'm headed there anyways."

"How many times do you need to get hit up side the head before you get some sense knocked into you?"

He took her hand and playfully swatted it against his head. "That makes two."

"Do you know how worried I was for you?"

"I didn't even know you were in town!"

"In town, not in town, there's a difference?" She stood and stepped away.

"Tell me where I can find you."

"I've got to go."

"You just got here." He leapt up and kissed her on the lips. "You're crying."

A church bell began gonging. Six A.M.

She turned and fled out the door, feet clattering on the steps.

"When can I see you again?" he called going to the window,

peering down the block, seeing only a lone storekeeper sweeping his walk.

There was no need to try waiting up for her. When Herman sat on his bedside expecting her to appear, he drifted off only to awaken to find her at his side with her palm against his cheek then fleeing as the bells set up their 6 A.M. chorus.

She told him of her childhood in Brooklyn, of her mother and father with their long, mournful faces that made Benny, when she first met him, seem like the most spirited and debonair of God's creatures. She told him how her first husband, Ike, a gambler, had been cold in his affections, and that the day she divorced him he was impatient to get back to the track. On her wedding night to Benny, she'd been "shocked and delighted" by her new mate's "love of pleasure."

She could tell Herman of her intimacies with husbands, but not why she had to leave nor where she went. She warned, "If you care for me, don't follow."

After her next visit, when she'd let him go so far as to kiss her on the neck before hurrying into the chiming dawn, he followed.

Through silent Atlanta streets he trailed, knowing that if she sensed him behind her she'd vanish for good. He suspected now it was to another man she headed: a worldly German, he imagined, who kept her unhappily in comfortable surroundings and would break the neck of any guy he caught so much as looking at her, much less welcoming her, however chastely, to his bed.

In his mind he confronted the Kraut at his sumptuous abode, proclaimed his desire for the beautiful aunt it was his role to protect and love. When the boorish patrician laid a soft, dull paw out to swat him Herman ducked, gave the man a sharp blow on the back and kicked him into the street, then swept in, taking Fanny and pulling her toward their joyful life together.

Instead of turning in the direction of Peachtree which led to the homes of gentry with their ordered privet hedges and kerchief-headed help mincing at the doors, Fanny turned the other way, catching a trolley at Fulton, setting a buzz in his feet to keep up.

As he ran a block behind the trolley the neighborhood fell away from rooming houses like his own to small, clapboard houses where white faces became fewer and black ones emerged looking back warily. Off the trolley, Fanny made her way down a dirt path between these houses.

Going where he knew he was not welcome, a few yards behind her now, Herman leapt behind a tangle of azaleas, hearing a baby's frantic cry and Fanny's voice calling out sweetly, "How's my darling little one?"

A girl stepped out of a door handing off a bawling infant the color of dark berries. First Fanny pressed the infant's cheek to her own, then unbuttoned her blouse and set its mouth onto her breast. The infant nestled in, making fists of its little hands, kicking its tiny feet, smacked, gurgled and hushed.

Ritual as prayer she came again that night but this time curled up beside him. "Herman?" She spoke so faintly that the sound of a truck rumbling through the night street made him bend to listen. "Are you awake?"

"Yes, doll," he said, remembering the word Benny had always used for her.

"You mean"—fainter still—"so much to me."

"Oh, my sweetheart."

They curled together, arms and legs entangling, her hand tracing the knobs of his spine, his fingers walking her shoulders, her palm sliding cool and soft to his hips, his circling the small of her back.

He felt her skirt rising, her knees brushing silkily against his. He tugged at her brassiere until she flicked her hand behind her back and released it and her breasts pressed warm and cushiony against him. But he said, "No," even as he held her tightly.

"*Not* no."

"I want to, God, I want to, but it doesn't seem right."

"It's been *four years.*"

His body hummed with the sweetness of her skin. "It's not about Benny."

"He thought the world of you," she said. "Benny would want this for us, he wanted me to be happy, you remember how . . ."

"But you've got a baby!"

"You did follow me."

"Why didn't you tell me?"

"You followed me, dammit." She leapt up; fastened her blouse.

"You think I disapprove? It's wonderful. A baby!"

"How dare you sneak behind me! Just like your Daddy, *just* like him. Oh, God, he was sneaky, too! Always following up behind me and Benny."

"You leave Daddy out of this."

"Every time we screwed he was practically *there.*"

"He opened my family's *door* for you. When y'all didn't have a pot to pee in he gave you and Benny a home."

"And Benny's blood money gave him the German's store!"

"Because Daddy protected him. They don't give insurance payments to suicides."

"You are a child! Still a big, naive child."

"I figured you came here 'cause you cared about me."

"I do care about you."

"Then why didn't you tell me about your baby?"

"Leave Shona out of this."

"*Mazel tov,* already! A baby girl!"

"Because I knew you'd judge me like everybody else."

"Because her Daddy's colored, you mean?"

"There! *There!*" she shrieked. "Scratch the skin and every one of you Southern Jews is a nigger-hating cracker underneath."

"Where *underneath?*" He grabbed at his ribs mockingly. "This isn't Abe you're talking to. What I tell you is exactly what I feel."

"Abe knows plenty you don't, like who the hell he is and what he wants."

"But you've got what *you* wanted, Fanny. Shona, Shonala. It's a real pretty name."

"But I wanted it to be mine and Benny's," she said, softening, "that was my prayer. Not a man's who'd keep me like a wife for two years—why else do you think I'd stay in this hick South, Atlanta's no better than all the rest of it—and then disappear. One died, one fled. All because of Fanny Bergman Weiss Chantell."

"A Frenchman?"

"His grandaddy was a slave in Louisiana took the name Chantell."

Fanny's eyes broke with tears, the years of her life from Brooklyn to Mobile to this Atlanta rooming house all running together across her face and, as he pulled her close again, onto his. On the bed together, clothes peeled away, he felt her breasts wet against his chest where they now leaked mother's milk, a high, sweet scent that made him touch her everywhere but that sacred place that was Shona's alone.

He shut his eyes to keep Benny from looking back at him, and shut them tighter to ward off Daddy's reproachful gaze. Fanny was over him, around him, carrying him far beyond this Atlanta room, beyond the Peachtree stores and Cobb County fields, beyond the Charleston and Savannah and Richmond streets where his classmates were already building their conventional lives, as far as the edges of the Atlantic Ocean where Fanny had once plucked Benny out of the surf and now set Herman in his place until he felt the shore streaming through him in sweet agony.

She left him as silently as she'd come, hurrying home to a hungry child.

When she did not come the next night he raced to find her, down the Peachtree Streets, down to where colored town started and the shanties began.

Hurrying up the walk past the thick azaleas he was met at the door by a sullen teenager, the same one he'd seen before.

"You looking for Miss Chantell?" the girl asked, her voice flat and hard.

"Where's Fanny? I must see her. Fanny!" he called.

"She gone."

"I'll wait, I'll just stand right here until she returns. I won't bother you at all."

"Then you gonna be standin' there 'til Jesus come, 'cause Miss Chantell she done took her baby and gone back where she come from."

"To Mobile?" he said excitedly.

"What Mobile? She gone back to her peoples. Up north."

Sweeping his walk, waiting for light to break through the mild winter sky, Morris goes beyond the boundaries of M. Kleinman & Sons and continues to the end of the block. He shakes his head, standing before a dead storefront where Eberhardt Karl's restaurant used to be. It is not Karl himself who has died—indeed, his German friend passes the store everyday to say hello—but his business. Another store, too, Pinkerson's Music, has folded up. Its windows stare blankly at the street.

Empty stores are a bad sign. Without chairs, tables, shoes, loaves of bread, people, business establishments are empty rooms filled with cobwebs and ghosts. They wait forlornly for new owners to create life again. Until then they are holes in the street that grow wider, waiting for the missteps of others.

He sweeps back toward the front of M. Kleinman & Sons. Does he hear noise upstairs? Abe, lazing through the morning, finally making a stir? At least this son is working at the store, making a try, doing his best. Herman? "He wants now to be a *gonif,* a thief!" he has told Pastor.

"Your Herman a thief, never," Pastor consoles him.

"A lawyer is a man who sits with paper and tricks people for their money. Or worse, makes criminals to go free. And this is what Herman wants now. More school he needs? Life is not with paper in an office high in a building where the millionaires jump when Wall Street crashes. 'Life,' I tell him, 'is in a store, on the street. With people.'"

"The children," Pastor concedes, "they do not listen."

"Your David works with you."

"My David"—Pastor smiles—"this is different."

Setting down his broom, Morris sighs. "Ah, sons." But without a store at all what can he give them when they do return home?

"Dear Lord," he says, breaking his vow never to petition God, Blessed be His Name, for such a mundane blessing, "please send me customers."

But an answer comes.

Dressed in blue once more, but this time silky blue and a broad-brimmed white hat, the *shayna madele* appears on the walk, hand outstretched to shake. "Mr. Morris, it's me! Betty Green!"

"Yes, Miss Green, of course, Miss Green."

"I'm here to extend you an invitation to our church. Might mean some good business for you!"

"What business can I make in your place of God? I am only a poor, hard-working . . .'"

"We're building a religious camp," she cuts in excitedly, "and need about fifty chairs and a bunch of tables, a big couch, beds. Folks there never met someone like you, like us, really, you know my grandaddy was Solomon Gruen. But you're the one out of the Bible. They just want to take a look at you, that's all. Preacher's already got a big collection to make a down payment if it's good for you."

Looking back at the empty storefront down the block, he shrugs. "OK, Betty Green. For business."

On Sunday he walks to the corner of Broad and boards a bus to Dog River. He knows well the downtown Cathedral, and the Government Street Methodist Church, and Christ Episcopal Church, but never has he seen so many small wood-frame country churches as now.

Out the window of the bus slide by the Church of Christ, the First Church of Christ, the Church of Christ Disciples, the Church of God, the Church of Latter Day Saints, the African Methodist Episcopal Church, the Predestinarian Baptist Church, the Land of Canaan First Baptist Church, the Riverside Free Will Baptist Church, the Church of the Redeemer, the Church of the Holy Word, the First Church of God's Holy Word, the Church of Apostles, the Church of Zion, the Church of the Holy Bible.

In each church, through open doors, he sees the heads of the congregants pious and bent, shiny pates and silver waves and thick nests and brown bobs all leaning into the voice of the preacher that rises before the cross that is stark and mournful in one church, bright-white and jubilant in another, thick and tall as the rafters in another, nowhere the body of Christ carved in anguish as in the Cathedral where, above a crown of thorns twist the letters INRI, King of the Jews.

What are they praying, Morris wonders, spying children hand-in-hand with mamas and daddies walking up the aisles, kneeling, sprinkled, blessed, rising, shouting for joy? What is it like to have a man's face deep in their heart, God's Son they call Jesus, with His dreamy gaze and woman's locks? Why would they not be blinded by the awesome light, like Moses on Mt. Sinai arrogantly seeking the Lord's visage?

How many of them might need tables and chairs?

Like a Jew in Piatra Neamt selling at the monastery door silken cloth for priestly robes, silver for reliquaries, leather for holy shoes, might he not supply, at pious discounts, simple furniture for a hundred meeting houses, camps, and retreats? He glances around, expecting the ghost of Lutchnik laughing at his unceasing enterprise, but sees only a dozen ladies in hats, pocketbooks on their shoulders, eyes fixed on his.

Off the trolley, pacing the final yards to the Dog River Church of Pentecost, he looks up to see the bobbing head of the minister: a lean, sallow-faced man, a gaunt Donnie McCall, welcoming him even before his feet hit the threshold, calling out, "Mr. Morris Kleinman of Dauphin Street, welcome to the House of the Lord!" as his boots hit the runner and three congregants lay their hands on his wrists and shoulders, and Betty Green is there wearing the dress Lillian sold her, her face as radiant as on that long ago day.

"Oh, Morris, thank you for coming!"

"Thank you," he says apprehensively, "for inviting."

"You're so very, very welcome."

The preacher's hands are in the air as though pulling down the very fire he extols: the Holy Ghost of fire, the spirit of fire, the baptism of fire. Morris feels the fire, a heat up around his chest and shoulders, a crinkling in his chest, and as he reaches for a handkerchief Betty Green has one at the ready, pressing it to his palm and folding his hand around it, although his hand doesn't fully want to close.

"The spirit inside here today is strong, so strong," the preacher effuses. "Let's show our guest, not just from downtown Mobile, no, all the *way* from the land of Canaan, what the spirit can do! It's alive here with us, today, alive, beyond the comings and goings, the risings and fallings, of our simple, meek lives. No, brothers and sisters, the spirit here is enduring, it is all powerful. Yahweh, our Hebrew brother calls this spirit. Yahweh, Jesus Christ our Lord! Glory Hallelujah! Let us, together, pray!"

Not Hebrew, Yiddish, Polish, Romanian, Russian, Serbian, Slavic, German, Swedish, or French, the voices of the congregants rise up, one after the other, in babble Morris has never before heard. Is it Japanese, Korean, Polynesian, Chinese? Is it of this earth, or some other? One woman, too fat for her yellow blouse, is rolling her head from side to side and jabbering; another, Adam's apple crawling up and down her throat, is hooting and hollering; two others, twin men with coronas of baldness atop full heads of hair, are whispering and stammering, the spirit streaming through them faster than tongues can follow.

He has seen men transported like this before: in the Piatra Neamt synagogue, after a day of fasting, the old men beneath prayer shawls beating their chests in atonement, their recitations tumbling from parched and weary lips. He has heard the incantations of the Hasidim in the Polish villages, the cock-eyed followers of the Baal Shem Tov leaping with prayer.

"Don't be afraid," Betty says lightly. "Those that feel the spirit let it talk. Scared me too, at first."

"Morris Kleinman, would you come forward?" The preacher extends his hand; it seems to reach right into Morris's chest, squeezing at his heart.

"He just wants to introduce you," Betty says, "that's all."

Flushed, sweating, Morris walks politely forward. "For business," he mumbles, emboldening himself.

Standing close, Morris can feel the preacher's stale breath palpitating the air, saying how "Morris Kleinman is a friend of ours" and "Betty Green met Morris Kleinman in his hour of need, sunk low with sorrow" and that "thanks to Morris Kleinman, we'll be outfitted for our holy camp in the beautiful Alabama woods," and, remarkably, he jams an envelope crammed with dollar bills into Morris's hand and says this is down payment—"a holy pledge"—against all the other payments to come.

Why is his heart wrinkling and tightening? Why here, God help me, among these exuberant gentiles with their hands weaving in the air? He falters; Betty Green is at his side, holding him up.

"The spirit is with us!" the preacher cries.

If the spirit manifests itself in tiny needles pricking his arm, then Morris feels it, too, but he knows this is something else, and when the preacher turns, nodding at him, reaching out to lay a hand on his head, he sees Donnie McCall's face again and understands how McCall must have dreaded drawing his final breath with only Morris there as witness.

It is not so much to die as to do so alone, without Miriam, whose name he is silently calling. He reaches out to touch Betty's dress believing it is the same one Lillian had sold her, finding his daughter's touch and lifting his hands to her thick head of hair where he weaves his fingers to try and save her one last time.

He knows now that he has prayed to God for customers, but God has rebuked him for this selfishness, bringing him to this stage with its naked pine cross and humbling him before the yammering devout. Was not the life he had been given joy and breath enough? Was it not enough that he should make a decent, honest living without riding past the houses of the Lord and seeing, in every one, a way to sell even more? *Dayenu,* he had sung at his daughter's bedside, but, like Moses feeling short-changed without a peek at God's face, he had forgotten how magnificently he was blessed.

"Forgive me, Lord," he whispers, and the preacher exults, "Praise God!"

When he slumps into Betty's arms she understands this is not how the Holy Spirit works and she summons the deacons who help carry him to the air, and she leans over him, her hand pressing to his chest.

When Morris opens his eyes, the world swirling around him, asking where's Miriam, and can he have his rocker, she answers, "You're gonna be all right, don't you worry. I'm doing just like Grandaddy Green taught me: Pray, but just in case God don't answer right off, call you a doctor."

Rose Wine

The doctor gave Morris a pale brown pill to take when his heart hurt. How could this tiny orb, no bigger than a button in Miriam's sewing tin, know where to go in his body? After a week in the hospital, he said he would do better to eat a good chicken liver sandwich chased by a glass of ginger ale. His heart, battered but in one piece, was like an old boot from the cast-off shoe box. It could still carry him where he wanted to go.

Back at home in bed, sipping Miriam's matzo ball soup and eating her pickled watermelon rind—the doctor had told him to swear off the chicken liver for a while—Morris discovered what was truly the best medicine of all. When Abe brought the ledger books upstairs and showed his father how effectively he had been managing the store, Morris felt renewed. He propped himself up against the pillows and praised, "It is good, very good, that you are selling."

"You can push some of 'em," Abe said, "who're sitting on the fence."

"But do not oversell," Morris warned. "Repossession, this is the saddest thing of all."

To Abe, though, taking back what a customer refused to pay for just made good sense. "There's nothing wrong in taking back what belongs to you," he instructed Chemenko the next day.

"To break the door," Chemenko agreed, "is good."

Abe's strategy was to stand politely at the threshold of a customer's home, explaining, "We're just here to have a friendly chat." When the door eased open, he wedged his foot under it, saying, "Now, we'll turn right on around and go home if you make some kind of payment in good faith." Often that would be enough to have a housewife scrabble through the drawers for a stray dollar or pull out a hammer to crack open the piggy bank, change cascading to the floor.

If the customer just stood there, silently blinking, Abe nodded to Chemenko, who stepped closer, leering his crooked grin until the door swung open and the customer pointed remorsefully to the bed or chaise lounge.

"Do I get back what I done paid?" one crochety grandpa asked, when Chemenko hoisted his sofa. "It makes near 'bout sixteen dollars!"

Abe shook his head. "How come none of you people ever *listen* to the agreement before it's signed? There's nothing in there about paying on the furniture 'til you don't want it anymore." Abe mimicked: "'Come to think about it, Mr. Kleinman, think I'd like my money back.'"

"I sure in hell's name would! All sixteen dollars' worth!"

"We've given you all the slack we can, but time comes, sooner or later, to pull on the rope."

"Well, you shore done choked me good if that's what you were after."

"What I'm after, *alter kocker,* is what's fair and just."

"Don't call me no filthy names!"

"Good day," Abe said, seeing that Chemenko got safely out the door without a stick cracking his head.

That next night Daddy summoned him to his room. "How did you mean the words you said to Mr. Robert Douglas?"

"You mean that old man trying to rob us of our couch?"

"Such a *grosse macher* you are now, a big shot, running the store. First you take a man's sofa, then you call him a bad name."

"I said, '*alter kocker.*' I wasn't using it bad. All it means is what he is, an old man. I'm tired of everybody taking advantage of us!"

"This year we are making a profit! This is your 'taking advantage'?"

"And you know how much bigger profit we'd have, Daddy, if we were paid all we're owed?"

"If you shear a sheep you cut all his wool and what is left? But if you clip a little today, next week you still have . . ."

"Why are you talking to me *about sheep?*"

"Do you want a customer back again? Do you want his brother, his cousin?"

"So the whole family can make us fools?"

"So we can make good business!"

"Aren't I doing a good job? Don't you *ever* give *me* any credit?"

"Do you know how my Papa's distillery was locked up by the Romanian guard? How I was sent to sleep on sacks?"

"You know how many times I've heard about all you learned because of those damn sacks on the floor? Me and Hannah?"

"Do not speak for Hannah."

"You won't let her speak for herself."

"Let Avraham speak for Avraham!"

"Then why not let me speak for the store?"

"Speak what? *Alter kocker* to an old man who thinks you are calling him son of a bitch?"

"I've heard you say plenty worse to troublemakers wandering in here stinking drunk."

"This *alter kocker* is a customer."

"Remember what Besser said, Daddy? We're not working for them. They're working for us!"

"Maybe you are right," Morris said.

"Well, yeah, of course I'm right. You got to go out and collect, be tough, if you want to get anywhere these days."

"No. Right about my Papa. He was robbed of everything, he had nothing, but what did he give me in a cold mat on a stranger's floor?

A schoolhouse. What have you learned with all I have given you?
How to hold up a whore like a queen? How to knock open the door
of a hard-working man?"

"I thought you were teaching me to make a living like a
Kleinman!"

"A living, not a killing."

Abe looked down. "Good night, Daddy."

"Come." Morris raised his hands. Abe walked forward. Morris
took his son's head in his hands and kissed his forehead. "*Langer
loksh,*" he whispered.

"That's when I was ten, Daddy!"

Down the stairs, past Mama making her way up to bed, into the
showroom of the store, Abe made his way, muttering, "Not a kid."
The furniture hunkered in darkness: a prison of floor fans and
dresser drawers and easy chairs. He paced past the mirrors and side
tables, came to the wall, peered out the window at Dauphin Street.
He thought of Suzy opening her arms to him in the backroom club.
Maybe she'd been half asleep, or drunk, or drugged by that cue-
ball-headed bastard. Maybe she was crying for him right now. "Too
bad," he said to the picture of her, scrawny and naked, in his mind,
"you had your chance." On the street passed Molly Gerson, arm-in-
arm with Isaac Kass—"engaged," Mama had told him. Let them
dance their feet to calloused nubs at a hundred B'nai Brith dances;
what did he care!

There were other stores on the street where he could seek work:
the new haberdasher's on the corner of Joachim, or the novelty
shop opened catty-corner from M. Kleinman & Sons. Wouldn't
they relish a young man with his vigor and drive? A businessman
of *this* century who understood, as Besser preached it, the gospel of
time?

He smacked his fist into his palm and turned to the office, going
to Daddy's chair and opening the first drawer: cigars. He pulled one
out, bit off the end and lit the tip, puffing the brash tobacco. Is this
what Daddy felt, feet on desk, chair tilted back, Cuban tobacco
swirling down his throat? The grandeur of being boss?

The Dog River Church of the Pentecost was behind in its payments—three months behind. "These Christians," Daddy had said, "they are good to us. Let them alone, they will soon pay." Abe looked at the calendar: eight more days and they'd be four months behind. Who were these Bible-shakers to receive special privilege? Just because a pretty Miss Green came to ask of Morris's health, they should be exempt from the demands placed on other customers? With their sermons about love and compassion, they were worse than deadbeats—*hypocrites,* yes, that was the word.

He heard the front door open; he got up and walked out of the office.

He saw his sister stealing toward the stairs. "Hannah!"

She looked up. "Good night," she said and put a foot on the first stair.

"Hey. What's . . . You're out awfully late, aren't you? Who've you been with?"

"Friends."

"Who friends?"

"Are you Daddy?"

"No, but I think I can speak for Daddy."

"Liar."

"What did you call me?"

"Oh, Abe, you heard me good and well. Daddy didn't give you permission to run my life anymore than to run this store."

"But it's sure damn my concern who you're out with and where this time of night."

"I was out with David," she said. "Are you happy?"

"*Pastor?*"

"He's just a friend. He understands me when I talk."

"You speak Spanish?"

"Not like you and Milagros."

"That's enough."

"Or what?" she said.

"Or else you'll be restricted to this house!"

"It doesn't matter what you say, you know that, Abe. I can go out when I want, and keep what friends I want."

"And what do you think Daddy will say?"

"He'll say, 'Mazel tov.' Because I've decided to go away—to college."

"To . . . Why, you can't go to college. You're a . . ."

"Girl, that's right. But there are colleges for girls, too, you know. I've written Herman and he thinks it's a good idea. A wonderful idea. In Atlanta."

"So Herman's behind this!"

"Thank God."

"Daddy won't stand for it."

"Yes he will because Herman will introduce me to some nice men to go out with, some may even be from New York, and who knows where I'll end up. I'm going to be a teacher."

"It's not right, Hannah!"

"To leave you here alone? Is that what you mean?"

Abe whirled to look toward the store window. David Pastor's shadow flickered there, was gone. He turned back to Hannah, seeing the hem of her skirt disappear at the top of the landing, heard her footsteps treading quickly to her room.

He went back to the store office, took his position up in the chair and put the ledger back in the drawer. Underneath he noticed another ledger and took it out. He opened it to see the name of Pablo Pastor followed by a long list of items purchased from the store—and payments received. He turned to 1917. A pair of shoes: one cigar. Workman's overalls: three cigars. He leafed through the pages: cigars for Easter dresses and cigars for boots and cigars for chairs and dressers and beds. He puffed furiously on the stogie, ground it out in the ashtray and tucked the ledger back where it belonged.

"*La vida*," Pablo Pastor said, walking to the edge of town, "*es breve*."

"Life," he repeated, uncertain if God heard him in Spanish anymore, "is short."

That Morris had suffered a heart attack and lay inactively above his store saddened him deeply. "The life in the city," he spoke to the smoke that curled from his stogie, "maybe is not so good."

"En la naturaleza se encuentra la salud," he remembered his grandmother used to say. In nature a man finds his health.

Everywhere, though, in or out of *"la naturaleza,"* Pastor whiffed only cigars. At the end of Dauphin where the dock's air was rife with creosote and fish, he breathed cigars. Near the Albright & Wood drugstore, only cigars. Even in Miriam Kleinman's kitchen, where he had first tasted the sweetness of corned beef and cabbage, he clicked his tongue on the abiding aftertaste of tobacco.

At the edge of town, satchel of cigars over his shoulder, he boarded the bus to Dog River. Morris had told him about the churches that lined this highway: he saw them as stations of the cross, markers in the journey of a man who must do penance for aggrieving his son.

As a result of his meddling, David had fallen ever more deeply under the spell of Hannah Kleinman, and no good could come of this. Years ago his son had first revealed his adoration of the girl, and he had promptly taken a strap to his arms and back. If he had ignored David then, would not the boyish infatuation have played itself out? The bruises had outwardly healed; beneath them, as Marta had warned, festered more intense longings for the girl.

During the last month he'd spied them conversing in the back room of the apartment among the tobacco leaves, and on one quiet Tuesday afternoon sitting in lounge chairs on the Bay Queen as it pulled out from the docks. When he saw David's face, though—eyes gazing off, mouth slack—he knew at once that his son loved a chatty and fetching young woman who offered him a heart of stone. David and Hannah might amble through the square talking about their lives, but afterwards, late, while David's head sank in sleep crazy with pictures of Hannah, two blocks away Hannah dreamed of anybody but him.

And if they did marry and have children? No matter that Pablo defended Jews loudly against those who believed them doomed to an afterlife of suffering; when he sat quietly rolling cigars, imagining a Jewish grandson of his own, he secretly worried that Christ might turn His back, in the Holy Kingdom, on an unchristened child.

"The Jews," he had once told David in words that haunted him, "they will break your heart."

But he would not send his only son to Cuba to hunt a wife! No matter how Marta argued that David must do like Milagros and go there to marry, he would not give up his son to an island that had paid him only in sweat and a growling belly.

"*La naturaleza . . .*" Perhaps out here he would find the answer, where the oak trees fattened like Cuban matrons in shawls and complicated hats. He climbed down from the trolley and walked in and out of churches, pushing pine doors open to show empty congregation halls, kneeling before each altar and folding his hands. From the crevices of his interlaced fingers came the smell of Havana cuttings. He raised his head and snorted; was there anywhere he could escape these crumbled leaves rolled from dawn to dusk, this life's trail of chewed and flaking cigars?

At the altar of the Holy Word Church, before the cross as bony and forlorn as an abandoned child, he found a Coca-Cola bottle holding flowers. He looked up at the cross, down at the flowers; he glanced back up. Had a rose-colored light flickered across the pale cross-tie? He thought of the painting in the hillside church where he'd taken first communion: Christ, arms wide, sacred heart rose-red and bleeding. Is this how Morris's heart had looked when it crumpled?

More brightly shone the red light and he sucked at the faint smell of flowers. "*Hijo de madre!*" he exclaimed, then crossed himself and tore at his chest for having spoken profanely before Christ. But he breathed deeply again, his head thrumming with the delirium of roses.

Not certain where he was going, but stepping with certainty there, he walked out of the church and along a road leading toward the glint of the river.

The air turned riotous with flowers.

The smells carried him back to the Havana markets as a boy when he'd wander with his father through the strings of chiles and bushels of plantains and clusters of red bananas Luis crazily called "love fruits" because they showed the time of month the banana plant, like a woman, need not fear making babies; nearby hung slaughtered hogs, bellies splayed open to show their bloody tangle of insides, so that one could understand, his Papa said, how the Hebrews recoiled from pork, never knowing the sweetness of sucklings revolving slowly on a spit with potatoes and apples.

The smells brought back the magnolias behind his room as a boy that dropped and rotted letting loose a cloying perfume the first time he felt his sex harden, the first time he dreamed a girl slipping through his window, the first time that dream changed to a real girl, Elena Ruiz, dressed in perfect white, buck-toothed and coltish, making his manhood on a wet night of his sixteenth year when flowers burned the air.

He came to a promontory near the river, gated with the sign, "Reed Gardens." "*Ah, jardines! Como el cielo,*" and as he said, "Gardens, like heaven," he looked up seeing the skies like those over the Cathedral the first afternoon he'd tramped down Dauphin. As he walked up a rise, the promontory changed colors. "*Dios!*" he exclaimed, thinking himself drunk on the smell so that his eyes were crazy, too. Reaching the entrance he dug in one pocket for the entrance fee, five cents, and in looking for his coins pulled out a fistful of cigars.

"Tell you what," a man's voice said.

Pastor saw a grizzled, smiling man.

"I work for old man Reed, it's his place. Name's Mel."

"Pablo Pastor."

"I see you got some mighty fine smokes there. How 'bout you go on in and look around for free, so long as you give me one of them beauties."

Pastor handed him a cigar.

Mel shook his head. "I wish we had somethin' good like tobacco growing here. All old man Reed's got is a bunch of flowers pretty enough to look at, but nothin' worth grinding up and puttin' a match to."

"*Estamos en el cielo aquí!*"

"You ain't from round here is you?" Mel asked, trailing Pastor where lilacs hung their sweet, pendulous heads and sunflowers bowed like humble men with sad faces.

"I am walking in Heaven."

"I hope not, lest you done died and I'm St. Peter, 'cause all I do is sit at the gate all day. Used to help old man Reed at his house but my back, it give out."

Pastor came to a path that passed beneath wisteria. The ground was a violet carpet. Farther on, a magnolia grove had dropped its creamy blooms; they curled and browned.

"What would you take for one more of them Havanas?"

At the end of the magnolia grove he'd come to a field planted with roses: scarlet, blood-red, deep-orange, pink, moon-white, yellow. He opened a gate and entered the path, a sleepwalker through lanes where thorns snared his pants and petals broke off and fluttered down.

He stopped, leaned over, and picked up a handful of the blooms.

"Don't worry 'bout it none," Mel said. "They don't last long, none of 'em do. I think any man's a fool for keeping a big garden 'cause nothing lasts more than two weeks before it dies, but that's flowers for you. You take me, why I'd go for a field of tobacco any day of the week."

Everywhere he looked rose petals were underfoot, crumpled and velvety, their aroma staining the air. He lifted another handful and held them against his nose.

"They could just about make you drunk, couldn't they?" Mel said.

All through him wove the heady scent taking him to the afternoon when he'd first held Marta and breathed her cologne and opened just one button on her blouse, nuzzling against the top of her bosom, and she'd sighed and said, "Pablo, no," and he'd reached down her skirt and laid his hand against the damp flower of her sex, and in the falling, flowered night took her feverishly, letting loose inside the soft warmth of her body; and when they'd waked together he said, "America. We will marry and go to America."

But even then he'd had no idea of how he might make the transit from Havana to New Orleans, except that his back was strong and his brother Luis said, "Cigars, you will sell cigars," and they struck a deal with a farmer to buy a bulk of leaves for Pablo to carry to America's Gulf Coast. Luis, on his way to Tampa, Florida, would ship his brother fresh leaves as needed.

The scent took him to the first evening in Morris's house, when Miriam had surprised him when she came down the hallway sweeping the floor; she'd just stood there, watching him naked to the waist rolling his fine Cuban cigars, and as she'd flicked perfumed water onto the floor he fantasized her crossing his threshold voluptuous and lemony. It carried him from there to the nape of newborn David's neck, and to the neck of Milagros, his own niece by marriage. God forgive him, the one time he'd held her longer than a usual uncle's embrace.

God sent a stiff breeze that made the petals flutter from his hands and Pastor knew this was another sign, too, like the sky above the Cathedral.

"Old man Reed, he sometimes make 'em into wine."

Pastor looked at the man.

"Ferments 'em, petals, hips, stems and all in a big old wood tub with some sugar, and *whooee,* he has himself some lip-smackin' wine. Too sweet for me, though. Give me corn liquor any day of the week." The man glanced around. "Here, I'll show you somethin.'"

They walked to a small shed, entered, and the man reached up to a shelf and brought down a few bottles. "Was a time you'd have had the temperance ladies coming here to bust us up, but we're home free now, ain't we!"

"I can buy this wine?"

"Reckon so. You want a bucket of them roses, too?"

"You will take five cigars?" Pastor reached in his satchel and brought up a handful.

"Guess I *have* died and gone to Heaven!" Mel put the bottles into a sack, then found a bucket under the table already filled with the cuttings for making wine.

Pastor envisioned a cottage by the water, David stooping and planting and harvesting alongside, the air free of seeping tobacco and rattling automobiles and throaty Dauphin voices.

He looked up at the sky flush with Christ's sacred heart and planted his feet against the plot of earth revealed as his destined home.

Three buckets of water, sugar, a strong oaken barrel, cheesecloth to let in the air but keep out the bugs—and roses. In the corner of his kitchen, Pastor set up the wine-making operation. In two weeks, having already drunk Mel's creation, he had his own bottles of rose wine. Accompanied by the stalwarts of Dauphin, he carried them to his friend, at doctor's orders still holed up in his bedroom over the store.

Morris did not even have to open his eyes to know them— Pastor, reeking still of tobacco; Pafandakis, overripe bananas; Sahadi, olives from the big vats that stood in the shadows of his store; Spicer, the constant hand-washer, Fels-Naptha soap.

When he did look he saw Lutchnik floating behind them. He blinked his eyes. No, it was only a Stetson on a hatrack, cocked toward the light.

"You are here for a reason?" Morris asked, sitting up, catching their high spirits, even Mirsky grinning, lips empurpled. "The doctor has sent you to say 'Shalom' to a man who does not have long to live?"

"We don't know who that man is," Pastor exclaimed, "but we do know a good friend who will live to one hundred. Morris, if I ever had a bad thought of you, God make pure my heart."

"Your heart, it is bad now, too?"

"No, *mi corazón está lleno.* Is full. We have brought you a gift"— he handed a bag out to Morris—"for your heart."

"The second million dollars."

"The first million."

Morris blushed. Had they taken up a collection of nickels and dimes for him up and down the street? Did they judge him some pitiable remnant of a once great storekeep?

"Take, take!" Pablo said.

Gingerly he slid three bottles out of the bag, one of them visibly almost empty. "Schnapps?" he said in disbelief.

"Read, read," Pastor said.

Morris held up the bottles to the sunlight and spoke aloud. "Pastor Gold. Rose Wine." He added, "*Mishuganah.*"

"That's 'crazy,'" Spicer laughed.

"Not to worry," Sahadi said, "it is sweet."

Taking the cork off the mostly empty one, Morris breathed in the strong, sweetish smell. He raised the bottle and touched it to his lips, then hiccuped.

Mirsky reached out and took it, lifting it to his lips. "They make wine from strawberries, apples, cherries, plums. Why not roses, Pablo."

"Rose tea's good for what ails you," Spicer mused. "Rose wine, too, I bet."

Pafandakis nodded. "In Mykonos, you drink *ouzo,* it is good for your heart, good for your lungs. Drink too much, though, and it makes your hair stand up straight!"

Spicer took a swig. "Straight as a preacher's dick?"

Mirsky bellowed.

"Hey Pablo," Spicer went on, "when you were picking these roses, did you get a prick?"

"With a good one already, I need a second?"

Morris took the bottle and sipped again. "I know why the man's *putz* is a *prick*. But why is it also called a man's good name, *Dick?*"

"You do not know a Mr. Putz?" Sahadi teased.

"I know a Mr. Krutz," Mirsky said.

"*Krutz,*" Morris explained, "in English means *scratch*."

"A man asked a lady," Spicer said, reaching for the bottle, "please to *krutz* his *putz*."

"Because Peter," Mirsky picked up, "went to buy himself a heater!"

"And when the cock crowed," Spicer began.

"Enough, enough!" Sahadi said, gasping for breath.

"It is the chicken who cries to the rooster enough," Mirsky said.

Morris threw back his head and felt the laughter run through him like the wine: sweet, heady, delicious in its freedom. "I have been too long sitting"—he grinned mischievously—"on my *burro*."

"On his ass!" howled Spicer. "I know Spanish and Jewish, too."

"But this is your *'culo,'*" Pastor said, slapping his rear.

"*Tuchas,*" said Mirsky.

"I got a *'burro,' 'culo,'* whatever you call it story for you," put in Spicer. "Young boy went hunting over in boss man's property. Caught himself a live gobbler and was carrying it slung over his shoulder down the road. The policeman grabbed him and said, 'Hey, young 'un, seein' as how you been trespassin', I'm gonna do to you just what you gonna do to that turkey.' The boy looked up and said, 'Well, sir, I'm plannin' to kiss *his* ass and turn him loose.'"

The men laughed, but Pastor said, "To me what is more funny is that you say bu*rro*.'"

The men sent up a chorus of lazy *r*'s until they sounded like a pack of dogs growling.

"Repeat, *el burro del barro en el ferrocarril*."

"We are saying what foolishness?" asked Mirsky.

"The clay donkey on the train."

"All that *r*'ing just to make nonsense?" Mirsky said.

"Better this one," Morris offered: "*Ashrechlecha, ashrechlecha! A shayna shiksa haut shtark geshussen a shaygets in die shnoogle!*"

Pastor opened another bottle and passed it around while Morris translated: "Terrible! Terrible! A pretty gentile lady shot dead a gentile man in the nose. '*Shnoogle,*' this is Yinglish."

The men back-slapped and chuckled and held their sides, trying to repeat the Spanish and Yiddish tongue-twisters. Morris laughed through the end of the bottle, and the beginning of the next, thinking at first that the sound of furniture being dragged through the doors downstairs was the sound of heavy items being shipped out until he went to the top of the steps, seeing Pavel Chemenko's beefy red face pass by, the claw foot of a table in his hand.

He started down the stairs and only halfway down the parade of objects became visible: two chairs, a table, chest of drawers. Abe appeared, glancing up at him, then continuing on to the back of the store.

"I collected on Pastor," was all his son said as Morris felt his knees tremble and he walked, feeling the heat rise through him, to the bottom of the steps. "We can't eat cigars, you know."

Morris made his way to where Abe was directing Chemenko to store the furniture for cleaning and stripping, and when Abe turned to him saying, "I don't think there's any question about it, Daddy. I can't stand somebody mooching and cheating us all these years, and . . ."

"Leave the store."

"The Pastors have been on our back since way back when."

"Out of this store."

"OK, I was going out anyway."

"Out of my store!"

"Can't I just get a quick bite of dinner? I mean, you and your cronies seem to be having a grand ol' time upstairs."

"Go!"

Abe stood tall and walked toward the front door. "You kick me out of here and no matter what you say, I'm not coming back!"

"I am not asking."

"No matter what you say."

"To you I am saying nothing."

The door slammed shut behind Abe, the greeting bell jangling. Morris heard the men's voices rise and break into raucous humor overhead. Taking a long, tired look around the store he summoned Chemenko and said, "Here, a dollar to take back what you have just brought here."

"But the boss, Mr. Abe, said."

"The boss his name is Morris."

It was enough that Abe should take a job directly across the street at Carnival Arts, a "*thotchke* shop," as Morris derided it, that tried to make its profits from craft items made by local folks—driftwood-mounted clocks, feathered Mardi Gras masks, carved walking sticks—but Miriam also insisted, seven nights a week, on carrying him dinner. She would not discuss Morris's "exile" of Abe, as Hannah termed it, nor criticize either husband or son. When time came for them to sit down to the table, Miriam set his plate out of steaming chicken and carrots and peas, then walked out to deliver Abe's. When Morris urged her to join him, she said only, "Eat, I am fine."

In the bed she showed him her shoulder, turned into her pillow. He reached out to touch her; she burrowed into the covers.

August 31: another bank payment was due the next day. The Dog River Church of the Pentecost had made good on its promise, Betty Green arriving with another envelope of cash the day before; but she'd left it with Miriam, hurrying away before Morris could come from the office to write out a receipt. As he'd stepped onto the street to call out to her, he could see from the angle of her neck and fury of her walk that she had not cared for the note he'd sent her: "Betty, please, we need money from your church. Thank you, Your friend, Morris." When he turned back into the store, Miriam, unspeaking, handed him a sealed envelope backed by Betty Green's name. "Dear

Mr. Morris," it read, "here's your money. We took this from the poor to pay you. Miss Green."

"You are welcome," he huffed, wadding up the note and tossing it into the trash can.

On the way to the office he looked into the shipping department to see Pavel Chemenko, in a stupor perched on a stool, giant hands hanging at his side. Miriam had opened the ledger book to farmer Jonas's account and circled in red his overdue payments on a chair, a table, and an additional bed to the one Morris had returned him as a gift.

He summoned the Ukrainian. "We are making a visit."

Out past Toulminville they turned the truck into the rutted road leading to Jonas's house. Chickens squawked and hogs lay sunk in mud, snouts lifting as the flat-bed truck kicked out its exhaust. "You stay here," Morris instructed Chemenko, climbing from the cab and going up to the porch to knock.

"What you want?" Mr. Jonas yelled through the door.

"Ah, Mr. Jonas, it is your friend, Morris Kleinman."

"I don't need no more furniture," Jonas called back.

Morris smiled and shook his head. "Do you think I come to your door to sell?"

"I have no durn notion what you're doin' at my door."

"Mr. Jonas." Morris waited. "Mr. Jonas?"

He heard the click and rattle of a shotgun being opened and loaded with shells.

Morris stepped back down into the yard. "I am only calling on a gentleman to make good on a sale . . ."

"Get off my damn property!"

Chemenko leapt out of the truck and came up behind Morris, fists clenched. "I will break in and take, I will make good for you."

"Mr. Jonas!" Morris yelled. "I am not here to rob . . ."

A powerful blast tore a ragged hole in the wood. Morris jumped behind the truck but Chemenko held his ground.

The door swung open and Jonas stood there, a withered stalk, shotgun broken open and empty shells on the floor. "If I had me more shot I'd fill your dirty ass with it right now!"

Morris stepped from behind the truck. "We are here to honor a contract, Mr. Jonas."

"Don't 'mister' me!"

"I take what is yours," Chemenko seethed, looking to Morris.

"What's mine," Jonas bellowed, pushing the door closed, "is mine!"

Chemenko stepped up to the porch. "For you, I take."

"Go on, Jews," Jonas yelled through the holes, "git!"

Morris took a deep breath, let it out slowly, and nodded, "OK."

Chemenko showed his sidewise grin, and with a half-dozen joyful kicks to the door and a few slams of his shoulder accomplished what his boss asked.

IV

1937–1945

Chicken Dreaming Corn

"A bastard they call me," Morris said to Pastor, holding the nub of a stogie, cold, between his fingers. "First, I am their friend, now a bastard. Why?" He put the cigar to his mouth, drew on the dead leaves. "Because I ask what they owe. This"—he lifted the cigar to the air—"is good business. What does it cost? Cheap. What does it give?" He sucked at the stub again. "Time to think. Furniture? It takes fourteen months to pay and is only a place for a man to put his fat behind."

Alone he stood, rocking on his feet, watching the silent stone. The angels of the Catholic Cemetery hovered rigid on tombs, hands folded in piety. Only three Pastor Golds were left of his cache, the last ones fashioned by his friend before his legs gave way and he'd crumpled to the ground among roses. The wine-making business had been a bust—Pablo barely managed to fill enough bottles to inebriate his friends again—and David had refused to move to the country to live among "rednecks," even after Hannah told him she was heading off to teacher's college in Atlanta. Young Pastor was content to pick up where Pablo had left off and roll cigars on Dauphin. Even so, his hands were clumsy and he resorted to using molds to shape the smokes. "Nobody does it like my father anymore," he lamented.

"So," Morris acknowledged, "say all the sons."

A manager his own ungrateful Abe was now at Carnival Arts

across the street, and he came nightly for dinner and talked about the thriving sales of the doo-dad shop. When Morris, in bed, asked Miriam why there should be honor in selling what people did not need—Christmas lights and carnival masks and costume jewelry— she said, "He is stealing from no one and will one day make a good woman proud."

"One day? We will live like Moses to be one hundred and twenty to see this miracle?"

"Too long you made him a boy but now he's becoming a man."

"*Mazel tov*," he answered drily.

He drew again on Pastor's cigar, sensing his friend's fingertips at the leaves. How long might pass before he smoked it down? The cigars would eventually lose their flavor, even in Pablo's humidor presented to him by Marta. When he'd smoked the last, would there be nothing left, at all, of his friend?

He cocked his ear at the noise of feet shuffling through leaves. "*Not to disturb another mourner,*" he thought, keeping his gaze on the etched whorls of his *amigo's* stone: "*Amor y paz.*"

Might it be Betty Green, who sought him out among final resting places? Was she coming to apologize for her lousy, Dog River preacher who'd called Morris "a modern day money-lender" because of interest on balances due? Didn't that Jeremiah-hollering son-of-a-bitch understand the meaning *terms*?

"Mr. Kleinman?"

He looked around to see Father O'Connor galumphing toward him, face wizened as a dried apple.

"*Shalom,* Father. You are thinking I am lost."

"Many are lost."

"My friend, Pablo Pastor ..."

"Was a good Catholic. Many years ago he came first to me, then God sent him to you."

"How we met, it was an accident, his cigars."

"You gave him shoes."

"My children"—Morris hesitated—"they gave him the shoes."

"It was God's holy hand, resting on his shoulder, that guided him to you."

Morris fell silent. Had God's hand pulled Lillian to the darkness, Benny into the waters, his own Papa, alone and frightened, into an anonymous grave? Had it been the same hand that had grabbed at Abe's lapels and yanked him out the door to a *gonif's* store?

"One more cigar," Morris sighed, "I would like to share with him."

"Where this journey ends another one begins."

"A journey, it is better to make with friends."

"God sends us on different roads to the same home."

"We have all come to Mobile."

"The home where we're headed is greater than a hundred Mobiles."

Morris glanced at O'Connor's fake right leg poking out from the bottom of his robe.

"Another place where God laid His guiding hand," O'Connor said, noting Morris's fascination. He inched up his robe to reveal a crude shaft of wood merging into a block-sized shoe.

"When I was a boy," the priest began, "in County Cork, we lived on a farm. At the time I was eleven and my brother Peter, nine. There"—he lifted his hand and gestured to a series of mausoleums against the fence—"he is buried."

A quarter mile farther was the Jewish cemetery. Hartwell Field, the new baseball stadium, rose in the field beyond.

"I am sorry."

"Oh no, no, he lived to be sixty-seven years old. God thought to take him earlier, but, instead"—he tapped his wooden shin—"he settled for this. My leg." He faltered where he stood, but before Morris could aid him, leaned against Pastor's headstone. "You see, Peter was a sickly child. Very weak. It was his heart. That spring it rained, a terrible, terrible rain, day in and out, with the wind knocking loose tiles from the roof and . . . Where was I? Oh, yes, my father called out, 'Peter, you and James run down to the barn and pitch more hay for the horses.'

"The rain was setting up a horrendous fuss, streaming down the barn walls. Creatures of all sorts were being flushed from their hiding places. Peter was right behind in the barn when I looked down and saw Satan's hand—a black rat—sweeping across the floor.

"But God touched me. Yes, Morris, He took my foot and set it down right in front of Peter's, and the rat caught me instead of my brother—Hosannas to the Lord—with its bite. Not leeches, nor quinine, nor healing salts, could cure me. Over the next fortnight, such swelling! A month later the surgeon was called. But God gave me strength. I was a little boy, but I knew His plan.

"You see, our dear Peter could not have withstood such an infection. His heart, so weak."

"My Lillian," Morris mourned.

"What was a leg that I should lose it next to Peter's young life?" Morris put his hands to his face. "I must go."

The priest reached out and touched him on the shoulder. "The Lord works in strange ways, my son."

He headed off through the narrow paths between the grave plots, gasping at the taste of plaster and gutter water in his mouth, hearing Lillian's frantic cry. He'd visited her gravestone before coming here: one lone pebble sat atop it, and he'd lifted a handful of rocks to spread, a sign that he, no, would not ever forget his beloved daughter.

What would it have cost the King of Kings who had rained manna and parted the Red Sea to have moved Morris's foot six inches to intercept the black death that ravaged his child?

He gazed up at the grizzled sky. "If I'm a bastard, what does that make You?"

He entered the field near the ball stadium, taking the short cut to the resting place of his own people. A cheer rose: God's taunt.

The baseball soared like a white bird over the stadium walls—

"home run" the crowd was chanting—landed on the scrub grass, bounded once, took a small hop, and rolled toward Morris.

Elbows pumping, knees scissoring the air, two boys came chasing the ball from the side of the stadium. It was at Morris's feet now and he reached down, intending to flip it toward them, but the first boy who reached him tore it from his hand, butting him to the ground. He climbed back to his feet, but the next boy came at him, shouting, "Where's the fuckin' baseball, old man?"

"I don't have . . ."

A fist slapped his nose and he tasted the blood curdling down into his lips. The boy pivoted and took off in pursuit of the other who waved the baseball triumphantly.

"More bastards!" Morris shouted at them. He yanked a handkerchief from his pocket, but tucked it back. Betty Green had given it to him years ago: it carried the whiff of another who'd turned against him for doing only what was required of a simple man trying to make an honest living. When he wiped his nose with his sleeve and blood streaked his shirt, he had a picture of Miriam bent over a washboard, scrubbing at the stain. He pulled the handkerchief back out and jammed it to his nose.

Head tilted back, chin pointing in the direction of home, he trudged back to Dauphin, making sure to hide from Abe's view as he reached his block and stole back into the store.

More than a decade had passed since a hawk-eyed crone had peered down at Morris as he'd made his way to Donnie McCall's house. He had to search his memory to place her: a hot afternoon, a street off the trolley line, the sidewalk to McCall's porch. High in a window her outline emerged like the faded postmark on a weathered envelope.

Blind in her last days, afraid to speak of what she had seen, she'd received Father O'Connor at her side for a deathbed confession and told him of what she'd witnessed: Morris entering the house of the man next door and leaving him for dead. Only one other person had been in the bedroom when O'Connor gave her last rites: her good friend, the mad airplane inventor John Fowler.

From behind his tangled beard Fowler had whispered to Abe what he'd overheard, and Abe had warned his mother about the rumor let loose: that Morris might be implicated in McCall's demise, just as Miriam had always feared.

When Miriam told Morris in bed that night what had occurred, this time it was he who mourned, "Maybe has come the time to leave this Alabama."

"That time is behind us."

"It is now."

"You did nothing to McCall."

"God does not want us here."

"Where does God want us, Morris? In the old country where they are breaking the windows of the Jews?"

"Those are the Germans."

"New York?" she cut back. "We will go to New York where is that woman who married my brother and then tried to steal my Herman?"

"What?"

"Hannah tells me, oh, how she tells me!"

"In Brooklyn was better. In Brooklyn. Why did I not listen to you many years ago?"

"Because I was foolish and you were wise. This is the home of our children. We live for the children."

"Oh," said Morris, "to be back in Romania before the soldiers came."

"They came."

"God . . ."

"Do not speak to me of God. Speak to me of Morris."

"I have cursed God," he said.

"You have cursed your son," she said. "That is what you have done."

"He can ask forgiveness."

"It is you who must teach him."

Morris fell quiet.

Miriam put her hand gently on the side of his face. "Who will believe what the *mishuganah* Fowler says, anyway? With his bird's nest beard to his navel? The priest? He will tell?"

"When did the old woman die?"

"Two weeks, maybe three it now makes."

He saw again the gnarled cleric perched by Pastor's grave, black robe billowing in the wind. Would he have heard the old woman's confession by then? Was this what he meant by his rabbinic talk of journeys and God's strange ways? That he would protect, despite all, his favorite Jew?

When he paced by Holy Cathedral on following evenings and heard Latin dirges rising through ecclesiastical caverns, he remembered the story Pablo had once told him about how Judas betrayed Jesus, pointing him out to his enemies; might Father O'Connor, turning the tables at last, do the same to Morris?

One night late there was sudden banging at the door, and Morris knew the priest had done so.

"Mr. Kleinman?" The voice rose from the street. "Mr. *Kleinman!*" A man's voice, urgent, demanding.

He leaned out and saw policeman Louie Flynn, son of Officer Sam Flynn: a youth, he'd learned from Herman, who'd once tried to beat up his sons in the docks alley. What was that piece of paper the anti-Semite was waving in the air?

"Your father in his grave," Morris whispered down at him, "is turning in shame."

"Stay here," Miriam said, "I will go."

"No, he is calling for me. I will go."

Down the steps from the bedrooms to the first floor of the store, past the clothes under dustproof cloths waiting for a day that might never begin, Morris made his way to the front door, drew a deep breath, and opened it to the man of the law.

"This came in over the Western Union from Europe. My

Daddy, before he passed, told me to give special mind to you people." He turned to go.

"Louie," Morris called.

"Yes sir, Mr. Kleinman?"

"Thank you." He turned to Miriam who'd come to the top of the steps. "You think I am being arrested? It is only"—he laughed once, nervously—"the mail."

"So important, at this hour?"

With heavy fingers he pried open the envelope and read the telegraphed news: MORRIS A MIRACLE STOP YOUR FATHER AZRIL IS ALIVE STOP COME TO PIATRA NEAMT STOP HE WANTS TO SEE YOU STOP BRING AMERICAN DOLLARS STOP PETRU EMINESCU.

From where he is perched on the stool in front of Carnival Arts, Abe glances over at Morris, who quickly looks away. Morris turns back, Abe gazes off; Abe sneaks a look back at his father, Morris hunches the other way.

Abe has offered to clean the walk in front of the shop, but its owner, Ed Canterbury, says, "Who the hell cares about the side-walk?" He has suggested different ways to arrange the displays to entice the customers, but Ed has shrugged and concluded, "People want junk. That's the great secret of the day. Charge them more, and they want it more."

"'*Thotchkes*,' my Daddy calls it," Abe says. "That's Yiddish for 'Odds and ends, knick-knacks.'"

"Enough with religion," Ed fusses. "We're selling the Fourth of July, Mardi Gras, Easter, Christmas, first communions, sweet six-teens and weddings. To *Americans*. Got that?"

"You don't like the way I manage the store?" Abe bridles.

"You're a dynamo," Ed says. "Let's keep it that way."

He sees how his father's shoulders are bent, how he wields his broom more slowly, like a tired sorcerer stirring his pot; how he clutches the telegram that has come from Romania, rubbing his fingers across it as if clearing a window fogged with ice.

When Asa Spicer comes in looking for streamers and balloons to throw a party in his office for the ninetieth birthday of Berenice McNulty Jones, Abe claps him on the back and pulls out the drawer filled with bright papers, but Ed summons Abe into the back and says, "You got to start charging them more."

"You can't raise prices in the middle of a transaction," Abe says in astonishment.

"I told you before, if niggers want to shop here it's fine with me. But we charge them the nigger price 'cause of the aggravation we put up with having them here."

"Dr. Spicer's my friend!"

"Give one a good price and what do you think the next one's gonna say?"

"You're a cheap, scheming scoundrel, aren't you?"

"Learned it from y'all."

"Not this."

He walks to the front and tells Asa he is no longer working here, and that he'd do best to put the money to a gift from Daddy's store that Berenice McNulty Jones might find useful like a wall clock, hell, Abe himself would even contribute, and he reaches into the register, takes the cash that is his weekly due, stuffs it in his pocket, handing a couple of dollars to the dentist.

"Don't you come back cross here looking for no more work!" Ed shouts at his back, but Abe, like a traveler fording a deep stream, is already on the bank dominated by M. Kleinman & Sons.

He takes his place in a rocker on the sidewalk and when Daddy appears, gazing down at him in weary puzzlement, Abe says, "If it's OK with you, Daddy."

"It is OK."

"Just tell me what to do."

"Take over the store. I am making a trip."

□

Behind the wake of the S.S. *Rex*, New York receded in the distance, the city no longer concrete and mortar but someplace ethereal, its banks and office buildings, its bridges and steeples, softened by the waterfront mist. As Morris stood at the stern, gazing back at the skyline, he imagined himself not departing but arriving again, a Romanian boy setting out to make a new life in America. As the vessel pushed by the somber walls of Ellis Island, beneath the regal gaze of Lady Liberty, through the Narrows and on to the mouth of the harbor, Morris spoke his beloved names: "Miriam, Abraham, Herman, Lillian, Hannah." Had he yet lived a life in Mobile, Alabama, at all?

A blast of the ship's whistle brought him back to the deck—not a stowaway put to work in steerage, but a businessman with a third-class stub in his right pocket, a money belt on his left hip. Up top in first class, where the streamers fluttered and a band already played, he glimpsed men and women in evening dress leaning over the railing, waving *adieu* to well-wishers no longer there. A ball-room, a billiards room, a dance hall, a swimming pool—the Italian steamship, like its French and Dutch counterparts, advertised luxury to the monied elite. "They should one day eat ice cream," Morris said to the wind, "at the Old Dixie Hotel."

To the ship's port side was the tip of Brooklyn, the looping tracks of the Cyclone roller coaster visible at Coney Island, the seaside hotels set like dominoes against the edges of the Atlantic. When Morris had courted Miriam they had visited the park, riding the Dragon's Gorge, a miniature train that circled the amusements. With her chaperone waiting for them on the ground, he had been so bold as to slip his hand into hers; she had not pulled it away.

He opened the basket now that she had prepared for him for his trip from Mobile—two chickens, a tin of rice, six boiled eggs, a mason jar of beet soup—and took the last, limp wing. "Out there you will find only *traife*," she had worried, stuffing the lunch box with the kosher victuals he had nearly finished by the time he'd reached Baltimore. On his morning in New York before the sailing, he had headed to a Delancey Street delicatessen, consuming a fat corned beef sandwich and two briny pickles.

But he yearned, already, for the flavors of Miriam's kitchen. He consumed the last morsel bearing her touch.

He walked to the bow of the ship and saw the endless stretch of ocean, only another steamship in the distance breaking the horizon.

"*Hola, Americano,*" a man said behind him.

He looked over his shoulder to see Pablo Pastor—no, not Pastor, but a slender Spaniard with a pencil-thin moustache and cigar stub in his mouth. He was on his way to Gibraltar perhaps, the *Rex's* first port.

Morris nodded.

The Spaniard stepped closer.

Morris pulled his coat closed and let his left hand fall over his hip.

"*Cuidado, amigo,*" the Spaniard said, nodding in the direction of the money belt.

Morris knew the meaning of "*cuidado*"—oddly spoken as though in Pastor's voice—so he turned away and, being careful, checked the catch on the belt. Inside was his return ticket and a fat wad of cash—enough for Papa's companion ticket home. He turned back to the Spaniard, but the man was gone.

He heard a whistle in the distance; the other steamship grew larger. Gulls dove and hit the water and rose straight up, noisy hecklers.

Soon the other ship was close enough so that Morris could see the voyagers crowding its decks. The gulls wove deliriously between the two ships, as though celebrating one's departure, the other's arrival. The passengers on the arriving ship were facing toward their long-awaited destination.

Near the smokestack of that liner the black-red-yellow of Deutschland's flag stood out, a tiny splash of color marking a German ship.

He could have booked passage on that line, taking him to Bremen-haven. At first Abe and Herman had encouraged him to do so, figuring that the voyage was shorter, the train to Bucharest more direct. But Morris reminded them of the newsreels they had seen of the Munich Olympics two years earlier, how the German Jews were not allowed even to compete, and how the Germans who did run and jump had been humiliated by the Negro born in Alabama, Jesse Owens. "You want I should be in a nation that hates me for who I am *and* where I come from?" he had said to his sons.

Then Herman changed his mind and called from his law school dorm in Atlanta, telling Morris how they had talked in class about laws in Germany called the Nuremberg Laws—excuses for laws, Herman explained, meant to rob Jews of their rights. "This news," Morris had assured him, "I have already heard in the *shul.*"

He clutched his chest, thinking with a rush in his heart of his sons: their smooth, youthful faces; their intent, dark eyes. Suppose they had left him at sixteen years of age, as he had Papa, not to return until they were aged, half-defeated men?

The approaching vessel gave another long blast, and Morris spied its second flag: the sharp-pronged Swastika.

The two ships passed and the *Rex* again pushed along on its own through unbounded waters. The ocean light pinkened and dimmed. Morris watched a scrap of moon, like a cast-off from the New Jersey junkyard, lift humbly into the heavens.

Facing east to his first home, its ancient synagogue closer with every league of the sea, he muttered the prayers of revelation and redemption and gratitude and, all alone in the thinning light, davened in first darkness.

He heard a voice at his side: "Go, look, he will find you."

He looked around; a shadow receded.

"Then," the voice said, "go back home."

"Lutchnik?" he said, calling after the figure.

A dinner bell rang.

He bundled up his belongings and, glancing around at the ocean, the deck, the portholes, went to his cabin.

The next morning he began a letter to Miriam telling of the two men he had encountered who reminded him of Pastor and Lutchnik, then told of the excitement of a whale that had been seen off the ship's bow. He kept the letter folded in his pocket, adding lines that next day about how the Atlantic reminded him of his first voyage to America and how he thanked God, blessed be His name, for all the riches he had been given. He told her that he had eaten boiled chicken in the third-class restaurant, prepared by a Jewish cook; it was only a small lie. He had eaten chicken, but a Basque chef, with a beard to the top of his belly, had prepared the simple fare.

On the third day of the voyage he added a note to Abe, instructing him to double-check the shipping list of the furniture from Besser, who'd joined forces with Shmuel the chair-maker and Gluchowsky the sofa king. Besser said big ticket items, which sold on time, provided steadier income than ladies' fashion, though he kept on with apparel, too. Every hour he checked his money belt, a gift from Besser, who'd said, upon giving it to him, that he wept to see his own father in Dorohoi, and would have accompanied Morris on the journey, but his own health was not so good.

The Lord God had made the world in six days, but during the week Morris rode the S.S. *Rex* he did little more than rest, and pray, and try not to worry about the ledger books and shipping crates and bedroom suites. Through solitary hours he watched the rolling waves of the ocean, the shades of blue and green shifting against the world's edge.

And one evening, as the ship see-sawed on stormy seas, he zigzagged to the third-class lounge where a three-piece combo played music for the couples who fox-trotted up the floor one way, down the other. He ordered a beer and sat at a table, alone, seeing Miriam turn before him, young again. He blinked; and, when he looked to see only a lone woman moping by the bar, he made a promise to himself that he would take his wife dancing at least once more in their lives.

It had not been until the seventh day that God rested, but it was the day of the voyage that Morris could not rest. Off starboard, faintly visible, was a vast stretch of land: the coastline of Africa. Within hours, the rocky edges of Portugal came into view.

By dusk the *Rex* came to port at Gibraltar, and after the traipsing on and off of passengers, the removal of cargo, the ship started off again, destination Italy. From the shore a man waved at Morris: Asa Spicer. Morris waved back and the image of Spicer was folded back into the crowded dock.

He could not concentrate to pray the next morning as Genoa came into view. His heart knotted up until he placed a pill under his tongue, and he paced the deck and slowly breathed in the damp salt air.

"Soon, Papa," he vowed, "I will be with you."

The train from Genoa bustled with soldiers with caps slung low over their eyes, carbine rifles over their shoulders. Morris squeezed into a car with old ladies carrying straw bags, children looking up at him wide-eyed, dull crosses hanging from their necklaces. As the Italian countryside slid by he nodded to sleep, his chin sinking down into his valise, his cap keeping from his eyes the sharp Mediterranean sun. It was late September, and getting cold.

When he woke he saw smokestacks and highways where toy-sized cars jammed intersections. "Milano!" the conductor called. He got down into the clanging, steaming station with train cars lined up on dozens of tracks.

On the connecting train he settled into a car with only one other man—a priest with a caged canary—but the door of the car abruptly opened and a soldier spoke to him, "*Dove vai?*"

"Romania," Morris answered, remembering his little Italian.

"*Venga, vecchio. Andiamo, andiamo.*" The soldier pulled him into the aisle, opened another door and shoved him into a crowded car.

He recognized these faces, starkly different from the lean, swarthy Italians: broad-faced, high-browed, eyes deep-set. Romanian.

They were not Jews, though, but countrymen from the domed churches set high on hills and from the rocky fields where farmers under metal skies dug their shovels into gravelly soil. How amazed they would be by the Alabama loam that sent lush collard greens into nurturing sun. An old man in a gray cloak stared at Morris. "You are not," spoke his hard gaze, "one of us."

When he first heard the conductor call out Trieste, he knew that Bucharest was not more than a day's ride away. It was late when they stopped in the Italian border city with its looming churches and gypsy families on corners sleeping three and four to a blanket in the Adriatic night. He thought of the Negroes back home sauntering into the store on a Friday after a docks shift, a few dollars in hand. Even broke they would never find themselves wrapped in a horse blanket on a city corner on a bone-chilling night.

As he watched the other Romanians sleepwalk across the drafty station to the east-bound trains, he felt the cold return to his body, wedging beneath his left shoulder blade. Wearily he climbed onto a new train—one headed not through Bucharest, but on a route through Moldavia to Bicaz, and on to Piatra Neamt—found a seat in a half-empty car, and sank into sleep.

At daybreak he was roused by border patrol to show his passport. As the guard studied his picture, Morris looked out to the first stretches of the nation he had fled: the lonesome farmhouses like abandoned shoes scattered across white fields, the drawn cattle, black and huddled near gateposts.

From the gray heavens swirled a million crystals, a snowfall the likes of which he had not seen since standing in a New Jersey junkyard the early part of the century, a snow he had not even thought of in his long years far south of the Mason-Dixon line where mention of the word sent brawny men shivering.

Through the snow he saw again Chaim, a bundled figure, hand flinging out, snowball let go, coming at him like the ball sailing from the Mobile ball field. Into his eye it exploded and Mama came running, yanking his brother by the ear as he screamed in outrage while Morris lay back on the icy walk, eye burning, ears stung with cold.

Like an empty place around his chest he felt where his brother had been, as close as the feeling of the snowball. He remembered climbing up from the ice and going after him, pummeling him to the ground as Papa came running out, shouting, "Never, never you will be fighting against each other."

As he and Chaim and Ben huddled in sleep, he heard Shayna Blema's voice saying, "Talk to them, Azril. Tell them this is not the way of brothers."

Peering through the snow, he made out the shapes of old women waddling out doors in heavy blankets and men, dark lines moving toward barns carrying pitchforks, who all became the good people of Mobile rising to slop their hogs and throw hay to their horses. From the cold arch of a Romanian Orthodox church appeared a priest, black robes billowing: Father O'Connor emerging from the Holy Cathedral raising his hands in a blessing toward the train.

Looking out the window, Morris saw Papa as a little boy outside the train window squatting next to a sick and dying horse, rubbing his little hand across the mane. He would be afforded less dignity than an animal when the soldiers came to shut down his business and pitch him out into the snow.

What had his father's face looked like as a boy? Strong and certain, like Herman's? Puzzled and hurting, like Abe's? Soft-eyed and amused, like Lillian's? Chestnut-haired, like Hannah's? Was his face that of the lost child, David, that clouded Miriam's eyes still at least once every year?

Other children appeared by the tracks, like the urchins who lined up to watch the Mardi Gras parades. These offspring of the Carpathian ranges stood large-eyed and gaunt, the passing train the novelty of their day. One boy on a single crutch raised his hand and saluted. Morris saluted back. A wide grin spread across the boy's face.

Across a field soldiers trudged, their helmets tamped down like barber bowls, their breaths making scythes in the air. Before them walked a man head bare to the snow. "*Garda de Fier,*" someone behind Morris said. The Iron Guard.

Morris pressed his face to the window. The man before the soldiers threw up his hands and collapsed to the ground. The train rounded a curve and a spruce curtain closed off the world.

When the trees fell away he saw a mountainside monastery, its turrets reaching into the sky, its walls stretching down the hill. Even from the train he could glimpse the mosaics of saints in its arched entranceways. As a boy he had imagined those saints watching him like hawks as he rambled along the Bistritia River with his brothers, ready to catch him in their spiritual talons.

The train rose through the mountains, chugging slowly, a gorge opening to the side. Below, the Bistritia River flickered silver, colder than the lazy Alabama that curled to the foot of Dauphin Street. "Dauphin Street." He spoke the words. They sounded like the memory of a dream.

So familiar was this boyhood landscape that he had to touch his own face to make sure it was a fifty-eight-year-old man's brisk with stubble, that he was not nine years old again, returning with Papa from Bucharest on a trip to buy supplies for the distillery, watching the silos and rugged fences and old farmhouses where smoke crawled into the sky.

He recognized the crumbled wall where he'd stopped to rest his second day of flight from the Eminescu farm, the centuries-old stones, hulking and dreary, a mere forty years older than they were that morning; eons ago in human time.

He felt again the oxcart he'd hitched a ride on to where it turned off up that hill, the shards of icy straw like broken glass beneath him when he'd dozed, thinking suddenly to return to Piatra Neamt, not even a good-bye had he given Mama and Papa. ("You will not come back to here," Papa had made him promise, "the soldiers will come looking for you.")

And he had waited in the berth of that wall for the flinty Romanian sun to dwindle down one last time before taking off toward the far stretch of countries where he would hitch rides and steal aboard trains and walk until the tongues flapped loose on his boots, making his way to where the German port looked out onto the shimmering sea.

As the train descended toward the river, the road leading to Papa's distillery slipped by and the edges of the town began—the white-washed building that housed the provincial capital, next the shabby park, then the rows of stone houses near the train station. That old crab, his heart, crawled sideways in his chest. He reached for his pills, swallowed two, turning his gaze to the town square, seeing the timeless ancients in berets and ratty wool coats leaning on canes, pushing checkers and rolling flaky cigarettes.

Over the market counters of Piatra Neamt were Friedlander and Reiss and Pastor, Sahadi and Zoghby and Mutchnik, Berson slaughtering his chickens, Pafandakis setting out his potatoes, Matranga readying his bread: the Dauphin Street faces transplanted to this Romanian village just as the faces of this village had once been transplanted to eight noisy, bustling, nickel-and-dime, special-price-just-for-you blocks in downtown Mobile.

Petru Eminescu was standing at the platform like the stone at Patriarch's Hill, unchanged save the scoring of the weather against his face: left eye gone, mouth pulled to one side, the symptoms of a stroke victim. As the train screeched and sighed, Morris's heart turned over once more, the engine of a worn jalopy unsure of the next hill.

"*Maybe I have come here to die. To join Petru and Papa and Shayna Blema and Chaim and all the others.*"

He fumbled at his pocket for the envelope holding the picture of Miriam and the children: a small copy of the portrait taken at Overbey Studios the day of Abe's high school graduation. Clutching his valise in one hand, the envelope in the other, he stepped down.

"*Buna dimineata, Moritz,*" Petru said, catching his elbows in both hands, telling him good morning in the familiar Romanian tongue.

"*Noroc, Petru,*" Morris answered.

"It has been so long."

Morris held out the envelope.

"American dollars!"

"No, my family."

"Oh . . ." Petru turned his head to one side and peered with his good eye. "God has been good to our Moritz."

Morris looked around, eyes darting from old man to old man in the crowd, fearful he would not know his own father, would mistake him for one of the eternal checker players in the park.

"Azril," Petru said, "is at the farm. He did not feel good for the ride to the station."

"But he knows I am here? That I've come?"

Petru nodded. "We said to him, 'Moritz is coming.'"

"And what did he say?"

"He said, 'I am waiting. For my son.'"

"*Baruch Hashem.* But who is staying with him?"

"My sister."

"Elena?" Morris asked, shaking.

"No," Petru answered. "The Lord Christ took her into his arms last summer."

"I am sorry."

"She is now at peace, with Christ. It was a fever." Petru touched the side of his mouth. "This happened to me the day after God took her. He struck me across the face." Petru looked down. "For being a sinner."

When he looked back up Morris glanced away.

Petru straightened his back, jutted out his chin and said, "To our home, yes?" and slapped Morris on the back, grabbing up his luggage.

Past the town square, by the rows of squat row houses with the charcoal chimneys, past the blackened churches with their mournful bells, past the alley snaking away to the holy synagogue that stood at the entrance to the Jewish quarter, the motorcar bumped and shook.

The Romanian sky welcomed him just as it had sent him off more than forty years ago, raining needles of cold.

He only half heard Petru's story about "returning to Christ" and "paying for his sins" as they neared the Eminescu farm. Even King Carol, he told Morris, called his Iron Guard the Legion of the Archangel Michael.

"*This Christ,*" Morris thought, "*he is making problems everywhere.*"

He imagined Betty Green at his side prattling on about her redeemer. Perhaps she would have found a worthy companion here at Petru's side.

Had Petru traveled to America, he might have made his way to the Deep South, too, might have ended up in the Dog River Church of the Pentecost clapping his hands and mouthing strange tongues.

He remembered the land surrounding the farm as rolling to the ends of the sky. Now the fields looked ragged as bunched wool.

The sight of the barn made him grasp his chest. He looked up at the broken-faced commander. Close, behind the pulled mouth and cheek, was still the lordly youth.

"Our Moritz," Petru repeated, "back home."

He saw his ancient father sitting in a chair, eyes in familiar dark circles, beard a white tangle. A cane in his hand pushed against the ground, his wiry arm raising himself up against it; his body was unfolding, one foot searching ahead, the other following.

"Papa!"

Leaping out of the car, tramping his way through the snow, Morris came to where his father reigned like a propped stick. He took the wispy, encrusted hands—he remembered in a flash the feeling of them large and warm enfolding his own—and, clasping them, bent and kissed them.

"*Mein zun,*" Azril muttered. "*Mein zun er ist gukumin tzedig.*" His voice fell away into a soft crying.

The words lingered in Morris's ear: My son has come back.

"*Haim, yah,* Papa," Morris answered, "your son is home," and climbed to the top step, wrapping his arms around him, falling into a wintry morning when the sun rose like shattered glass and the square churned with the frenzied tracks of men running and horses galloping and a spill of blood like a wound in the snow, Papa comforting him, saying, "No, I will not stay here afraid, no, I will not let all the blades and muskets in the world keep me from my duties, keep me from going out this door, on to work, managing the distillery as my father did, and his father, too, on back to the first of us to drop a pick into the stony soil."

And they were falling back to another day so windy it knocked the skullcaps off their heads as they hurried to synagogue, the fast beginning, the cantor's voice already chanting the Kol Nidre, and he'd wedged himself between Papa and Chaim, glancing up at his mother in the balcony: Shayna Blema, pretty rose, strong jaw, almond-shaped eyes, lips parting in silent recitation of the prayers, widening into a smile seeing him.

"Shayna Blema, look who has come to see us! Look who has come home!" his father called.

Morris stepped back, looked around. "Papa?"

"Shayna Blema? Ach, the woman, always hiding back in her kitchen."

"Papa," he said, holding up the photograph, "I have children, you have grandchildren. Look how big they are, the *nachas,* the joy, such handsome and beautiful children. I wrote to you and Mama, how I miss Mama. My wife, my Miriam, she is from Iasi, we will travel to see her cousin there."

Azril gazed down with milky eyes, then back to his son.

"Shayna Blema!"

A stout, gray-haired woman was gazing out shyly from the foyer.

Azril turned to her. "You are not Shayna Blema. What have you done with my wife!"

"Our Moritz," the woman said.

"Theodora Eminescu!"

"How American you look." She repeated softly, "Our Moritz."

"A good boy," Azril said and lifted his cane into the air. "He has come to tell his Papa good-bye before the soldiers come. I will not tell them where he is going." He brandished the cane at Petru. "No matter how they beat me, I will not tell. Not a word. He is my son!"

Petru drove a Studebaker, a wireless radio buzzed opera, and water ran through a pipe into the kitchen, but the heat came as it always had—from logs thrown into the fireplace.

Papa huddled close to the fire, lost in blankets. Theodora, in a gray shawl, color of her thinning hair, leaned against a corner. Petru poked the skittish flames.

In their first two hours together they had exchanged the news of forty years: the births and deaths collapsed into strained words of comings and goings. Papa had called repeatedly for his reluctant bride, gone to God now for thirty years, and Theodora had stood quietly at a room's distance, only saying, "Our Moritz, like yesterday, our Moritz."

"He thinks you are here to tell him good-bye, that you are a boy on your way to America," said Petru.

Morris nodded. "I never came back from the farm to tell him."

"Yes," Petru said, "I know."

Azril's ragged beard draped over his chest and spilled into his lap. He was asleep, snoring, sitting up to cough then falling back asleep, snoring again. Morris shifted him in the chair, propping his head on a pillow.

"A kind son," Theodora whispered.

"I told them where you were!" Petru said to Morris's back. He stood without moving. "I told them you were here, at the farm."

Theodora left the room. Her footsteps passed back and forth upstairs.

"I knew how you felt about her," Petru said. "I saw it in your faces, the way you looked at each other. My father said, 'Let him sleep in the house, what trouble can he make?' But I said, 'No, it is better in the barn.' But I think that made her dream about you even more. 'My poor little Jew,' was all she said.

"She told me, 'Our Moritz'—it was she who began to call you that—'he had a dream about traveling far away to a house on the water, a warm place, the sun always shining. Our Moritz. How good it is to have someone to talk to when he climbs up and down the grain cellar, our Moritz, do you know when the sun goes down on Friday, the very moment that it sets, he lights a candle like a little boy and prays to his God?'

"If I'd said to my father, 'Theodora and the Jew,' what would he have done? Sent you back to your family. And raised his horsewhip at Theodora."

He paused. Morris kept his back to him, still facing the fire, feeling the heat of it like he had felt as a boy briefly warming himself while waiting for old man Eminescu to finish his breakfast and give him orders for the day.

"The time I rode into the barn on my horse—what a grand stallion he was!—I saw the two of you there. The little figure you had whittled for her. I decided, 'I will tell Poponescu, the commandant. How he loves to lay his hand on the Jews.'

"Then I told him about what a hard worker you were, about what a good soldier you'd make, and he sent two men to come find you. Fifteen years they would have kept you, more than enough time for my Theodora to become a good wife to a true Romanian, and a good mother. I wanted only for her what was good.

"Poponescu came to me when you had fled. Tell us where he has gone. Moritz, what choice did I have? Go to Azril Kleinman, I told them.

"He sent a soldier to your house. Your Papa, Christ wash me clean, your Papa said, 'You have taken my distillery, you have taken my work, you have taken my livelihood. But you will not take my Moritz, he is gone into the wind. 'Another son here,' the soldier said, 'he will do. They are all the same.'

"'You will not take my sons!' your Papa shouted and he reached behind the door and grabbed up a poker and raked it across the soldier's face. With the butt of his rifle the soldier beat your Papa to the floor. 'We will come back and kill you,' he vowed. 'Tonight, we will ride through your *shtetl* and kill you all.'

"But, God's mercy, a blizzard that night froze the world. The next night came, the next. Poponescu and his regiment were ordered to a peasant uprising a hundred miles away."

"You call that mercy?" Morris asked. "That my father was whipped to the floor?" Morris turned to his father, stroking the sleeping head. The hands that had once wielded a poker with the force of an axe lay delicate and small in his lap, folded together like a child's.

"Our Moritz, I have suffered, too."

"I am not your Moritz. I am a man nearly sixty years old with four children, a store, a street called Dauphin, and a home called Mobile."

"*This* is your home."

"And a father still living by God's blessing, who will go back with me to America."

"Azril can walk as far as the barn."

"Is this where you make him sleep, too?"

"We care for him because of you, our Moritz. *Moritz.* Could we not have left him muttering in the sanitarium?"

"Why have you told me all this? Why have I crossed the ocean to come hear how you betrayed me, how you betrayed my poor Papa!"

"Because Christ spoke to me from the cross and said, 'You must ask Moritz his forgiveness.'"

"Ask my Papa." He heard footsteps passing overhead again. "Ask Theodora. Do not ask me."

He slept in a cot alongside his father in the room closest to the fire. When Azril woke in the middle of the night asking about Shayna Blema, Morris knelt by his side and told him of Lillian, Abe, Herman, and Hannah. After Azril drifted off to sleep and woke a few hours later with a sharp cry, Morris told him of early morning on Dauphin Street, of the sweepers and looping swallows and shop-keepers cranking out their awnings. When Papa arose, together they said their matinal prayers and he looked up to catch Theodora's passing gaze.

Although he exchanged few words with Petru, and only formalities with Theodora, he relented to letting them drive him and Papa into the center of town, to the old Jewish quarter, watching the ghosts of boys run wild through the near empty streets. No wonder his father stayed in the last century. In this one the once lively streets teeming with angry and sad and festive voices were swept with the monotonal wind.

Near the synagogue a soldier stopped them and asked the identity of Morris and the old man. *"Prieteni,"* Petru said, *"American."* American friends.

After they had pulled away Petru said, "It is not a good time, Moritz, to be a Jew in Europe."

"Tell me, Petru, when has been a good time?"

That night, when Petru had gone outside to fetch firewood and Papa had nodded off, Theodora eased up behind Morris. "Can I be of any help with your Papa?"

"These are the first words you have spoken to me since when I arrived."

"What am I to say?"

"You are to say how you have been all these many years."

"After what Petru has told you, I am ashamed."

"It is not your shame, but your brother's."

"It is my family's."

"That Petru would say these things? About you, about looks on my face, about some piece of wood that I made, about this and that! Who is he to make up those lies?"

"They are all lies?"

"What do you mean?"

She was silent.

"Theodora, I am an old man married more than thirty years."

She averted her gaze. Head turned against the flickering light, eyes downcast, her skin glowed like a girl of seventeen again, a profile somber in the fire glow.

"I cannot remember all," he consoled.

"Then my shame, it is even greater. It was I who told him, 'Yes, it is true, there is something'—she touched her chest—'something here for our Moritz.'"

Morris looked at Papa, head rolled back on the chair, breath rattling, the butt of a rifle against his head like a violent black wing passing over him.

"Why would you say this?"

"I did not know that Petru would do such a thing! 'He will understand,' I thought. 'He will tell me it is a good way to be, that father will approve.'"

"I was a dog on whom they had pity."

"I watched you run across the field that night," she said. "I prayed for God to watch over you and I prayed for Him to bring you back. My prayers were answered."

Two nights later, when Azril waked at dawn's first hint calling for Shayna Blema, Morris reached out and took his chill hand.

"She is outside, Papa. Feeding the chickens."

"Such noise they are making. *Pasarea malai viseaza*," he said in Romanian.

"Yes," Morris said. "We are all like the birds—the chickens, says my Miriam—yearning for their bread, dreaming their corn."

"This is good," he whispered. "Thank you for coming to tell us good-bye. You have a long journey ahead. Go, before the soldiers come."

When Morris woke next, clutching his father's cold hand, Papa's soul had fled and swooped and turned like a starling toward the World to Come.

He did not know the rabbi at the synagogue. Indeed, not one Jew was left in the *shtetl* he recognized, though some remembered his father and formed a minyan, and two of the eldest said they remembered Morris himself as a little boy.

Where Ben lay buried he knew not, only that it was far off in France; but Chaim and Shayna Blema lay waiting for Azril to join them.

Standing beneath the nickel sky, Morris felt the ground tremble as the Kaddish prayer passed his lips, an aged son's tribute to a father who may have returned to his life once, but would not come back again.

Like a wife, Theodora stood by his side, and when they returned to the farmhouse she draped cloth over the single mirror in the great room. "I will sit with you," she said.

On the first day he telegraphed Miriam to tell her the news; on the second he arranged with the rabbi to place Azril's headstone one year later; on the third and fourth, Morris sat hearing Petru out the window talking in low tones with soldiers.

When the hour came to roll back the cloths and Petru announced he must be away for one day, Theodora went alone to her room and, through the wooden slats above his head, Morris heard her crying.

He went to her room and knocked softly at the door.

"You will soon leave," she said.

He fished in his pocket for a handkerchief to give her; it had the crisp, familiar smell of Miriam's iron across the kitchen table. He closed his eyes, hearing the hiss of metal against cotton.

"You are thinking of the way I was, long ago," Theodora said.

"Yes," he lied.

He handed her the handkerchief.

"You are going soon."

He looked at the fair blue eyes of a teenage girl looking back at him from the weary, lined face of a woman whose years had taken her no farther than a few miles from this farm. The lantern flickered against the rough pane window, and he saw himself, in a moment too, the wary look of an ardent boy; a child's eyes looking back from another tired, gray head.

"Thank you for all you did for my Papa. Theodora, you are"—he chose his words carefully—"the angel of God I saw in the barn that first time you entered."

"Oh, Moritz."

The way she said his name took him back to that evening he stood outside her window, her hand reaching up to brush out her rich red hair, her gown slipping off her shoulders. She touched his shoulder and he remembered coming up from the cellar, his heart beating wildly as she brushed against him.

"I wanted to go with you. You were running across that field and I thought, 'He is going where I should be going. He is flying away but I am pinned here. I want to fly, too!' What was there here for me? A drunk old man who father had picked for me because he had a plot of land where I could be as lonely as my mother had been before she died. When you came here, to this farm, and became our Moritz, I knew God had sent you for me."

Theodora moved her hand away and looked out the window. "Petru, he has left us alone."

"He had to go into town."

"He made so he had to go into town."

"Why would he do such a thing as this?"

She turned to him again. "Would you have turned back for me if I had called out to you?"

He was running again across the wintry field, turning to look up at the young woman whose gown was slipping off, shoulders rising in amber glow, hand pushing open the window and her voice sending his name through the starry night. He was turning, racing back the way he had come, barreling into the house, by the fire, up the steps, old man Eminescu right behind him wielding a poker. Morris was grabbing Theodora's hand and facing down the toughened Romanian with one eye straying across the room, the other fixed on him as they prepared, willful lovers, to flee. They started out the door and into the crystalline night.

"No," he answered softly, "I would not have come back."

With her silence filling the room he went outside and stood on the icy breadth of earth where he turned and looked up at her window. Her face was a drawn mask set toward the black horizon.

Overhead the stars crackled—he knew it was the crunch of his boots on the frozen earth— but he imagined it the heavens on a bitter cold night.

Out of habit he moved his fingers to check his money belt. A wad of cash—gone! He tried to peer down into the pouch, blindly sifting through its contents. Only a few bills were there but—he clasped them firmly—the return tickets, too.

He was too old to run off hitching rides on the back of hard straw wagons, but he would make it out somehow.

Theodora's light went down.

All around him darkness and cold and endless, foreign land.

He felt a prickling at the back of his neck, a trembling down through his body, not his heart giving out but blood surging through his limbs. He remembered the sensation from long ago standing beneath these same frozen skies—the raking need, no matter who was left behind, to move on.

This harsh place imprisoned by mountains and scoured by wind had claimed his Papa, Shayna Blema, Chaim, Golda, Ben, Petru and Elena and Theodora.

But never him.

Over the Store

Wedging one bare foot between the box springs and mattress, lifting herself up, Lily peers at Granddaddy on his back, cigar stub at his mouth, belly rising and falling. She reaches out and brushes down his thin crown of hair; eyes still closed, his lips curve in a faint smile around the cigar. She pats him lightly on the bald spot at the top of his head.

"Are you all better now?" she asks.

"Yes, I am only taking my beauty nap." He removes the cigar and plants it on the bedside table.

"This medicine is pretty!" She reaches for the candy-colored pills on the bedside table.

His hand surrounds hers and gently pries them loose. "These are Granddaddy's. I will keep them here to make sure they are safe." He puts his hand over the bedside and jams them beneath the mattress. "Our secret."

"Oh, a secret!"

He nods.

"Granddaddy?" She drags her palm across his stubbled chin. "Are you making a beard?"

"A bum does not shave in the morning," he says. "Every day I do not work in the store, it makes me a bum."

"I want to be a bum, too!"

"Your daddy, he was good at this when he was a boy. But not my Lily."

"You're funny."

"And you are a *'shayna madele.'* Do you know what this means?"

She shakes her head.

"A pretty girl. Like your Aunt Lillian." He reaches up and weaves his fingers through her hair. "She had curls, too."

"Daddy's name is Abie and Mommy's name is Molly!"

"Also a pretty girl!"

"She's not a girl." She crawls over him, spraddling his belly. "She's a lady!" Against the insides of her bare knees his white cotton shirt is smooth and warm. "Giddy up!"

He bucks once, twice, pushing the squealing three-year-old into the air. She reaches down and grabs his nose.

"*Schnozzle,*" he says.

She squeezes.

"Honk honk."

Her laughter ripples through the air.

"You have a shiny ring, Grandaddy."

"One day your Daddy will wear this ring."

"You don't like it?"

He holds up his hand; his fingers shake. "Oh, I do like it. *Gelt,*" he says. "Money. When I came to America I made five dollars. Will I buy a fancy hat, I asked, or go to a big hotel and live for one day like a big shot?" He shook his head. "No, I said, I will buy this ring. If the day should come, God help me, when my family has nothing to eat, with this ring I can get money for food on the table. First, always, food on the table."

"Food on the table."

"Do you know how many times I have taken this ring to a shop for money?"

"A hundred times!"

"Not *one* time."

She begins to bounce on his tummy again.

"Obey your mama and daddy."

"Mommy and Daddy," she says.

"Follow God's law."

She bounces higher.

"And protect your *gelt*."

"Protect your *gelt*," she peals, and she feels him reaching up and cupping her face in his large hands and pulling her close. Against her cheek his own is scratchy and he smells like tobacco and rumpled cotton shirts.

She does not want to let go but he urges her off, picks his cigar stub up from the bedside table, and, plugging it into his lips, sinks his head back in the pillow, his snore sawing the room.

In and out of naps he drifts, a bum, he thinks himself, a *nebbish* whose cranky heart will not let him pound down steps, broom flying, this week or the next, but lie in bed, whiskers wild as a Hasid's, until Abe drives in from his fancy neighborhood to open the store for business; until Herman walks the two blocks from his law office and helps him shave; until Hannah, a solitary school teacher in Atlanta, comes to tell him that she will soon marry Edward Galleano Del Fuente, a moustached Spaniard, at least a Sephardim, blessed be His Name; until even Pavel Chemenko comes shuffling in, head bowed, to admit he has stolen a radio, a lamp, and a recliner and please Mr. Kleinman to call the cops he will pay penance in the county jail. "You will keep these things," Morris says, "and work to pay what you owe for them." Chemenko's face, long and slack-jawed on top of his vast body, scrunches up and he weeps like a boy.

Even with his heart a cracked melon, Morris might say, "*Dayenu*," for returning both Abe and Herman from their tours of duty, for helping America beat the Germans once again, but has God delivered his children at all? If Morris had once called God a bastard for letting his precious, rich-haired Lillian marry the darkness of Mobile soil, what should he say to Him now?

Iasi, Dorohoi, Piatra Neamt. He whispers the names of the Moldavian villages where some Jews had clung to the vestiges of the long-ago *shtetls* when he'd journeyed to find Papa. Some, being rounded up by the Romanian army, had been gunned down right away, others delivered to the hands of the Nazis to be carted to the ovens. Had Petru silently witnessed this horror from the front seat of his Studebaker? Had Theodora, on the steps of the farmhouse, pined still for "our Moritz"?

What Creator of the World would be so callous as to turn His back on a million children throughout Europe who'd one evening sat lighting Sabbath candles in loving homes and the next were shunted into cattle cars for trips to Buchenwald and Bergen-Belsen and Treblinka? Who'd held hands like his family on a hundred Sunday strolls around Bienville Square, only to find themselves in guarded compounds, gas filling their lungs, their songs of prayer snuffed to silence? Their once vibrant bodies heaped onto pits of the dead?

When he'd fled the Eminescu farm as a youth he'd traveled through Germany, and had slept by the roadside one night in Dachau. He remembers the clear Dachau morning, the clatter of goat bells, the shepherd's son who approached him and offered him a flagon of milk. A boy with a pure, red-cheeked face, the lad had squatted next to Morris as he'd drunk the milk. Had the place where he'd blithely breakfasted been the very ground where other Jews would one day be herded moaning prayers, their bones, after months of scant food and senseless labor, turning to knives inside their own skins?

"My trouble," he whispers, tearing his buttons and making a fist, knocking it against his chest, "it is nothing."

"*Dayenu,*" Miriam says at the *seder* when the Passover air is rich with wisteria and honeysuckle explodes along the eaves and Morris has taken his place again at the head of the table, reclining in an easy chair Chemenko has carted upstairs.

But when it comes time for Morris to close the prayers, and he recites, "*L'Shanah Haboah Beerushalayim,*" he does not translate for Molly and Abe and little Lily and Marta Pastor as the text has read for centuries, "Next year, Jerusalem." He speaks instead the only truth he knows, the hope of the displaced throughout the Old World he has left far behind, its carnage just ending: "Next year, America."

A month later, being wheeled along a hospital corridor on a gurney, after repeated heart pains, he looks up at the doctor and says, "I want to go back home."

"But you just got here, Mr. Kleinman. We're going to take good care of you, so don't you worry about a thing."

"I have a family, I have a store. I cannot stay."

The doctor smiles.

As he lies beneath an oxygen tent, Miriam sits by his side through long nights and he talks about expanding the office for a second desk now that he and Abe will be working side by side; switching the repossessions with the showroom of couches; buying the empty back room of Molyneux's drugs, knocking down the wall, and setting up a special room for a display of radios and fans.

He stops talking and looks up at his wife. Her eyes are red and wet.

"You are sick?" he asks.

She reaches through a zippered opening in the tent and takes his hand.

"You are thinking, ah, this Morris, he is not a good prospect?"

She kisses her fingers and reaches back in to touch his lips.

Abe joins them and Morris instructs, "Make an advertisement that will make Lutchnik himself jealous."

"But Lutchnik," Abe says, as though Morris has lost his senses, "has been gone a long time, Daddy."

"Do you have a pencil? 'Kleinman & Sons has the best fans in town. Ceiling fans. Basement fans. Attic fans. Window fans. Any fan even a baseball fan.'" He cranes his neck from the pillow to see if Lutchnik has appeared at the door.

The figure that materializes at the threshold is only the doctor, opening his hand to show a fist of pills. "Playing hide-and-seek with us now. Don't you want to get well, Mr. Kleinman?"

"Who can get well in a hospital?"

Indeed, it is not the mandatory bed rest and oxygen tent that make him feel better—he still feels as lousy as a mildewed couch—but the thought of a triumphant return to Dauphin.

Next to the window looking out onto Bienville Square, near the sign, "Herman Kleinman Attorney at Law," Herman scratched through his third attempt at the letter, then started again, resolved to abandon the effort if he did not finish this time:

Aug. 1, 1945

Dear Fanny,

I can imagine your surprise that I have written to you. I hope above all that you and Shona are well. We are all doing fine in Mobile, and have survived the terrible war intact and all together again. Mama is well, and though Daddy has had a rough time of it, humor and 'chutzpa' will probably keep him going longer than any of us.

Now you are wondering, how did I find you to start with? I saw you in New York!

There you were, passing right by me near Pennsylvania Station, and with your lovely Shona at your side. Much as I wanted to stop and embrace you both, I knew that the greatest joy I could have would be to keep a picture of you both in my heart, in that very moment, like a portrait inside a locket.

I was just another soldier on the street, on leave from Washington where I'd been stationed. I followed you for a block into the crowd, but then turned away and went to a telephone booth where I rang the operator who gave me your address. It would be best, I knew, to write.

And where am I writing from? My own legal office. I

*know hearing this will make you proud. Thank you,
Fanny, for reminding me many years ago that I had more
to give the world with a book and pen and paper than
with a shovel and pick. I am married for several years,
too. In a little while I will end work for the day and go
meet up with Iris for a movie down at Arlington Pier. The
war done, we hope to start a family soon.*

*This morning I was thinking about all the wars, even
at my age, I have seen. When I was a boy I saw Civil War
soldiers marching in front of our store, and remember the
very day that the Great War ended. Now we have seen
World War II come and go. G-d willing, that will be the
last. The ship yards brought many new people to town,
and for Daddy and Abe many new customers. For that, at
the least, I am grateful.*

*Please tell Shona she has an older cousin in Mobile
who hopes one day to become her friend. If there ever
comes, out of the blue, a knock on my door one evening,
even if it should be twenty years from now, I will welcome
her as my Yankee* mishpocah. *Yes, family, no matter what
color our skins. The South has not changed very much in
that regard, but in my home we live in our own special
corner of the South.*

*With fond regards always,
your Dixie* mishpocah, *Herman*

He started to read the letter over, but changed his mind. He
slipped it into a readied envelope, stepped outside and dropped it
into the mailbox.

Three weeks later, daydreaming of Fanny opening the letter,
Herman's office door jangled as he swiveled about to catch first
glimpse of a young man, no older than twenty-five, easing in and
looking about warily.

"Yes sir!" Herman said, leaping to his feet to shake the man's hand. "What can I help you with today?"

The man's skin was the color of Shona's—light-brown. He had crinkly dark hair and hazel eyes.

"Help me with a lot," the man said quietly.

Herman offered him a Coke, but the man declined and continued standing. Herman pulled over a chair and urged him to sit. "Thank you, sir," the man said, as Herman returned to his swivel chair.

"You the Jew lawyer, ain't you?" the man said.

"Yes, that's me. That good or bad?"

"Good if you willin' to help me. They said you would."

"Who's that?"

"Some of the other lawyer men I been to. They said it was best to try you."

"What's your name?"

"Donald McCall."

"Pardon?" Herman sat up straight.

"Donald . . ."

"No, no, I got the name. I . . . go on now, tell me what's eatin' at you."

"I got some property due me. That's all. I got a wife, two boys, and my granny with us too. It's a fine house not too far from the Avenue. My daddy died in it long time ago."

"Tell me about your daddy."

"Not much to tell seein' as how he never give me no claim on him. My mama she, my mama." McCall fell silent. "She passed."

Herman rolled his chair a few inches closer to McCall. "She work," he said gently, "in your daddy's house?"

"Yessir."

"What'd your daddy look like?"

"I never seen him 'ceptin I know"—McCall looked down, then back up, shrugging—"he was white."

"I'll help you, sir."

"You will! You"—he slapped his hands together—"*believe* me?"

"It's my job to believe you, Donnie McCall, but more importantly, I think you're telling the truth."

"How you know folks call me Donnie?"

Herman smiled. "We start going after your white daddy's property now, you know there'll be a fuss."

"I ain't worried about no fuss. But I ain't got much money to pay you. Just not right now, that is."

"Your wife cook?"

"Yessir."

"She fix chicken and black eyes and collards?"

"Oh, yes sir."

"Tell you what, that's my fee. You bring me two big plates of that every Friday, about 3 o'clock, enough for me, my wife, my Mama and Daddy, too. That's what you might call our church night."

"Thank you, Lord," McCall whispered.

Herman took out a legal pad and wrote at the top: "Claim of Donald McCall, Jr., on the Estate of Donald McCall, Sr."

"Now," he said to his new client, "let's kick us up that fuss."

Down the steps from the bedrooms to the floor of the store, onto the walk, Morris made his way, broom in hand, buoyed to be working again. Already the swallows were coursing their manic alphabet against the pale Mobile sky, and Abe was nowhere to be seen: still in his seductive bed, Morris figured, no alarm loud enough to wake him from wasteful slumber. Sure, you could manage a store by wheeling in by car in time to greet customers, but could you know it like a woman without sleeping next to it every night?

Foil gum wrappers, Coca-Cola tops, plastic chip bags: he whisked away last night's debris. Where the Dauphin Street trolley tracks had long been ripped up when he was not even looking and used for scrap iron by the military there were now ever more automobiles, even in early morning, grinding and belching. America may have won the War, but it was dirtier than before. All the more reason to dance his broom over the walk until the mica glistened.

When he leaned over to pick up a yellow button for Miriam's scrap box he felt his body stop a moment—the old fist grabbing hard at his chest—and broke into a sweat.

He stood up; Dauphin Street turning around him, the street rising and falling. Falling.

"Morris!" Miriam's voice was clear and lovely and far away even as he felt her close, under his arm, urging him to take his pill. "So much work," she commiserated. "So much and you are not well! Let Abe do . . ."

Then he saw it: the store that had been Matranga's bakery now empty, "For Sale or Lease" on its door.

"We will expand," he whispered exultantly. "One store is good, two stores better. Why not the whole block? A store for furniture, a store for ladies, a store for men, coats and ties in the front, the ladies very fancy, the tables and chairs . . ." He stumbled backwards but latched onto the arm of his rocker. "What times does the First National open? We will tell them our plans. A loan, who can refuse? It is good business."

"Sit, sit!" Miriam pleaded.

He shook his head. "Upstairs," he uttered.

Upwards they trudged, step by looming step, his left arm slung over his bride, his right hand fumbling for the button in his vest pocket, no, in his shirt pocket, no, he could not find it but wrapped his fingers around hers, warm and tight, as she led him to their bedroom over the store where her touch, like Shayna Blema's, like the Mobile morning, like the Piatra Neamt sky, all too soon slipped away.

Acknowledgments

It is a long way from my grandparents' nineteenth-century birthplaces in Romania and Russia to a novel published in the twenty-first. Inventing this work has been made easier, and sweeter, by the sustaining love of Nancy and Meredith, my wife and daughter, always there for me outside the study door; the soulful, late-night dialogues with my sisters Sherrell, Becky, and Robbie and their families, including the much missed Charlie Grean. My Mobile and Memphis cousins over the years, and aunt and uncles, the late Goldie and Abe Walter and Louie Hoffman, added to the conversations. My parents, Evelyn and Charley, have been close to the heart of my writing from the time I first seriously set pen to page. My Dad, who grew up over the real Dauphin Street store, is a superb raconteur.

Although this tale is imagined, I gathered insights from many wise people. Medicine in history: Dr. Sam Eichold and Dr. Matthew Mosteller. Judaism: David Weiner, for his close reading of the text, and Rabbi P. Irving Bloom, for his teachings over many years. Yiddish: Elaine and Bernie Sherman. Spanish: Orlando Rodriguez.

I've heard expressive stories of the past from many people, including my in-laws Dr. John H. Mosteller and the late Janet "Gran" Mosteller; my cousin Ronnie Hoffman, who knows downtown; Ruth Lamensdorf and John Strauss, who helped bring to life old Dauphin Street; Ernest Edgar Jr., Sam Brown, and the late Robert Adams for recollections of Armistice Day; the late Joe Bear and Alberta West, for taking me way back; and many older folks I've interviewed for articles encouraged by *Mobile Register* editors Mike Marshall and Dewey English, and my city desk colleagues.

My friends Professors John Hafner and Walter Edgar had me read from the novel, respectively, in Mobile at Spring Hill College and in Columbia on South Carolina Public Radio (where a listener wrote in with the Romanian derivation of this novel's title) and at the University of South Carolina–Beaufort. Professor Marc Raphael invited me to the College of William and Mary. My gifted friend, the late Bailey Thomson, always welcomed me at the University of Alabama. Others have promoted my work: Kathleen Driskell of *Louisville Review*, Suzanne Hudson of Tulane's alumni magazine, Professor Bert Hitchcock of Auburn, Professor Sue Walker of the University of South Alabama, Joyce Dixon and Pam Kingsbury of southernscribe.com.

Sena Jeter Naslund had me debut the novel and brought me into an inspiring circle at Spalding University's brief residency MFA in Writing program in Louisville. My colleagues include Karen Mann, Luke Wallin, Ellie Bryant, Melissa Pritchard, Connie Mae Fowler, Crystal Wilkinson, Dianne Aprile, Greg Pape, Rich Goodman, Jeanie Thompson, Bob Finch, Kirby Gann, Brad Watson, Elaine Orr, and Charles Gaines.

I owe much to Eli Evans. Through his encouraging words and searching books Eli, in humor and friendship, has propelled me to seek out the crossroads of the two grand American literary traditions we share, the Jewish and the Southern.

Many others have been supportive, including John Sledge, Karl Hein, Charles Salzberg, Diane McWhorter, Lincoln Paine, David Alsobrook, Michael Garin, Bob Wilson, Stan Tiner, Connie Rosenblum, Dana Jennings, Andy Antippas, John T. Edge, Gene Jones, Bill Baker, Eugene LeVert, Charlotte Cabaniss, Jake Reiss, Byron McCauley, Garry Mitchell, Sam Hodges, Tom Mathison, Bill Pangburn, Barry Silverman, and William Oppenheimer. At the University of Georgia Press John McLeod, Allison Reid, Sarah McKee, and Mary Koon have been of special help.

Without my literary agent, Joelle Delbourgo, and University of Georgia Press director, Nicole Mitchell, this novel might be a manuscript forever hopeful in a box, and I, rather than this book, would be the chicken dreaming corn.